BIRTH OF THE GATOR

THE DISTURBING HISTORY SAGA

KAMI BOLEY

www.boleybooks.com
9919 Boxelder Blvd.
Pensacola, FL 32526

Edited by Spencer Hamilton
Cover design by Damonza
Interior design by Sandeep Likhar

Published by Boley Books LLC
Printed in the United States of America

ISBN: 978-1-947898-01-1
ISBN: 978-1-947898-00-4 (ebook)

With much solidarity to my wordplaying cohorts and
my shenanigan-seeking story lovers.
Keep those pages turning—read on, my friends, read on!

Contents

Monday, July 7, 1958 13

Friday, August 23, 1940 14

Saturday, December 7, 1940 20

Sunday, December 8, 1940 28

Monday, December 16, 1940 30

Friday, February 21, 1941 35

Sunday, February 23, 1941 37

Saturday, August 23, 1941 39

Monday, February 2, 1942 42

Thursday, February 26, 1942 48

Monday, July 13, 1942 52

Friday, July 31, 1942 58

Tuesday, February 8, 1944 65

Friday, November 24, 1944 66

Wednesday, August 22, 1945 70

Friday, September 3, 1948 73

Tuesday, July 12, 1949 75

Wednesday, July 13, 1949 82

Saturday, May 6, 1950 92

Sunday, May 7, 1950 99

Monday, November 13, 1950 107

Friday, November 24, 1950 112

Sunday, November 26, 1950 115

Sunday, December 3, 1950 118

Tuesday, January 2, 1951 122

Wednesday, January 3, 1951 127

Wednesday, March 7, 1951 133

Wednesday, August 8, 1951 137

Friday, August 10, 1951 141

Sunday, January 20, 1952 146

Tuesday, January 29, 1952 148

Wednesday, January 30, 1952 150

Saturday, February 2, 1952 152

Friday, March 7, 1952 155

Saturday, March 8, 1952 158

Sunday, March 16, 1952 160

Thursday, March 20, 1952 164

Friday, March 21, 1952 172

Friday, September 12, 1952 176

Thursday, September 18, 1952 179

Tuesday, November 4, 1952 181

Sunday, March 1, 1953 195

Monday, June 29, 1953 199

Sunday, October 18, 1953 202

Tuesday, October 20, 1953 208

Friday, October 23, 1953 217

Monday, November 2, 1953 223

Thursday, November 12, 1953 225

Thursday, November 19, 1953 229

Friday, November 20, 1953 232

Sunday, November 22, 1953 239

Saturday, November 28, 1953 243

Thursday, March 18, 1954 246

Friday, June 18, 1954 247

Saturday, January 1, 1955 249

Monday, January 3, 1955 251

Thursday, January 6, 1955 255

Monday, January 10, 1955 259

Thursday, January 13, 1955 265

February, 1955 267

Thursday, February 24, 1955 268

Saturday, June 4, 1955 273

Friday, August 12, 1955 278

Monday, November 7, 1955 282

Tuesday, November 8, 1955 289

Sunday, September 2, 1956 291

Saturday, December 8, 1956 293

Sunday, March 3, 1957 298

Tuesday, March 12, 1957 302

Thursday, April 4, 1957 305

Friday, May 3, 1957 307

Monday, June 17, 1957 312

Tuesday, July 2, 1957 321

Thursday, July 4, 1957 326

Sunday, October 20, 1957 332

Friday, October 25, 1957 335

Thursday, November 14, 1957 341

Friday, November 15, 1957 345

Saturday, January 25, 1958 347

Wednesday, February 12, 1958 351

Tuesday, March 4, 1958 354

Saturday, April 5, 1958 356

Friday, June 20, 1958 359

Friday, June 27, 1958 360

Saturday, June 28, 1958 361

Tuesday, July 1, 1958 365

Monday, July 7, 1958 368

Wednesday, July 23, 1958 370

Wednesday, August 13, 1958 373

Friday, September 5, 1958 378

Saturday, September 6, 1958 382

Afterword 389

Acknowledgments 391

About the Author 395

BIRTH OF THE GATOR

The mounting of strategic deception calls for the close cooperation and high security of all parts of government engaged in the effort.

—Allen W. Dulles

The Craft of Intelligence:
America's Legendary Spy Master on the Fundamentals of
Intelligence Gathering for a Free World

Steer minds and money and you will control the world.

Governments old and new, both legal and illegal, both foreign and domestic, both public and private, understood this to be the cornerstone of any and all endeavors—the power to rule. Emperors, kings, queens, presidents, bankers, and big business owners all vying for a resource that can only be given through cooperation, all asking for the same intangible currency: Give us your energy! your hours! your loyalty! your *life*! Slavers and slavery, a Neolithic construct that never seems to end, a global plan re-invented and re-packaged under new management, as each generation is ensnared by a net that only becomes harder to see.

A strategic catastrophe, a well-orchestrated panic, was levied on an unprepared public in 1907; it wasn't the first time an aristocratic hierarchy conspired to deceive and manipulate the public, and it would not be the last. Out of a secret meeting at Jekyll Island, an idea for a seemingly heroic fiscal solution—a central banking system—was born, and in 1913 the Federal Reserve was presented like a gift to Woodrow Wilson.

It's relatively easy to endear yourself a hero if you extinguish a large fire, even when your treacherous pockets are heavy with matches.

Environmental destruction, caused by over-farming and economic dominoes set in place across the years by concentrated wealth, tipped and crashed in October of 1929, launching America into the Great Depression. This man-made disaster delivered years of upheaval and despair. An opportunity for government to dig their poisonous fingers deeper into the backs of struggling businesses and the less fortunate, breeding weary puppets for their ballot boxes.

Many significant streams of consciousness and consequence tore their way into existence in 1938; some were born fully formed entities and some were still abstract and malleable after birth. Nylon was manufactured, the first minimum wage was established, Seabiscuit was winning, Hitler was rising, oil in Saudi Arabia was discovered, Snow White was on the screen, *War of the Worlds* was broadcast, *Superman* was in print, and innocent babies divinely entered the universe.

In the beginning, the potential impact of any one of these things was incalculable, subject to variables beyond average human cognition. A small secret faction of US national intelligence—one that had not yet been sanctioned or even given a name—was gathering awareness of the few citizens that could manifest special abilities beyond the average. Scrying, telepathy, clairvoyance, pyrokinesis, telekinesis, and various other extra sensory perceptions and projections were of critical use to those who sought global influence and power. People with these supernatural gifts of cognition were to be collected, studied, harnessed, exploited, or extinguished in order to serve and protect American idolatry.

There is always someone wanting to change the world—some for the betterment of all mankind, some to satisfy a monstrous ego. In a world full of chaos and hard choices, where the lines and colors overlap and blur, it can be difficult to tell the difference between a violator and a victim . . . a villain and a hero.

Sometimes, they're both . . .

Monday
July 7, 1958

re you watching?

The boat's engine goes quiet and the propeller is still. Nature's orchestra begins to play with a chorus of excited buzzing and chirps. Floating along peacefully in the black midnight waters of the Pontchartrain Basin, passing a bank littered with storm-tossed limbs and twigs, a man playfully slaps the side of a boat to call up a dear friend, the big boy of this neighborhood, a cold-blooded apex predator that shares his namesake.

The gator hears that dinner bell ring.

His formidable red glowing eyes approach, eerily spaced eyes that glide along the murky water's surface, followed by bony armor that slices a serpentine line through a thin carpet of duckweed. He opens his broad, powerful snout and gives a slow, angry *Back off!* hiss to the smaller sets of eyes that gather round, those lazy swamp dwellers hoping for a taste of his meaty treat.

Both the beast and the man hone their talents in the wild.

Intense.

Solitary.

Deadly creatures who master the dark.

Friday
August 23, 1940

I n sweat-drenched pain, an overly pregnant woman waddles over to answer a knock at the door. Her wince is replaced by a grin as she welcomes a dear friend and her two-year-old son.

The quiet child partially hides his smile behind a small, treasured, stuffed gray mouse their hostess had gifted on his last birthday to remember her by. Standing in the doorway, he turns his bright eyes up to her own.

"Oh, Beulah," she says, her voice a soft little squeak, "thank you for coming! How did you know?" She struggles to breathe, huffing and puffing in her advanced stages of labor, two days overdue.

Beulah's café au lait skin shimmers in the August heat. She gives a sarcastic smirk and raises her chin. "How you *think* I know, Mouse?" she asks, gently helping the pregnant woman to sink down into a nearby chair.

"Silly me." Mouse has known for quite some time about Beulah's clairvoyant abilities. Yet still it manages to catch her by surprise.

Mouse measures harsh breaths between her gritted teeth. She embraces her tightly swollen midsection, sharing a smile with the handsome toddler through her pain. He shadows his mother like a baby duckling, but with more of a scurry, reminding her of how she became branded with her own affectionate nickname.

"So far de only people I can't read at all is my son and mahself," Beulah says, pouring water in a pot and setting it to boil on the stove. "I came as soon as I could, and I tell you what"—she shakes a finger at Mouse and her extended belly—"dat baby girl ain't gonna wait much longer." She steps out of sight to run a warm, soothing bath, which will hopefully take the sharp edge off of Mouse's escalating contractions.

Mouse raises her voice just above the sound of the rushing water. "I called for Vinny. I hope he gets here in time . . ." She frets as she watches Beulah rush back into the kitchen, hunting around for Epsom salts and herbs to add to the bath water. "Are you sure it's a girl?"

Beulah snaps a mock-angry look in her direction. Mouse leans back, rolling her eyes, and bites down hard on her bottom lip in self-deprecation. Beulah smiles, pouring a glass of orange juice. She adds a dash of a powdery substance and a splash of mineral oil, and places the glass on the table by Mouse's chair.

"Chug it," she demands, before going to check the water level. With a sharp squeak of the valve, the loud rush of water ceases, leaving that incessant drip that no fix has ever mended.

Mouse frowns as she picks up the glass. She wrinkles her nose at the smell. "I won't mind a girl at all," she says, stalling. "It's just that Vinny has been dreaming of a son. You know how very fond he is of your well-behaved Jack." Mouse upends the nasty mixture down her throat and shivers.

Returning from the now-ready bath, Beulah reaches down to muss

Jack's soft, wavy hair. "Lil Jack here lit up like the sun when I told him we was goin to Mouse and Vinny's place."

Mouse pecks Beulah's cheek as the Creole woman pulls her arm over one shoulder for stability.

"To the tub with you," Beulah says with a blend of warmth and worry.

"It might be because Vinny likes to horse around on the floor just to hear Jack laugh," Mouse says, reaching over with her free arm to nip the tip of Jack's button nose as she struggles to find her feet. He giggles, squeezing his stuffed toy a little tighter.

Beulah snorts. "Or . . . might be 'cause Vinny spoils him with dem damn cherry tart cookies-a his."

Mouse giggles and dips when her shaky legs give way a bit.

"I got you," Beulah says, fortifying her hold.

"Do you think you can want someone *so bad* that you dream them into being?" Mouse says, and looks to Beulah with a frightened pool of tears forming in her eyes. "Will she love me?"

"Oh, honey, o' course she will," Beulah says, her strong arms keeping Mouse on a steady keel. "When a heart is brave, de bonds of love *can* be forged befo' two people meet."

Once Mouse is settled in the tub, glistening with sweat from the effort, Beulah attends the steaming pot in the kitchen. Jack knows better than to go near the hot stove, so he stands at a safe distance, watching his mother's soft facial features become stern and tinged with dread as she drops a knife, a spool of thread, and a curved upholstery needle into the pot's turbulent water.

"Oh, oh, oh!" Mouse's painful moans echo from the bathroom, and Beulah runs to her aid.

Jack stays guarding the angry, murmuring pot but squeals when Vincent suddenly flies through the door, past him, and into the bathroom without a word.

Vincent's anxious lips land on the thrashing, feverish forehead of his beloved Mouse. "I made it," he says, exhaling in relief.

"It hurts! It hurts so much!" Mouse squeals.

"You better wash dem hands good if you gon' stay," Beulah tells him, checking the progress in the birth canal. She sees a small head of hair crowning and leaves in a rush.

Vincent rolls up his sleeves to scrub his hands, but before he can finish, Beulah is back, standing tub-side and wielding a sharp sanitized blade. Mouse would have screamed, but in a blessed moment of fateful timing, she has lost consciousness.

He turns off the sink faucet, eyes wide as he gapes at Beulah. "What the hell do you think you're going to do with that?"

"I'm gon' save dis baby, and her mama too . . . hold this!"

Beulah forces a cloth filled with the sanitized needle and thread into his hand. Frozen, Vincent holds his hand out like a coatrack, tears running down his petrified face; he knows better than to question her or get in her way.

Drawn by all the excitement, his pot-watching duties fulfilled, Jack peeks into the bathroom to see what the fuss is all about. He witnesses the forced, scary, slightly surgical, bloody birth of a purple baby girl. He watches his mother dig bloody mucus out of the still-attached baby's mouth and nostrils with quick, jerking movements. She braces the purple baby on her forearm, turns her upside down, and rubs her back like she's buttering a large ear of corn, trying to get her to breathe.

Vincent falls to his knees on the bathroom floor, in awe of Beulah's calm, praying for miracles.

After an intense moment that feels like an hour, the baby's chin quivers and out comes the beginnings of a wail. Beulah quickly cuts the cord, swaddles the baby tight in a towel, takes the tools from Vincent's still-rigid hand, and shoves the baby girl into her daddy's stunned and fearful arms. He stares down at his new baby, speechless, as she continues to fuss about being yanked from her cozy womb.

Beulah pulls the plug from the drain and swats Mouse on her face, trying to bring her around. She turns the bathtub faucet on and flings some cool water at her.

"I need you to wake up now, Mouse," Beulah says, her voice loud and clear.

Mouse is pale. Unresponsive.

Jack becomes upset. Tossing his stuffed animal aside, he runs and puts his little hands on his friend's cheeks. "Wake up, Mrs. Mouse! Pweeze wake up!"

Mouse, perhaps having heard his small baby voice, begins to stir.

"I need you to wake up and push, Mouse!" Beulah shouts with urgency. "We need to get the afterbirth out."

"I . . . can't." Mouse's voice is barely audible.

"You can and you will!" Beulah demands. "Right now—push, dammit!"

"Try, Mrs. Mouse! Pweeze try!" Jack begs, dancing on his short legs.

Mouse's eyes search and then settle on Jack's tear-stained face. She musters what little strength she has and squeezes as best she can.

"That's good. You're doin good," Beulah says, her voice now soothing. "Take three slow, deep breaths, then give me one more good one."

On the third breath, Beulah readies the cord. "Okay—push, push!" Beulah coaches as she helps to pull the rest of the placenta out. She turns to Vincent. "Give dat baby to her mama and go fetch me some ice."

He lowers the infant down into Mouse's upstretched arms, disappears from the room, and returns momentarily with a small bowl of cubes as instructed. The precious new arrival is just the distraction Mouse needs while Beulah numbs and places a few painful stitches to bind her slashed perineum.

"What's the baby's name?" Jack asks the beaming parents, who are staring down at their pink and wiggly bundle.

"Camille," Mouse answers, looking up to Vincent for approval.

He kisses his wife's forehead.

"Camille Nicole Smith," he announces proudly.

Saturday

December 7, 1940

A **harsh winter** wind blows across the Atlantic, sending a shiver up President Roosevelt's spine. *Great Britain's democracy is doomed to Nazi conquest* and other indelicately chosen words prove fatal to the public aspirations of ambassador Joseph P. Kennedy Sr. as the Second World War continues to pelt Europe.

Due to wartime rationing, Beulah and Mouse string popcorn and cranberries on floss during their morning visit, crafting a garland of Christmas cheer. With a belly full of popcorn, and now all caught up on the recent woes of politics and cloth diaper laundering, Jack ignores the hens in conversation to curl up beneath the warmth of his mother's hand as a series of soft strokes lulls him off to sleep.

Mid-stroke, Beulah inhales sharply when Mouse opens her house coat to reveal the dress beneath. Beulah playfully rubs her eyes. "Is that a *waist* I see?"

"It is . . . isn't it?" Mouse squeaks, marveling at the elasticity of her midsection, the high-pitched noise causing Jack to stir.

"Shhh, let's not wake little Jack. Let him nap." Mouse pulls Beulah from the couch and into the kitchen. "It won't be long before Vinny is home," she adds, checking on infant Camille sleeping in her mobile bassinet. "His extra Saturday shift at the shipyard ended at noon."

Beulah smooths her skirt and glances at the clock on the wall. "All de more reason for me to get out-a your hair. I just come to see how you were gettin on."

Mouse's shoulders slump. "But he will be so disappointed if he misses little Jack, Beulah . . . we're going down to the farmers' market when he gets home—why don't you come with us and stay for supper?"

"Only if you sure," Beulah says, then, smiling, adds, "and you let me do some-a da cookin."

"Then it's settled." Mouse smiles back and takes a deep, satisfied breath.

"What's settled?" Vincent asks as he closes the door behind him.

"Vinny!" Mouse says in hushed excitement. She flies into his welcoming arms and hugs him tight. "Beulah and Jack are going to spend the day and stay for supper. If that's okay?"

Vincent looks over Mouse's shoulder at Beulah with bright, comforting eyes. "The more the merrier," he says, and tiptoes to peek in on his baby girl.

A light, misty rain begins to fall as the group meanders around the open-air pavilion. There are tables and booths adorned with an abundance of fresh local produce and spices. The rainy backdrop locks in all the enticing aromas and enhances the lively colors. Mouse feels as if she is walking inside a kaleidoscope.

Holding the bag of mustard greens she just purchased, Beulah walks slowly beneath the sheltering canopy roof of the farmers' market, drawn to a pile of beautiful root vegetables. The healthy display of turnips, beets, and carrots is bordered by glass Mason jars filled with a syrup.

She picks up one of the jars and sees a few pieces of thick honeycomb suspended in amber. Beulah's mouth waters, thinking of all the recipes and all the ways she could put that jar to good use. She looks up to ask how much it costs, but is confronted with a glaring frown of disgust from the man guarding the honey. She carefully places the jar back where she found it.

The man watches her step away, his top lip lifting in a sneer. "Who's gonna want to buy that, now that a *zebra*'s touched it?" he snarls under his breath, shaking his head. Still glaring after her, he grabs the contaminated jar and wipes it down with a small towel.

The merchant's demeanor changes suddenly when Mouse drives her pram stroller up to the table. Developing a sunny grin, the man greets Vincent as he approaches with little Jack in his arms. "Good afternoon. What a lovely family you have here. Let me get your son a sample of my delicious clover honey."

Without waiting for a response, the man twirls the top off of a jar, dips a graham cracker deep into the sweet nectar, and brandishes it before the boy.

From a short distance, Beulah's jaw falls open in shock at the sight of the man licking a tiny drop of honey from his finger after touching her son's hand. She has always known that Jack is an even lighter version of her own diluted bloodline, but it has never occurred to her that he could pass for anything other than what he is—what the merchant would call a "zebra."

"Thirst-*yyy*," Jack says, reaching for his mother after finishing his sweet and salty treat.

Beulah smiles, hesitantly taking him from Vincent, and carries him over to the public water fountains. She stands for a moment in serious contemplation—should she allow him to drink from the fountain on the left? She eyes the sign above the fountain to the right.

COLOREDS

ONLY

Graciously unable to read, Jack hungrily slurps the forbidden water to relieve his thirst. When he is finished, Beulah allows him to wiggle and slide down out of her tender hold. Jack's short, chubby, wobbly legs run away from her to catch up with Vincent and he takes Vincent's hand.

She blinks slowly, watching her son, staring at her friends, while the wheels of her mind become greased with strange and fanciful wishes.

Later that evening, in a patch of silence after dinner and with a small glass jar filled with homemade apple wine, Beulah takes a deep breath to ask a scary question of her friend.

"Were you two serious about wanting to have another child? To have a . . . son?"

"My answer is still *yes*, Beulah," Mouse answers enthusiastically.

She tops off all three wine jars, and looks at her husband. Vincent is holding Jack, who is fast asleep against his right shoulder. Her smile falters. "But Vinny's answer has changed, I think."

Vincent shrugs with his left shoulder. "No . . . I still want a son." He nuzzles his nose in little Jack's soft wavy hair. "I'm just too scared to lose my wife. I don't know if I can let her go through that again." The memory of that August night flashes in his eyes.

"What if . . . ?" Beulah starts, but then isn't so sure how to finish. Uncomfortable, she looks down at her lap. Her face contorts in anguish. Her mouth goes dry. Her hand trembles, reaching out for the wine glass, and she takes another gulp of courage.

Vincent leans slightly forward in his chair and exchanges a look of worry with his wife. Mouse lays a caring hand on her shoulder.

"What if *what*, Beulah?"

"What if . . . what if you could have a son and not have to face de scary part?"

"And what if pigs had wings," Vincent scoffs.

Mouse flashes Vincent a reprimanding look and turns back to Beulah. "You mean like *adoption*?"

Beulah nods. "I know both of you love my Jack—" She pauses to swallow back the tears. "But do ya think ya could love him as your own? To raise him as your son?"

Stunned, Mouse and Vincent fall back in their chairs. There is a moment of silence in which they grasp at each other's hands, searching their hearts for an answer.

"You can't be serious . . ." Mouse mutters, eyes round and wet.

Beulah takes another gulp of wine, but her voice is stone-cold sober. "You both know how I got pregnant wit' Jack . . . and dat I never thought being a single parent was a good idea." She bats away the tears as they come. "But I saw you as a family today at de market, and . . . I realized my Jack would have a life wit' you that I simply cannot give."

Mouse sits in silence, tugging her bottom lip, her gaze lost in a series of hypothetical situations.

Vincent shakes his head. "I don't understand. Do you need money?"

"Dis ain't about money. Don't you see? Even if I had me a million dollars, I still can't give him de chance dat you can."

In her wicker bassinet nearby, Camille interrupts the conversation, beginning to whine and fidget for a late-night snack. Mouse jumps into action, lifting her fussy baby and readying her to suckle at a milk-swollen breast.

"But . . . we're so average," Vincent says.

" 'Average'?" Beulah repeats. She sighs and shakes her head. "My kingdom for your average. What is your heritage?"

"My dad was from England, and my mother is Italian."

"I see you go 'round and people just treat you like da white man. No need to explain anyting to anyone."

Vincent blinks, taken aback. "I guess it never occurred to me in quite that way."

"To boot, my boy looks like he could be *your* boy. Maybe he could be treated like a human instead of some half-breed mongrel. I grew up 'round here," Beulah says, the bitterness clogging her throat, "not white enough to be white and not black enough to be black. You can't please any of em and I know now not to try, but I had to learn it all de hard way. I don't want that for my son."

Vincent squeezes and rocks little Jack, hating the thought of anyone treating him badly.

Beulah sighs and rises from her chair, setting her wine aside. "I really should get him to bed. None of us gonna make any decisions tonight." Her arms reach out to lift Jack from Vincent's shoulder.

Vincent turns away from her, covering the young boy with his arms, a pained look on his face. He can't stomach letting the child go back to a reality he had never been aware of before now. "You can't leave right now. I want to talk about this some more. I have questions. When? How?" He squeezes his eyes shut and shakes his head. "So many questions."

Beulah sits back down and lowers her head, realizing she has yanked a veil away from their eyes without any warning or remedy at hand.

Mouse, still standing and feeding Camille, says, "I know how much you love him. How could you bear to leave him with us?"

Beulah straightens her back. "It is *because* I love him dat I would even consider it. Take a look at dat baby girl in your arms and tell me you wouldn't sacrifice for her to have everyting. Don't you see? With you, Jack would have more than I could ever give him. He would have two parents, a sister . . . and the life of an average little Caucasian boy."

Many complex questions are posed, with all three parents exploring the sides and angles to each painful, guilt-ridden issue. Just before midnight, Vincent spreads out a sheet and a blanket, making a comfortable space for his guests to sleep on the living-room couch. With heavy eyelids, and even heavier hearts, they put the discussion on hold, with plans to resume after a few hours of soaking their minds in dreams, possibly allowing a change in perception.

Beulah holds her son close with tear-filled, restless eyes, searching the dark for absolution, her mind fighting a battle that could rival any unrest the world over, a mother breaking her own heart for the noblest cause of them all.

Sunday

December 8, 1940

The matter quickly settled after a good night's sleep, as most matters are.

After a painful second morning suckle, Mouse hands Camille over to Beulah. The baby lets out a satiated coo and a hearty burp of approval over Beulah's shoulder.

"So we're really going to do this," Mouse says, refilling the coffee cups.

"Sooner rather than later," Beulah says, nodding. All three parents glance at Jack, still enjoying an oblivious slumber. "He's a smart one . . . and growing fast."

"I agree with Beulah," Vincent says, pushing his scrambled eggs and peppers around with a fork. "The longer we wait, the more explaining we will have to do."

"Potty," Jack pleads, sliding off the couch and rubbing the sleep from his eyes. Both Mouse and Beulah stand to answer his call.

Feeling the full weight of her decision—a heaviness so much stronger than gravity—Beulah lowers back into the seat and gently pats Camille. She begins to rock the baby, humming a song of love and hope.

Mouse touches a peck to Beulah's tear-stained cheek and leads the little man to the bathroom. The privilege of her assistance is not completely foreign to him, so Jack is playful and cooperative.

When Beulah's melody has ended, Vincent asks, "What now?"

Her gaze drifts, her mind searching the past for a place and a time best forgotten. Finally, she says, "There's someone I will need to see . . . someone who can iron out the details."

Monday
December 16, 1940

"Oooh-*weee*, I see me some light brown sugar coming up the walk," says a dapperly dressed middle-aged man as he rises from a stool outside the Brown Bomber Bar. His thumbs slide along his suspenders and he spreads his thick chocolate-brown lips into a welcoming smile, revealing nearly every shiny tooth in his mouth. "My, my, Miss Beulah Laveau! What brings you ova here to Gretna?"

"Hiya, Joe," Beulah replies, returning his smile with a demure one of her own. "Is the bossman here?"

Old Black Joe drops his smile, crosses his arms, and narrows his eyes at her for a moment. "And here I thought you done come to see Ol' Joe after all dis time."

Beulah gives him an apologetic rub on his narrow yet ample shoulder. "I'm sorry, Joe—that was rude-a me. How you been? How's ya mama an' dem?"

He melts. "I'm fine and dey good." Joe laughs and swats a hand in her direction. "I'm just funnin' ya, pretty thang." He purses his lips, turns his head, and pats a finger on his cheek, soliciting payment for any further information.

Beulah's smile broadens. She makes show of rolling her eyes and obliges him with a soft peck on his smoothly shaven cheek.

"Yeah, he in there. Hold up a second," Joe says. "Lemme make sure he in the mood for company befo' you go in." He spins fancily in his two-tone wingtips and disappears into the dark belly of the bar.

She waits outside for permission to enter, glancing nervously at a cherry-topped police car parked down the street.

Joe emerges. He also looks in the direction of the cop car and gives a short, curt wave. The car's engine starts and a uniformed hand raises out of the rolled-down window in response. The car pulls away from the curb and drives off.

"You can go in now." Joe pulls a homemade cigarette from a rolled sleeve and lights it from a match that he strikes against the wall, his eyes trained on the car as it rolls slowly around the corner.

The barroom smells of a busy weekend crowd throwing away their paychecks on intoxicants and gambling, à la stale cigarettes and piss.

"Have a seat," a short, muscular man says to Beulah. He wipes down a barstool with a white cotton rag, removing the thin, dusty film of blue pool-cue chalk that inevitably coats everything in the room. "What can I do you for?" He steps behind the bar to pour a nip of Four Roses bourbon in a short glass and slides it to her.

She looks at the booze and considers accepting the gesture, then raises her eyes to meet his.

He gives a quick one-shoulder shrug. "For old times' sake."

She puts her hand up. "No, thanks, Carlos. I don't touch *that* stuff anymore—not since . . ." She trails off, looking away, and clears her tightening throat with a sharp cough.

He leans against the bar in a wide stance, his face blank, but she still knows what that expression says: *Get to the point.*

"You told me once that if I ever needed anything, I could come to you," Beulah says, absently drawing a small heart in the blueish dust on the bar.

He cocks his head. "What is it that you think you need?"

"A favor . . . or two."

"What kind of favor we talkin?"

"The kind that only *you* can get done without anyone noticing."

His eyes twinkle with curiosity. He moves into an upright position and folds his arms. "What's in it for me?"

Beulah taps the side of the glass with her nail and raises one eyebrow. "You could do it outta da kindness of ya heart," she says.

Carlos snorts at the sentiment.

Her face brightens. She says, "Or you could call it an early Christmas present," followed by a timid chuckle.

He pinches the bridge of his nose and tightly squeezes his eyes shut. She can see he's losing patience. "Tell me what this favor is, Beulah, and I'll decide the cost."

Beulah's levity dissolves. She slumps in her chair and stares at the bourbon. "The first thing—" She pauses to swallow her heart back into place. "I need Jack's birth certificate removed from any and all official records, and a fake one put in its place." She carefully pulls out a folded sheet of paper that was pinned beneath the shoulder strap of her brassiere, and hands it to Carlos, keeping it away from the cloying blue chalk.

Having held items pulled from less savory origins, he is unfazed as he studies the paper. It lists exact instructions for all that is to be done to alter her son's future. He scans the paper, refolds it, pulls out his wallet, and tucks it safely inside. Then he levels his gaze back on Beulah.

"You sure about this?"

Beulah frowns, bows her head, and nods. "Now, what's your price?" she asks, feeling like he will ask for her soul.

Carlos licks his chops and replies, "You know what I want. What I've always wanted from you."

Without raising her head, she flashes her eyes on him. She knows. And what he's asking for is far too much. And she also knows, just as he does, that she'll give it to him anyway.

"I want the goddamned keys to the kingdom," he says, patting his middle with a satisfied grin.

After the specifics of their pact are ironed out and the deal is struck, Beulah walks out of the dungeonesque bar into the bright noontime glare, clutching Carlos's spare handkerchief. She stands defeated, and squints in Joe's direction. He jumps up from his stool as if she were a drill sergeant arriving for a field-day inspection.

Joe smooths his high-waisted pants. "It musta gone well. Didn't hear no hollering."

"It always goes well when he gets what he wants, Joe," she says, her voice thick with resentment.

He raises his eyebrows high as if slapped. "Well, ain't dat da truth," he agrees with an understanding nod, rubbing the back of his neck.

Joe's body is filled with nervous twitterpated energy; he's searching for a way to keep her from leaving.

With her sad, vacant eyes, Beulah looks at him, envious of his vivacity.

"Hey, I'm hungry . . . you hungry?" Joe asks. "You should let me buy you some lunch."

"Nah, I can't think about food just now. I'll be back in a few weeks. Can I get a raincheck?"

"Sho' 'nuff, doll, sho' 'nuff," he replies, thumbing the end of his nose in an attempt to look cool and hide his disappointment. He reaches into his pocket, pulls out a five-dollar bill, and holds it out to her. "Why don't you go ahead and take dis here Lincoln to buy some groceries wit' yo little boy."

Beulah winces. "I don't have no boy, Joe. You been misinformed."

She presses the handkerchief to her face to hide her shame and leaves as fast as her low-heeled T-strapped shoes can carry her.

Stunned and confused, Joe watches her disappear, his greenback flapping like a flag in the cool breeze.

Friday
February 21, 1941

Trying to teach someone the subtle arts of a natural-born ability is like trying to teach the deaf to sing opera, Beulah decides as she forces the whistle into Carlos's hand again.

"No one said dis was easy."

"I still don't understand why I got to use this damn thing. You didn't need no dog whistle," Carlos complains, sitting behind his desk on the last day of his tutelage. His lips pucker into a full-blown pout as he studies the four-and-a-half-inch metal device.

Beulah folds her arms and taps her foot. "You want to learn dis or not?"

"How will I know if it's working?"

"I guess you gonna have to test it out and see." A terrible thought suddenly crosses her mind and she sticks her long, elegant finger in his face. "But don't you dare ever think about using dat ting on my son."

Carlos leans away from her threatening finger with an affected hurt look on his face. "I would never do that."

She grabs his shirt collar and pulls him in close to her flushed, worried face. "I need you ta promise me. I need you ta swear!"

Carlos looks deep into the fire of her dark, glossy eyes, but doesn't answer.

Beulah gives him a hard shake to let him know she means business.

"I promise! I swear!" he says with his hands up, this time sounding sincere. "I will never use this on Jack or let any harm come to him." He leans into her menacing embrace and lightly rubs his nose across her velvety cheek, smelling her sweet clove-scented skin.

She pushes him away. "I taught you all ya need to know. I don't want be involved in all de trouble you 'bout to cause."

" 'Trouble'?" Carlos laughs, sounding like a CBS radio hour villain. "Me?" With a playful grin, he reaches into his desk drawer for a celebratory cigar. "Where you running off to, woman? Stay and have a drink with me." He snips the end off of the cigar with a guillotine cutter, then pulls a bottle of brandy from a shelf behind him.

"I can't."

"Why? You got to go cast a spell on a Louisiana Supreme Court Justice or somethin?"

"Why? You worried 'bout a case?"

He smiles wide with the cigar in his teeth. "Not anymore."

Beulah is headed for the door; she stops, looks back at him, and narrows her eyes. When she speaks, her words are slow and ominous.

"Don't go fiddle wit' every swinging ting dat cross your path now. Use what you know wit' some care, or it will turn around and bite you in de ass."

Sunday

February 23, 1941

Nothing bonds family like a hearty meal . . . and nothing angers the master chef faster than interrupting its creation.

"You get outta my kitchen, Vincent, before I bust-a your butt!" says a short, thin woman with her graying center-parted hair pinned in large coils at the back of her head. She smacks his hand with a wooden, tomato-stained spoon.

Vincent laughs, dropping the perfect al dente spaghetti noodle he'd just fished from the pot. "But, Mama, it smells so good in here," he says, giving her a smooch on the cheek.

She giggles and waves him away. "Go set-a the table and tell-a my new grandson Jack that I make for him da spaghet and I bake-a da thick cherry pie."

"Anything for you, Mama."

She puts her spoon down on the spoon rest and lovingly squeezes his face. "That's-a my good boy . . . and send-a Miss B to me." She lightly taps his cheek twice.

With his brow wrinkled in confusion, Vincent hesitates to leave.

"Shoo-shoo," she says, giving him a nudge.

A moment later, Beulah tentatively enters the kitchen. Her nose instantly fills with a lovely bouquet of garlic and herbs. "You asked to see me?" she says stiffly.

The small woman bangs her spoon hard on the edge of the pot, wipes her hands on her apron, and places her hands onto her frail, aging hips. "You come-a here and give Mama Rosella a hug."

Beulah breathes a sigh of relief and steps forward to receive her acceptance into her extended family.

"I keep-a dis beautiful secret and thank-a you for making the family so happy. You are welcome in Mama Rosella's house anytime." The small woman releases Beulah, pats her hair, and picks up a dishrag. "Except-a da kitchen. Now *shoo.*" Mama pops the towel in her direction.

Beulah smiles and joins the others at the table for a family meal, with a parade of food and laughter that lasts for hours. With full hearts and full bellies, any concerns the members of this newly formed family still had were completely absolved by the sacred ways of pasta, wine, and thick cherry pie.

Saturday

August 23, 1941

Missing those precious snuggle moments each night, Beulah has taken to sleeping over once a week to read storybooks aloud and hold the children close. She continues to visit the Smiths' home often, as the close family friend she has been to Mouse for years. She is both hurt and glad to see that it didn't take long for Jack to follow his new mama duck around the house. He has also bonded with his little sister Camille, and thoroughly enjoys his role as a helpful big brother. He likes making silly faces that send her into squeals of joy and laughter.

Camille sits with a gummy smile, slapping the tabletop of her wooden high chair, trying to reach out for Jack, who is playing peek-a-boo with her from Beulah's lap.

"So what's in store for us this next year?" says Mouse.

"Funny you ask me that. I've been meaning to tell you dat I can't get a read on you no more . . . none of you," Beulah replies, watching Mouse as she smears vanilla buttercream icing over a sheet cake.

Mouse straightens up and looks at her with shocked eyes. "Since when?"

"Ever since that first family meal at Mama Rosella's."

"No kidding! That's so strange . . . after all this time?"

"I still can't believe our Camille is a whole year old already,"

Beulah says, bouncing Jack in her lap.

"The year did go by fast, didn't it?" Mouse puts the finishing touches on the thin white topping of the birthday girl's cake, and celebrates by licking her finger.

Jack's three-year-old face lights up when Mouse hands him the sugary remnants of icing left on the stainless steel spatula. Delighted at seeing her baby so happy, Beulah kisses him on his still-chubby cheek.

Mouse rinses her sticky hands in the sink and says over her shoulder, "Oh, I didn't tell you! There's a huge project at Vinny's work and he got a raise. He is Higgins Industries' newest welding supervisor."

"Well, ain't dat sometin'." Beulah's eyes are round with surprise. "He surely deserves it for workin so hard as he do."

Mouse nods enthusiastically, drying her hands with a dish towel. "We saved up and bought a new radio with a phonograph that actually works."

Beulah turns to study the new piece of furniture that aligns the wall. "Ah, I see. It's smaller dan de old one."

Mouse rushes over and turns it on to watch the dark shellac disc spin around. "I told the salesman that Camille loves music, and he threw a couple records in with the deal."

She gently sets the needle down on the grooved surface. It pops and crackles through the intro music, and Bing Crosby's smooth voice begins to float through the speaker. Mouse lifts little Camille from her chair and sways back and forth. Beulah smiles and hums along, little Jack bouncing in her lap. The women get so lost in the music that they don't notice Vincent sneaking in the door.

"Daddy!" Jack says, wiggling down from Beulah's lap. As he runs to greet Vincent, waving the nearly cleaned spatula triumphantly, Mouse lifts the needle and turns the machine back off.

Vincent snickers and lifts him high in the air. "What do you have there, little man?"

"A treat! Mommy gave it to me." The women smile at each other, Beulah's smile vaguely heartbroken yet happy nonetheless. Mouse giggles as Jack holds the spatula out to him. "You want some?" he asks, licking the last traces of icing from the end.

Vincent laughs. He sets Jack back down and pats his tush. "No, thanks, pal. It's all yours."

After Mouse kisses him hello, Vincent takes Camille, raises her in the air above his head, and says, "Happy birthday, baby girl. This has been the best year of Daddy's life."

Monday
February 2, 1942

World **War II** rages on half a world away. While no one in power will admit that war is sought after, it sure is good for business. Erecting Higgins' boats by day, Vincent enjoys the spoils of war in the shipyard and a cherished peace at home by night—too bad that, with an ever increase in production, the days are stretched longer and the nights nearly nonexistent.

In wartime, many are tapped to serve in whatever capacity they are willing and able. For Beulah, her call to duty at the Smiths' is a welcomed one. Being mistaken for a live-in maid is a small price to pay for the joy of her son's bright future and her days well spent with him and Camille. It has been a while since Beulah gave baths and fastened diapers, but to her surprise her nimble fingers instantly remember the task of folding and securing each side of the cloth with a safety pin. That saying, "like riding a bike," holds some wisdom after all.

She raises Camille to her shoulder and pats her tiny butt for good luck, releasing a cloud of cornstarch into her face that ignites a coughing fit.

"Are you okay?" Mouse calls loudly from the kitchen.

Beulah is choking but manages a weak "Yes." She can hear Mouse's worried footsteps growing closer.

"Are you sure?" Mouse asks, arriving with a glass of water. She takes Camille and says, "Here, drink this."

Beulah sputters a bit, trying to wash the airborne cornstarch from her throat. "Thank you," she says hoarsely, sipping more water with relief. A burst of levity escapes Mouse's lips and surprises them both, igniting a cleansing belly laugh—much needed relief from somber times.

"No, thank you for staying with us for a while. You have been so much help. Vinny isn't going to be home hardly at all. They've doubled, almost tripled production since the Pearl Harbor attack."

Beulah places a hand on Mouse's weary shoulder. "You know I enjoy bein here. How many times I got to tell ya it's no bother?"

Mouse lifts her shoulder and embraces Beulah. Her face brightens. "Let's go eat," she says, making her way back to the kitchen. "I just put out supper on the table. I hope you don't mind that it's red beans and rice again."

Beulah can smell pepper and herbs as she follows close behind. "No, I don't mind at all." She stands in the kitchen doorway a moment, smiling at Jack's messy face. He is shoveling in his second-to-last bite already.

"Mum-mum . . . ma-ma-*deeee*!" Camille yells angrily, gumming on her finger after Mouse sits her in the highchair.

Beulah jumps into action, mashing a batch of unseasoned beans for her at the counter. "It's comin, little one."

"Can I have some more?" Jack asks his new mother, showing her the cleaned plate.

"Did you say grace before you started to eat?" Mouse says, taking his plate for a refill.

He plops his embarrassed face in his goopy hands. "I forgot, 'cuz it's a war out there," he says, pouting.

Beulah and Mouse share a look and try not to laugh at his cuteness. Sadly, Jack is more right than he knows. There is too much evil going on in the world to fuss little boys for being in a hurry to answer the call of their growling bellies.

"Well, let's hope God doesn't get mad for just that once," Mouse says, placing his new portion in front of him.

Jack bows his head over his clasped hands, wanting to perform a do-over. The women bow their heads, too.

"God, thank you for this food we are about to receive, Amen," he says with a respect seldom seen from a toddler, before beginning the meal anew.

After the shock of Pearl Harbor—an attack that sent all of America into a wild froth of activity, setting aside their previous anti-war sentiments in favor of vengeance—with exhausted souls, Beulah and Mouse ignore the war propaganda, growing anti- Japanese xenophobia, and the buzz about proposed internment camps to instead sit relaxed, enjoying cups of coffee and the soft, smooth sounds of Billie Holiday on the radio.

As the clock strikes eight, they both jump to their feet when a hard, rapping knock pounds the door. The meal is over; the dishes are all put safely away, and so are the children.

Mouse pulls her dress up closer to her neck, in reaction to a sudden chill in her blood. "Who on earth could that be at this time of night?" she squeaks.

"Let me answer it," Beulah says, waving at Mouse to stay back. Mouse sits back down but stays erect and perched at the end of her seat, her eyes blinking rapidly with fear.

Beulah opens the door a few inches and shrinks back, listening to a man's hushed baritone voice state his reason for the disturbance. She nods, lowers her head, and opens the door for the man to enter.

The policeman removes his hat, revealing his roughly handsome face, and places it in the crook of his arm. He coughs into a closed fist to clear his throat. "Are you Mrs. Vincent Smith?"

Mouse licks the salty tear that falls on the corner of her lip. She rises unsteadily to her feet and meekly answers, "Yes."

"Ma'am, I'm here to inform you that your husband has been in an accident at the plant."

Mouse's shaky hand rises to cover her mouth and stifle the horrible squeal from her strangled throat. She rushes to the officer and stumbles. He drops his hat to catch her in his muscular arms.

"Please take me to him!" she begs him with wild eyes.

The officer looks over at Beulah, who is backed into the corner of the room. *"Is he okay?"* she mouths at him. The officer grimly shakes his head, trying to hand the upset woman over.

Beulah takes Mouse into her arms and holds her tight. "He gone, Mouse . . . Vinny gone."

"Noooo!" Mouse screams a long bloodcurdling scream, her face buried in Beulah's shoulder, her tears soaking Beulah's dress. Beulah can hear the sanity being ripped from Mouse's head. Out of breath, Mouse lets go of her consciousness, and her body hangs limp.

"Where do you want her?" the officer asks, lifting Mouse as if she were a feather.

Beulah feels numb. She answers without thinking. "The couch."

He deposits Mouse's small frame onto the cushions. At first it seems she has followed Vincent into the afterlife, looking like a beautiful princess overcome by an evil curse in a fairytale. The officer places his finger to her nose and his ear to her chest to feel for her shallow breaths and her heart's broken beats.

Beulah gasps when she hears her son sniffle. She looks to the kitchen doorway to see Jack crying.

"Is God mad at me now?" he says in a jerky whimper.

She runs to scoop him up. "No, honey, no! Dis is none of your fault."

The officer stands, puts his hat back on, and shrugs. "You can call a doctor, but I think the best treatment for now is to let her rest." He pulls a printed square of cardstock from his pocket. "She can reach me at the station when she recovers."

Beulah nods in slow agreement with the officer's brief assessment. His only personal experience with people darker than himself has been forcing them into handcuffs and hauling them off to jail. With a biased opinion, pre-formed in skewed inaccuracy, he finds himself uncomfortable to be speaking friendly with a person of Beulah's ancestry. He hands the business card off to her—more accurately, he tosses it, and abruptly decides to remove himself from the bothersome interaction.

She examines his name on the card and her worry lines deepen. "Thank you, Officer Richard. I'll be sure she gets this."

But Officer Richard is already gone.

Thursday
February 26, 1942

Mama Rosella would have no less for her son than to have his remains be put in a vault in the affluent cemetery on Metairie Road, spending all the money she had in her safety deposit box. Beulah accepted a decent offer on her old home so she can stay and help Mouse indefinitely.

Three short weeks after the funeral, a neurotic, greasy-headed Mouse, unable to bring herself to step outside, still skittish and fragile from the loss of her beloved husband, has latched onto Officer Adam Richard. She contacts him for every noise and worry.

Mouse wrings her hands when he enters with the bag of groceries she requested. "I'm scared, Adam. I heard on the radio news that there was some kind of skirmish in California. You think it was the Japanese or a UFO like they said?"

The man eyes the radio in its corner and sighs. "Yeah, I heard about that, too. I'm not exactly sure what to think of it. The details about the incident just don't add up. If I hear of anything concrete, I'll let you know. I'm sure if it were a serious invasion of any kind, they would tell us what to do."

She nervously tugs at a thick terrycloth robe that she has taken to wearing over her clothes, shuffling alongside him in her slippered feet.

Trying to not let her trip him up with her clinginess, he sets the paper bag on the counter and looks around. "Where are the kids?"

Mouse frets. "They were upset because . . . well, I couldn't stop crying this morning, so Beulah took them to spend the night at my mother-in-law's."

"You do look a little rough. When was the last time you took a bath or brushed your hair?" he asks, leaning in to give her a sniff test, which, judging by the way he wrinkles his nose, she fails miserably.

Embarrassed, she looks down and runs her tongue over her furry teeth, unable to recall the last time she brushed them.

He looks down on her with pity. "I don't have anybody to go home to, so why don't I whip us up something to eat, and you go clean yourself? I think it'll make you feel better."

She goes back to wringing her hands as she looks up at him. "I have been asking so much of you . . . I couldn't ask you to entertain me, too."

"Ma'am, I'm trained and paid to protect and serve the community. I will protect you while you bathe, and serve you up some grub. Now go."

Mouse obeys.

When Mouse, smelling of rose water, sets her spoon down after two bowls of hearty potato soup, it is the first time her belly has been full in almost a month.

"Thank you . . . I truly needed this," she says to Adam, patting her lips with a thin cloth napkin.

Adam smiles and takes away her dishes. "Glad to be of service—but you should be used to being served with that maid of yours."

"Beulah?" Mouse laughs. "She's no maid! She's my friend."

Adam drops the dishes in the sink with a clamorous racket and one of the glasses shatters. With her frazzled nerves, Mouse covers her mouth and cowers in her chair. Picking the glass shards out of the sink, Adam looks over his shoulder at her, almost groans at the sight of her cowering, and asks, "Are you all right?"

"What's going on?" she asks, rising cautiously out of the chair. "Are you angry?"

"No, the damn thing just slipped out of my hand," he says, placing the pieces in the garbage. Then, abruptly: "I think I'd better go."

Mouse resumes the wringing of her hands. "Why? What did I do?"

"You didn't do anything. I just think it would be best to find yourself someone else to do this with. You're still fragile, and I'm not looking to take care of anyone right now."

"Do *what* with?" she asks, blinking. "I thought dinner was nice . . . that we had become friends."

He turns to face her, his gaze harsh. "Sounds like you already have a friend. What would you need me for?"

Mouse's face melts into a hysterical cry, thinking about her very best friend lying stiff in a cold box miles away. She wants nothing more in this moment than to claw her way through a layer of cement and lie down beside her Vinny.

"Awww . . . come on, don't do that," Adam says, reluctantly letting

Mouse put her wet, snotty face on his shoulder.

"Right now, I need all the friends I can get." Her voice is a muffled cry through his uniform shirt.

"Shhh . . . all right, all right, kid," he soothes, patting her back.

He inhales the fresh scent of her skin and nuzzles her close as his friendly touch wanders. A tear spills when she closes her eyes and welcomes the kisses on her exposed neck. Sometimes an ailing body needs what the heart just can't provide.

Monday
July 13, 1942

"**J**ack's birthday was *yesterday,*" Beulah says in a voice that she tries to make sound sarcastic but is actually sullen. Her arms are folded as she walks along the sidewalk in the back of the group.

Adam shrugs, leading the pack. "I had things to do yesterday. So what if it's a day late?" He leans over and whispers in Mouse's ear, "The kid is four years old—like he knows the difference."

Adam opens the door to the ice cream parlor, letting out a blast of cool vanilla-scented air, and raises his voice to announce, "Sweets are good any day of the year!" He clears his throat to get Mouse's attention, showing her his expectantly raised eyebrows as he holds the parlor door open.

"What do you say to Mr. Adam for bringing us here for milkshakes?" Mouse urges Jack and Camille softly. She turns her gaunt face and mouths *"I'm sorry"* to Beulah, who must wait outside according to the sign posted in the window that says:

NO

COLOREDS

"Thank youuu, Mr. Adammm," the kids sing in an obedient half-hearted chorus.

Having witnessed Mr. Adam's unpredictability, Camille hides her face in her mother's blouse; the bells on her toddler shoes jingle. Jack grips Mouse's skirt as they enter, partially hidden behind her far-too-thin frame.

Standing to the side and in the heat, Beulah frowns from having to bear way too much of this conniving weasel's presence for the sake of her fragile friend and her four-year-old son.

"I can bring a milkshake outside if you'd like," Adam tells Beulah just before he steps through the door, surely to let her know that he sees her disapproval. "Let me guess—" He raises his chin in the air and taps it jokingly. "You want yourself a nice cold . . . *black-and-white*, don't ya?"

He snickers, letting the glass door close behind him and stemming the flow of cool air.

Unable to stand any more abuse, Beulah tearfully walks back to the house with pounding steps. "How could she let that man in?!" she huffs, shaking her head.

In Vinny's chair? In his bed? Near our children?

She sheds all her hurt feelings and powers of reasoning onto three pages of paper, and packs her bags. On her way out, she leans the letter against Mouse's favorite coffee mug.

Hoping to still have some contact with Jack and with no home to return to, Beulah heads to Mama Rosella's, who is happy to have company to feed. Mama Rosella welcomes her into the laboratory, better known as her kitchen.

"Please sit down and tell Mama what the bad man did now," she says, pouring Beulah a glass of lemonade.

"He is simply a snake in da grass," Beulah says, shaking her angry head as she sits. "Mouse tinks da badge on his chest will keep her and de children safe? Bah!"

Mama pours herself a glass and sits across from Beulah, nodding. "She look-a so sick the last time I saw her."

"Yes . . . he keeps her and de kids so nervous wit' dat explosive temper he got."

Mama slams her arthritic hand down on the table. "My Vincent would break-a his neck for this!"

Beulah sighs. "I tried to tell Mouse dat Adam is de bad news, but she won't hear it." The letter she left for Mouse flashes in her mind. Maybe this time will be different.

"Beulah?" Mouse calls through the house when she returns to find all of her friend's things gone. "Beulah . . . ?"

While she puts the children down for their naps, Adam finds the letter Beulah left for Mouse and crumples it, folding his hand into a triumphant fist.

"I can't believe she left like that," Mouse says, dissolving into a chair at the kitchen table. "She was so much help to me . . . I don't know what I'll do without her."

The doubled paper bag serving as a trash bin crinkles when Adam grabs it from under the sink and stuffs the letter inside. "The trash is full. I'm going to take it outside. Don't worry about a thing, doll. You have a man around the house now."

She lifts her head out of her hands. "Do I?"

Adam hesitates, rolling the top of the bag. "Sure," he says with a shrug. "That is, if you want one."

Her brows draw together and her stomach flutters with moths. "Oh . . . Adam . . . is that a proposal?"

He shrugs. "I don't have a ring or nothin, but yeah, sure, we could get hitched."

Mouse bites her lip, looking down at the golden band that her Vinny put there the spring of '34 with so much love, and cocks her head. "I hadn't really considered it before . . ."

"I'll let you think about it, but don't take forever and a day. You're getting long in the tooth with two extra mouths in tow," Adam says, and leaves to get rid of Beulah's last effort to thwart his presence in their lives.

When he comes back inside, Mouse is back to searching high and low, picking up various items around the room.

"Did you lose something?" he asks.

"I just can't believe she left without saying goodbye or leaving a note . . . or something."

"Face it, doll. She left your ass high and dry. It's time you learned that you can't trust those kind of people."

She turns to him. "And what kind of people would that be?"

"Don't be naïve. You know exactly what I'm talking about."

Mouse musters up the courage to do something rare—she scowls at him.

He takes no notice, instead clapping his hands together and exclaiming, "We should drink a toast to our engagement!" Adam pulls the last jar of Vincent's homemade wine from the cupboard, spins the metal ring of the lid, pops the seal, and pours them both a glass. He shakes his head and laughs. "Hell, my friends already think I'm a saint for helping you out as much as I do. Wait until they find out we're gonna be married." He offers her one of the glasses with a scary, wide grin.

Mouse moves to take the offering, then stops; her face goes slack and her eyes blink rapidly. "But . . . I didn't say yes yet."

"In this economic weather, combining our households makes solid practical sense. What's there to think about?" He shoves the drink into her hand and forces their glasses together with a dull clink. "Cheers!" he says, knocks back a swig, and wipes away a drip by his mouth with the back of his hand, like a kid enjoying the first taste of sweet tea on a hot summer afternoon.

Mouse doesn't take a drink. "I . . . I have to see what Beulah thinks."

His face and his throat go tight as he turns to set his celebratory drink on the countertop, hands drawing into tight fists. "Why do we care what *she* thinks? This has nothing to do with her."

"Of course it does! You don't understand."

Adam wags a finger in Mouse's face and snarls, "*You* need to understand *this.*" He plants a hand on the table and leers above her. "We don't need that stupid high-yellow bitch hanging around here no more."

Her face flushes red. "Don't you call her that!" she yells.

Her eyes grow big as saucers moments before Adam's open hand strikes her cheekbone and knocks her out of the chair.

"Don't you ever raise your voice to me like that again!" He kicks the chair and paces in front of her. "Why are you always trying to ruin our special moments?"

"I'm sorry," Mouse whimpers, cowering on the floor with her eyes closed, listening to his raging footfalls until the front door finally slams and the house falls into silence.

For a while, Mouse is relieved. After some time, she can finally hear the quiet ticking of the clock over the heartbeat in her ears. She hopes he stays gone, never to come back—until she spies an envelope on the floor containing a milk delivery bill that is already past due.

Friday
July 31, 1942

Beulah knocks on Mouse's front door. No answer except from the neighborhood dogs barking in the distance. She cups her hands over the pane of a nearby window only to see that the curtains are drawn tight.

"Is anybody home?" she calls out and knocks again, then presses her ear to Mouse's front door to listen for signs of life inside. She can hear Adam's deep voice telling Mouse to shut her trap. Having given up perhaps too easily on the other attempts, Beulah bangs her fist hard on the door with a renewed determination.

"I'm not leaving until I see my family, *ree-Shard*!"

Adam opens the door as far as the newly installed chain lock allows. "You don't have any family here, half-breed. Leave."

Beulah's eyes dart around his bulk in the doorway, searching for a glimpse of Jack. "It has been weeks now. Please let me in. I need ta speak ta Mouse."

"She is my wife now, and I say she don't need to see your kind."

Adam smiles in satisfaction at Beulah's horrified expression, her eye bulging and her hand having flown to her mouth. Nauseated from the shock, Beulah fans her face and lets out a long, shaky exhalation. She tries again.

"I need ta know dat she's all right. Please let her come to de door and talk to me," she begs with glossy eyes.

"And what if I don't? You gonna call the police? Bitch, I *am* the police."

"Please, Adam. I only need to see her for a minute, and den I will leave."

"One minute?" he repeats, rubbing the back of a finger along his lower lip in itchy contemplation of her terms. "And then you'll leave?"

"Yes, sah," Beulah agrees.

He leaves the doorway.

Mouse soon appears in the crack of the door. She is sweaty, shaky, and pale.

"What de hell were you tinking?" Beulah hisses, shaking her head. "You a grown woman making some bad choices. You need to give me dose babies. I want my son outta dere right now! Let me take dem wit' me to Mama Rosella's!"

Unable to look Beulah in the eye, Mouse blinks, and a few silent tears fall to the floor as she listens.

"You don't even need to pack em up!" Beulah presses. "Just give dem to me . . . right *now*!"

Mouse nods and leaves the door to comply. Beulah dances anxiously at the door, waiting to lay eyes on her son for the first time in a month.

A moment later, the door closes, making Beulah's heart flutter . . . followed by the sound of the chain dragging and unhooking before the door opens again.

"What the hell are you trying to do now?" Adam pulls Mouse away from the door.

Behind them, Jack herds Camille to the corner of the room and stands guard in front of her. The sight of this breaks Beulah's heart.

Mouse raises her hands, head down, and backs away in learned proactive self-defense. "Let Beulah have the kids. I'll stay . . . but let her have the kids."

Like a red-assed primate bowing up for a fight, Adam's chest inflates with outrage and he bares his teeth to Mouse. "Those are *my* kids now, woman! I'm going to adopt them and give them my name."

Beulah's nostrils flare, and she boldly enters the house against Adam's wishes. "Over my dead body!" she replies with an animalistic growl in her throat.

"Trust me, lady—that can be arranged."

"Let her have Jack and she'll leave!" Mouse says, lowering herself to the floor, trying desperately to turn down the heat in the room.

Adam stops and jerks his head back. "What? Just Jack?" he asks and clinches his jaw, looking to every pair of eyes in the room for an answer that would clear up his confusion. "Why in the world would you let this crossbreed woman have Jack? My son?"

Mouse bites her lip and buries her face in her hands, unable to answer. Adam watches Beulah's face flicker with worry as he walks over to the boy.

"Don't you dare touch him!" she warns, inching closer, ready to pounce at any second.

Little Jack stands with small fists wide in front of Camille, for all his size managing to look like a vicious bulldog ready to attack.

Adam laughs nastily at Jack while rubbing his stubbled jawline. "You're a tough little fucker, aren't you? You sure don't get that from your mother," he says—and then it hits: an inkling of recognition, noticing an identical fire in Jack's and Beulah's eyes. "Or maybe you do . . ."

Mouse sits on the floor, useless, peeking through her laced fingers.

"Come on, Jack, let's go," Beulah says, her hand reaching out for his.

Jack's fierce eyes never leave Adam as he slowly shakes his head. His lip curls in defiance and he says in a voice that somehow no longer sounds small, "I'm not going anywhere without Camille, Miss Beulah."

Adam casually tosses an object out at Beulah, as if he were pitching her a softball. She reflexively catches it and looks down—his brown leather wallet sits in her hands. Adam uses the distraction to suddenly point his cocked service revolver at her.

Everyone freezes. The loud whining sound of a siren approaches.

"Oh, did I forget to mention I called for backup?" he jeers. "Over your dead body, was that how you put it? Happy to be of service."

The gun is steady in his hand, still trained on Beulah's face. Beads of sweat break out on her forehead.

Adam raises his voice theatrically. *"Please, don't hurt my family!"* he yells—

And pulls the trigger.

As he fires, Adam feels Jack's canine's clamp down on his

outstretched arm. Furious, Adam scrambles after the agile and slippery boy, planning to pistol-whip him to a bloody pulp; but before he's able to exact any harsh punishment, two officers arrive breathless in the doorway.

Beulah has vanished, leaving splatters of blood on the floor where she was shot.

Mouse, Jack, and Camille huddle together on the floor, crying.

"The guy must have dropped this on his way out," a tall, thin officer with a large beak-like nose announces, handing Adam back his wallet.

"It was a female perp," he corrects, adding, "with a knife."

"Really?" The officer raises his eyebrows.

He lowers his beak and his pen to begin recording the details of the crime as Adam concocts the perfect scenario, rewriting history to cover his own sneaky coup.

Hours later, in the Brown Bomber Bar, Adam rakes his fingers through his hair as he nervously paces, facing the expectant bartender.

"Where's my goddamned money, Adam?"

Carlos impatiently taps his fingers on the bar. Behind Carlos, Old Joe is listening as he slowly counts the money in the drawer, making sure there is plenty of change for the Friday night crowd.

"I picked up the haul from the runners, like I always do," Adam says, trying to repeat his lie again from the beginning. "I'm still on my honeymoon, in case you forgot—and as such, I went by the house to check on my wife. Out of nowhere some mongrel bitch with a knife shows up and takes the bag. I tagged her ass on the way out of my house. We have all of our guys on it, so she won't get too far."

Carlos's fingers stop their tapping. "First of all, why was my money sitting idle at your house? And secondly, do you really expect me to believe some crazy dame stole a whole week's take?"

"I swear," Adam says, pausing from his pacing to place a hand on his chest. "You have to believe me! Ask anyone in the department. I'm going to nail her to the wall for you, Carlos. That half-nigger cunt won't get away with this!"

Angered yet keeping his cool, Old Joe slams the drawer closed and moves toward Adam, licking his lips, ready to teach him a lesson in respect. Carlos reaches out, holding Joe back with his arm.

"Sorry, no offense, Joe," Adam says, raising his hands and shaking his head. "I'm just so upset."

Carlos taps Old Joe on the back and tells him, "Go walk it off." Cocking his head at Adam, Carlos says, "So wait . . . do you know this dame who ripped me off?"

Adam, caught off guard by the question, lifts a shoulder. "She's that spooky Laveau lady."

Before he walks calmly outside, Old Joe hears Carlos ask, "Don't you dare yank my chain on this, boy! Are you sure?"

Once outside, Joe breaks into a full run for the drugstore several blocks away.

Old Joe grips the phone in the booth at the drug store. "You gonna be all right?"

"Yeah," Beulah's voice soothes through the receiver. "Luckily de bastard only nicked mah shoulder. Mama Rosella wrapped it up for me. It should heal up fine."

"I gotta get back befo' we open. But I needed you to know right away. I want you to leave right now, ya hear? And stay good and low for a while. Having Carlos after you is much mo' dangerous than any iron box the police can put you in."

"I know. I wanta avoid dem bot' if I can. I'd be dead either way."

"Take care of yo' self. I'll see what we can do to fix this."

"I'll find a way to keep in touch. Tank you so much, Joe. Bye," Beulah says in haste, and hangs up.

Old Joe lingers on the phone with a painful lump in his throat, wishing he had said more . . . so much more.

Tuesday
February 8, 1944

When the policemen sent to track down Beulah cannot get any information out of Mama Rosella, she finds herself detained for eighteen months in a large internment camp for foreign undesirables in Crystal City, Texas, where she dies, on this unusually cold, rainy day in February, of pneumonia and a lonely broken heart.

Friday
November 24, 1944

For two years, unable to psychically read any information concerning the members of her family, and her usual clairvoyant insights refusing to shed any light, Beulah eagerly grasps at updates about her loved ones from Old Black Joe each week, either by phone or in person.

Joe, eager for his own reasons, often fictionalizes what Jack is up to. Ferreting clear intel on the boy isn't always possible, but the meetings must continue, he decides . . . they must. Besides, hearing little crumbs (no matter how small) of positive news about her boy does Beulah a world of good.

Mouse, meanwhile, has fully embraced her name—she scurries about in her daily chores, delicately avoiding traps set to spring at every turn, her presence rarely seen or heard by neighbors in the stark light of day.

Jack, rapidly approaching the malleable age of seven, goes about his days seeking Mouse's approval, avoiding his stepfather's wrath, and attempting to find answers to Camille's endless barrage of questions (followed by her inevitable and sometimes infuriating Whys?).

Adam's psyche spirals out of control after losing his position (lucky that was all he lost, but he doesn't see it that way) in the

Marcello organization—expelled from his main income source because of the missing money and unsolved status of the so-called "robbery." Amidst his steady slide into an alcohol- and drug-enhanced psychosis, he suffers an embarrassing demotion at work for reasons he refuses to disclose to Mouse, concealing as best he can the increasingly bizarre depths of his depravity. After he whores, gambles, and gobbles his way through the money he's kept hidden beneath a board in the closet, he lashes out at Mouse and the children, making a new malicious decree with every sullen mood swing.

At Adam's insistence, Mouse takes a laborious, sweaty job surrounded by large machines in the Hotel Monteleone's linen-management department. He also convinces her to allow six-year-old Jack to hand out a stack of newspapers on the corner for three cents a pop every weekday morning before school.

Today Jack's loud, hungry belly rumbles for whatever breakfast he can find when he walks back into the house. Startled by Jack's unannounced arrival, Adam readjusts himself on the end of the couch and yells, "Scram, kid! Go play in traffic or something!"

Acclimated now to his stepfather's constant abusive ways, Jack ignores the hurtful words and makes a beeline for the kitchen. Once there, he smears a pat of butter on some cold, stale bread left over from yesterday's pitifully small Thanksgiving feast.

What Jack does pay attention to is the strange vibration of suspense in the living room. He takes a bite and looks around, noticing Camille's motionless figure on the opposite end of the couch from Adam. Messy hair covers her face as she stares down at the empty, open hands in her lap. Jack's heart aches; he can't remember the last time he heard his little sister's giddy laughter.

Adam rises from the couch and takes a few steps to click the knob on the radio. "Don't you have somewhere to be?" he says to Jack, sliding the tuning dial across the airwaves and back again.

"No school today. I go back on Monday," Jack replies, his right cheek bulging, working his jaw against the unrelenting crust.

Ignoring him, Adam clicks the radio back off and grabs his pea coat. "Your mom will be back soon, princess. Daddy needs to run an errand," he says, waving his fingers in Camille's direction. She doesn't look up.

Adam gives a stern glance of warning to Jack as he exits. If anything were to happen to Camille, even a denial to play teatime with her, there would be hell to pay. Today Jack would gladly play teatime, even wear a silly bonnet, if it would make his sister smile. He slowly moves to the couch and sits beside her. Camille throws herself across his lap and begins to bawl. Not knowing what else to do, he hums a lullaby and smooths her hair, like their mother might have done if she were there. He doesn't ask her what's wrong, and she doesn't tell him.

Camille's tears have all but dried by the time Mouse comes home with a smorgasbord of Thanksgiving leftovers she has skimmed from the restaurant at work.

With memories of better times, Jack helps set the table with Mama Rosella's good china and bows his head in prayer for his small fractured family before passing the ham. The air seems easier to breathe as Mouse and Jack begin to recall this and that, unpacking the past and sharing some joy-filled laughter with Camille. A few treasured moments of peace and normalcy without Adam.

Wednesday
August 22, 1945

Earlier this month the namesake of Enola Gay Tibbets—a Boeing B-29 Superfortress bomber piloted by her son—unleashed "Little Boy" on the Japanese city of Hiroshima, quickly followed by "Fat Man" on Nagasaki (this one dropped by the B-29 christened *Bockscar*). Two atomic bombs aimed at one enemy, deemed a necessary evil by many, a righteous wrath exploding with radioactive fury, the delivery of swift devastation in lieu of negotiation.

Jack now reads and comprehends the papers he dispenses, extrapolating that surprise attacks and heavy-handed punishments seem to be a growing trend the whole world over—surrender or be annihilated.

On this muggy Wednesday afternoon, banished to the outside for talking back again, Jack watches his wide neighbor, Mrs. Eleanor, rock her way down the street on two sore hips, carrying a brown paper sack of groceries. She once told him the story about how she loved an ornery horse named Bucky, but he didn't love her back . . . or her hips, for that matter.

Jack bounds from his punishment on the stoop to help her the rest of the way.

"Oh, thank you . . . kindly, young . . . man"—Mrs. Eleanor huffs and puffs, out of breath between words—"I don't know *what* I was . . .

thinking going out in the heat of the day. Let's go . . . inside and have a glass of lemonade . . . shall we?"

He sits the heavy sack on her counter, as he has done many times before, and looks at the shelf of figurines—mostly flowers and animals that she carves out of soap.

"What did you do this time?" Mrs. Eleanor says, handing him a glass of lemonade. She rubs his sweaty head affectionately.

He sets his drink on the counter untouched. "What's a"—Jack wrinkles his nose—"a 'nigger'?"

She chokes on her lemonade. After recovering, she replies, "Why the heck would you ask me *that*?"

Jack reaches out to feel the grooves on the back of an Ivory soap turtle. "My dad calls me that sometimes when he's mad, but I don't know why." He crosses his arms behind his back and lowers his head. "Is it a bad word?"

She pauses before saying, "The word itself is just a word . . . but the hate that most people throw around with it is the meanest kind. The next time your dad says it, young man, I want you to pretend he called you a professor."

Jack lifts his head and cocks it. "You mean like a teacher?"

Mrs. Eleanor smiles. "*Better* than a teacher," she says, and lifts a finger in the air. "A teacher of teachers!"

He snorts. "I'm not that smart."

"You are what you believe you are, young man. Whatever you tell yourself over and over again will come to pass . . . good or bad. Let's make it all good things." She pokes a finger in his side. "Shall we?"

"I guess so," he says unconvincingly, squirming away from her finger in his ribs.

Mrs. Eleanor picks up a carved alligator from the back of her collection, knowing that it is his favorite. She places it in his hand and folds his small fingers around it. "This is yours now, Professor. Keep it close. Mama gators protect their young with ferocity."

"What's fur-ocity?" he asks.

When she laughs, Jack's cheeks burn, and he flashes Mrs. Eleanor a harsh squint.

"I'm sorry! The question struck me as sincere in a funny way, that's all. 'Ferocity' means that mama gator loves them young'uns a whole bunch," she explains, and lowers her eyes, adding, "She loves them enough to *kill*."

Jack's mouth twists in a mope. "I wish *I* was a gator," he says with eyes that become cloudy with introspection as he rolls the figurine in his hand. Adam's voice from outside startles him; his head pops up and he moves to leave, then turns to her and says, sincerely, "Thank you."

She winks. "Remember what I told you—*professor*, you got that?"

"Yes, ma'am!" he calls, scrambling out the door. He stuffs the soap alligator in his pocket—next to the red Lifebuoy soap rose he swiped as a present for Camille's birthday tomorrow.

For the rest of the nation and most of the world, the war is coming to an end; but Jack, clever and ever more devious, begins mentally and physically fortifying himself for the war—*his* war, waiting on the horizon, yet to be officially declared.

Friday
September 3, 1948

"**We need a** thirty-pounder," Big Lou calls out to the ambitious and muscular ten-year-old summer hire, recently turned full-time assistant, in the rear of the delivery truck.

"Yes, sir." Jack quickly bites into the sides of a slippery block of ice with a sharp set of tongs and slides it to the outer edge of the truck bed. When Big Lou takes over and swivels the heavy block around, Jack flashes the man a look of disappointment.

"Boy, you know damn well this block weighs more than you do," Big Lou says, chuckling good-naturedly. "I'll let you bring the tens, maybe even a twenty, but anything more than that is too much for you. I don't care how strong you think you are." He slings the block of ice over his shoulder, where it lands with a soft *thud!* on the leather pad he wears to keep from getting soaked. "Don't worry, you'll keep your job. I'll tell the boss what an eager helper you are."

Big Lou knows most of his words fall on deaf ears when it comes to Jack. He has been unsuccessful in convincing him to go back to school. Jack the truant wants to be a grownup; he refuses to be young, equating it with being weak and vulnerable.

Jack pushes his hair away from his stubborn, defiant face with his forearm, watching Big Lou trudge up the driveway of an affluent house in the Garden District. He leans against the interior wall of the truck; with brooding eyes—so much darker than a boy's eyes should be—he stares at a bag of the sharp cutting tools of his new trade, imagining how many alternative uses they could have.

Tuesday
July 12, 1949

Big Lou gives Jack the day off, and for the first time in months, the sun wakes him up instead of the other way around. He stirs in his bed, and a brilliant beam of morning light streams through the window and stabs him in the eye.

Happy birthday to me,

he thinks, shielding himself from the sun as he blinks the sleep away from his eyes. Mouse checked herself into the looney bin over the weekend and sadly, that isn't the only reason Jack will not be interested in an eleventh birthday celebration.

He rubs his face and hears a rustling noise in the kitchen, followed by Camille's distressed and whiny *"Nooo!"* It takes a minute for Jack to remember: he'd promised to take her swimming this morning.

But when he enters the kitchen to find Camille sitting in her peach one-piece suit on the kitchen counter, he's surprised to see Adam, partially in uniform, looming in front of her. It doesn't matter what Adam is saying to her; he's saying it too close, and so disgustingly low and intimate that it turns Jack's stomach.

"What's going on?" he growls.

Startled, Adam backs away from Camille with his hands up, busted. "Well, well, well! If it isn't the birthday boy," he slurs, and wobbles, reeking of cheap whiskey. "Here to crash the party." Still obviously caught by Jack, he sets to wiping imaginary crumbs off the edge of the counter.

Jack moves to Camille and lifts her chin. "Are you okay?"

She says nothing, pulling her chin from his grasp. Clearly embarrassed and ashamed, she slips off the counter and runs out of the room.

"Oh, *now* look what you did!" Adam says. He steps forward and knocks the wind out of Jack and then yanks him back up by his wrists.

"I'll get you fired for this!" Jack yells, fighting uselessly to get away.

"Joke's on you, kid. I can't be fired twice."

With one hand, Adam pulls handcuffs from his belt and locks them above Jack's elbows, then drags him to the coat closet. Jack kicks as best he can, but the door closes anyway, shutting him inside, in the dark. Jack stops struggling to think, and that's when he hears Camille's screams.

"No! Please! Stop!"

He kicks with renewed vigor. The solid door does not give. He lies with his face to the floor until his eyes adjust to the bar of light. Hot, angry tears stream down his face as he wiggles, tugs, and eventually scrapes his skin bloody and raw to get the cuffs to move until his hands are free. Instinct takes Jack over; he's wide awake inside the nightmare, every muscle in his body thrumming with adrenaline as he pounces to the bedroom.

Many hours Jack has spent shivering in the back of the delivery truck, staring at the tools of his trade, imagining how he would play out this next moment—and here it is, finally, *finally*, and he sinks nine inches of a steel icepick deep into the back of Adam's head, as Camille lies helplessly beneath him, her torn bathing suit shoved into her mouth.

A fan of blood spews and splatters across Jack's face. Camille hears a sick gurgle in Adam's throat when Jack removes the gore-coated pick. Adam reaches behind to try to defend himself against Jack's attack, but already his movements are slowing.

Relentless in his frenzy, Jack stabs Adam in his cheek, then in both of his eyes, and rolls him off of Camille. Smeared in the man's blood, she whimpers, pulling herself into the corner of her mother's room, where she barricades herself with a large pillow and removes the cloth gag. Her breath comes out in jagged sobs.

After Jack makes double-damn-sure that Adam is dead, he proceeds to work as if it's all old hat, just another normal day at the office. He gently coaxes Camille from the corner and scrubs her down in the bathtub with soap and water, checking her for blood, while she shivers silently, still in shock. Constantly hyperaware of the clock, he dries Camille off, helps her step into her underwear and her favorite dress, and lovingly combs her hair, whispering soothingly to her.

Jack then turns Camille around, takes her by the shoulders, and looks into her eyes.

"Nothing happened today, okay?"

Camille looks back at him and nods.

"We went swimming and that's all," he says. "I want you to go over to Mrs. Eleanor's house. You're going to be fine now. I need you to stay there."

"But—"

"What did I say?" Jack says, giving Camille a gentle shake. "You're safe now! I need you to do this. Okay?"

She nods, kisses him on the cheek, and does as requested.

Jack picks up the phone and dials the number to the main office at work.

"Icehouse, Mike speaking."

"Hey, Mike, it's Jack. Did Lou come by to refill the truck yet?" he asks, crossing his fingers. "I need to tell him something important."

"Lemme check," Mike says, and makes a rustling sound with the receiver. "Anybody seen Big Lou? Jack's on the phone," Mike hollers out into the truck yard. "He's coming," Mike says into the phone, and places it on the desk.

After what feels like a week of listening to papers rustle and Mike fart away his breakfast, Lou picks up the receiver. "I thought I told you no work today, birthday boy."

"Listen up, Lou. I'm in big trouble."

"What kind?"

"The messiest, go-up-the-river-forever kind."

A pause. "Where are you?"

"Home."

"Stay there," Big Lou says, then presses firmly on the switch hook for a second or two to disconnect and get a new dial tone. Lou's hand shakes as he dials the number of an old friend, knowing he can help, but also knowing that in the end, Jack may not be all that grateful.

Within the hour, there is a knock. When he opens the door, it isn't Lou. This man makes Big Lou look like Medium Lou. Jack's jaw drops at the large, bald, muscular man filling the doorway, wearing white clothes covered by a white blood-smeared apron, and carrying a big black tool bag.

"I'm the Butcher. Show me the problem," he says, devoid of any emotion—or hair, not even eyebrows.

Jack just blinks, staring at the blood on his apron. It's much darker than the blood he's just scrubbed from Camille.

The Butcher shrugs and enters. "I work at a slaughterhouse. No one ever questions the blood." He puts his tool bag down and pulls out two pairs of rubber gloves, tossing a pair at Jack and rolling the other set onto his large, smooth hands. "We aren't going to be friends, so we don't need to know each other's names," he says, clapping his gloved hands together, snapping Jack out of his stupor. "Let's get to work!"

"Yes . . . yes, sir. This way," Jack says, fumbling with his own gloves. He sharply inhales, wincing from the pain his biceps cause beneath his torn skin. He opens and closes his gloved fists, thinking:

All Adam's fault . . . but I'm not done with him yet.
Not done at all.

Fascinated and inquisitive, Jack pays close attention to the step-by-step instructions, gorging himself on all the vital information that the Butcher divulges about the process of stubborn pest removal and cleanup, more focused than on any lesson he was ever taught in school. Together they transfer Adam's body to the bathtub for de-identification and limb separation. The Butcher explains how and where to cut, and which tools to use.

"Always work from top to bottom. We will knock out all the top teeth, then remove the bottom jaw bone. Then we cut through the neck, the wrists, the shoulders, the hips, the ankles."

"Can I start it off?" Jack asks, holding a hammer and chisel. His wounds throb and weep with every movement, still seething with vengeance as he climbs into the tub.

"Sure, just work fast," the Butcher says, tossing in a bonesaw before taping the shower curtain to the wall and the tub, sealing Jack and the bloody mess up inside the small containment area.

You brought this on yourself, you son of a bitch!

he thinks, spitting in the face of a tyrant who had caused so much pain.

It takes hours of careful cleanup and preparation to be ready for nightfall. All evidence removed, Jack feels as if his decency was dismantled along with Adam's evil flesh, his innocence liquidated and rinsed down the drain along with blood evidence, learning that to expel one demon is to unlock all of hell. His body is squeaky clean, his soul permanently stained.

Slowly closing the cargo door to the unmarked truck, the Butcher wipes his brow and looks down at industrious little Jack, impressed with the boy's skills at having powered through nearly half the work himself. "It's Tuesday. My mama makes meatloaf on Tuesdays, and we need to eat. Get in the cab," he says, and it sounds more like an order than a friendly offer.

After the day he has had, Jack considers becoming a vegetarian, but his tummy puts up a strong argument in favor of Mama Butcher's Tuesday meatloaf.

"I don't know how to thank you for this," Jack says as they climb into the truck cab.

"I wouldn't thank me just yet. I haven't been paid, and I don't work for free." The Butcher cranks the engine and checks the gas level. "I own you," he adds nonchalantly.

Jack is too tired, hungry, and curious to be afraid of the consequences ahead. "Couldn't we have just taken him somewhere whole or buried him in the backyard?"

"Too risky. I like to spread it out. I never leave a body to be found and identified—unless I'm sending a message and there is some kind of art in it," the Butcher professes with an air of pomposity, rolling out of the driveway before turning on the headlights. "And I never leave a trace that will lead the cops to me."

The house is left sparkling, cleaner than it has ever been before, bleach fumes strong enough to make the air sting and the paint curl. Body parts have been removed under the cover of darkness, unwrapped from layers of thick butcher paper, deposited in various vats of sulfuric acid, the task complete.

Wednesday
July 13, 1949

Barely nine in the morning, the tree in the yard is still twittering with birdsong. Fresh bandages hide beneath the long sleeves of Jack's shirt as he walks gingerly on the concrete driveway that is already steaming beneath the summer sun's relentless rays. He listens to the truck's engine running with an impatient purr, and the horn gives a short blast, making him jump. Every muscle and injury, even ones he didn't know he had, screams out in pain when he lifts himself back into the cab of the truck after a decent night's sleep—or what might be better described as an after-work coma.

The Butcher sits in the driver's seat, eating a cold hunk of leftover meatloaf between two pieces of bread. "You sure you don't want any breakfast?" he asks, muffled by his full mouth.

Jack's stomach lurches seeing the Butcher's tongue-tossed meal in all its glory. "No, thanks. I'm good."

"Suit yourself," the Butcher says with a one-shoulder shrug. He throws the truck into gear.

Jack's mind wanders, imagining a peaceful new life, until he looks around and doesn't recognize his surroundings. "Where we going?"

"To see the man who hired me and get my money."

"Good." Jack sighs with relief. "I need to thank Big Lou for saving my ass."

The Butcher's hairless brow creases. "Who's Big Lou?"

Jack glances at him. "Don't go breaking my balls."

"Trust me, I'm not. I was told to deliver you for payment as soon as I could, so that is what I'm doing," the Butcher says flatly, watching the road ahead.

Jack's hair rises at his nape and along his arms.

"*Deliver* me?" he whispers to himself.

He hopes for an opportunistic red light along the way, and rolls down the window, watching the pavement pass by in a blur. He grows considerably more anxious with each mile, playing around with the idea of jumping from the moving vehicle, when the truck slows down and pulls behind a shiny burgundy Cadillac.

The car is being wiped down with a cloth by a nicely dressed black man who stops, looks up, and lazily walks toward the truck.

Jack's hand is poised on the door lever, ready to make a break, when the Butcher wraps his large fingers around the back of Jack's scrawny neck. "Don't even think about it, boy. Old Black Joe there can run as fast as Jesse Owens."

"Dis here's the package we expectin?" the black man says, looking in at Jack with disappointed recognition. He scratches one of his graying temples. "Kinda small, ain't he?"

"It is what it is," replies the Butcher, letting go of Jack. "Keep your eye on him, Joe. He's a flight risk." The big man steps down from the driver's seat and slams the truck door behind him. Jack feels the Butcher's eyes cut into him before he disappears into the Brown Bomber Bar.

Jack's shoulders slump as Joe opens the passenger door. "Looks like you done peed the carpet, Scruffy," he says, reaching out to ruffle Jack's hair—just like Vincent used to do.

Jack pulls away with an angry pout and smooths his hair back down. "My name's not Scruffy."

"Well, excuse me," Joe laughs. "What should I call you then?"

Jack hesitates, missing Vincent—Vinny—missing the kindest man he ever met, the only man he ever trusted, the only man he ever loved.

"Vinny. My name is Vinny."

"Mmm-hmmm," Old Joe vocalizes sarcastically in the back of his throat, knowing different. "Are you a good worker, Mista Vinny?"

"The best," he replies with confidence.

Joe hands him the polishing cloth. "Show me."

Baptized by bleach and blood, newly christened *Vinny* hops out and steps over to the Cadillac. He takes over rubbing the water speckles from the Cadillac's hide and metal to a clear mirror finish. Joe sits on a barstool in the shade beneath the roofline of the bar, his arms folded, watching the sore-muscled boy wince and grunt through the assignment.

Inside the Brown Bomber, behind the closed office door, Carlos Marcello is captivated by the Butcher's briefing on the previous day's events. He tosses a wad of cash on the desk.

"Good riddance. You can have him," the Butcher says, counting his pay. He stuffs the money in his pocket, watching Carlos pour him a nip of cheap whiskey. "That kid scares me. When he took the bonesaw to the subject . . . I ain't seen nothing like it my whole life." He pauses to throw the shot down his throat, and shakes his head. "The boy spit in his father's face and then hacked him to pieces. It took me years to get that cold."

"What's his name? The kid?"

"I don't know and I don't want to know," the Butcher admits, clearly ready to conclude the transaction.

Carlos chuckles, rubbing his dimpled chin.

"What's so funny'?"

"I can't tell if you're really afraid of him or if you're just a bit jealous."

"Jealous?"

"You said it yourself—the boy's already a few years ahead. He might put you out of business when his balls drop."

The Butcher shakes his head. "There's something off about that kid. If you get him into this business, the devil himself will be afraid."

Outside, when the heat becomes too much for Vinny, he rests his body against the car.

Joe lights up a cigarette. "You best stop leanin on dat car, boy—it jus' got cleaned."

Vinny snaps up straight away from the car. "It's so hot out here."

Joe opens the door to the bar and calls into the darkness, "Hey, somebody in there bring me a pitcher of ice water!"

"Why do they call you Old Black Joe?" Vinny asks. "You don't look all that old."

"That's so folks don't go gettin me confused wit' Old White Joe down the block." He laughs, pointing to a corner down the road.

A tall female opens the door. She has long eyelashes and the front of her wavy red hair pinned neatly in victory rolls. She hands a glass pitcher to Joe. Wowed by her good looks, Vinny tries to look cool and leans against the car again.

"Well, who do we have here?" she asks. Stepping out onto the sidewalk, she bends down a little as if she were talking about a puppy. Vinny gets a closer look at her smooth, milky skin.

"Peggy, dis here be my new friend, Vinny Car-lean-o," Old Joe says with a wink and a smirk. He walks over to Vinny and hands him the ice water. Vinny narrows his eyes and purses his lips, taking the pitcher. Joe bends closer to his ear to whisper, "Your last name's gonna be Mud if you don't stop leanin on dis here car."

In a few minutes, Carlos emerges with the Butcher behind him. When Carlos lays eyes on Vinny, he starts to laugh and point. "*That* kid? That kid right there?"

"Don't say I didn't warn you," the Butcher mutters under his breath. He walks to the truck and refuses to make any kind of eye contact as he drives away.

Dehydrated, abandoned, and a little bit scared, Vinny gulps down half of the ice water, experiencing the stabbing nerve pain of a frozen brain.

Peggy saves the pitcher from the boy's hands as they go slack. She rubs his back and says, "Oh, honey, you shouldn't drink so fast."

"Who's your friend, Peggy?" Carlos asks.

"We just met. This is Vinny Carlino," Peggy announces.

Vinny's head pops up to glare at Old Joe, who hides his giggle behind his hand and shrugs.

"Well, hello, Vinny Carlino. I'm Carlos," the man says, holding out his hand. Vinny gives it a firm shake. "It looks like you owe me some money, pal. Let's go inside and talk shop."

"Ya'll play nice and I'll go pick up some sandwiches for you boys. It's almost lunchtime," Peggy offers, batting her lovely eyelashes. Carlos frowns, but digs in his pocket and hands over the car keys anyway. She squeals, kisses him on the cheek, and wiggles off to climb inside the newly sparkling Caddy.

Vinny follows Carlos into the office. "Have a seat," Carlos orders, and sits on the corner of the desk facing him. Carlos studies the boy's face, knowing he has seen those features before . . . but where?

After a few minutes, Vinny squirms under Carlos's scrutiny and in the intense, uncomfortable silence.

"You're gonna have to disappear," Carlos says finally, and reaches for a fat, document-sized envelope. "Don't worry. It's all been arranged. A job is waiting for you in Arizona."

Vinny leans forward with pleading eyes. "But . . . sir, I have a sister to take care of."

"You won't be able to take care of her from Juvie, son." Carlos puts a hand on his shoulder. "I'm going to make up a good story and sell it to the cops. You gotta skip town until this thing blows over.

Everything you need is in this envelope." Carlos stands up, places the fat envelope on the desk in front of Vinny, and raps his knuckles on the desk.

Vinny stares warily at the envelope as if it might bite him. "I don't think I can do this—not without knowing that my sister will be all right."

"The way I see it, you got no choice," Carlos says, sniffing the length of an unlit cigar. "You're gonna catch the two o'clock bus to Phoenix and you're gonna do what you're told until your debt to me is paid."

"But Camille is only eight years old," Vinny pleads, and rakes his fingers through his hair.

Carlos exhales in frustration, reluctantly sets his cigar down, picks up a tablet and a pencil, and tosses them to the boy. "Write down whatever I need to know about this kid, and I'll make sure she's properly looked after while you're gone. Scout's honor."

Not exactly relieved, Vinny scribbles the information as fast as he can.

"Yoo-*hoo*, boys," Peggy sings from just outside the office. "I have some delicious muffulettas out here for you."

Carlos looks at the busy pencil in Vinny's hand. "Wrap it up. You heard the lady. Lunch is ready."

Vinny lays the pencil down, rises from the chair, and picks up the envelope.

Carlos folds Vinny's note, puts it in his pocket, and sweeps his powerful arm. "After you."

"Sit here, Vinny," Peggy says, patting the span of bar in front of her.

His eyes light up as she places a large, pie-shaped slice of the thickest sandwich he has ever seen, so thick he imagines having to unhinge his jaw to take a bite. Famished, he slowly works his way through his first muffuletta, savoring each and every crumb. Last one to finish, he is suddenly embarrassed when he feels all eyes upon him, having an audience of three as he licks the savory remnants from his fingers.

"Man, you was hungry," Old Joe says to Vinny. "Look like a stray that ain't been fed in a week."

Carlos grunts, picking at his teeth with the tine of an olive fork.

Peggy giggles, takes his empty plate, and asks, "What grade will you be in this fall, Vinny?"

Vinny squirms and looks to Carlos for the answer.

"He don't *need* school, Peggy," Carlos says, playfully hooking his elbow around Vinny's neck. "This boy has been in school since the day he was born. He knows the game, don't you, boy?" Carlos knocks Vinny's chin with a soft mock punch.

Vinny grins, feeling accepted by this man—as is, warts and all.

Carlos frowns, looking down at his watch. "It's about that time. I have some calls to make this afternoon," he says, and pats Vinny's note in his pocket. "So, kid, Old Joe is going to drive you over to the bus station, and make sure you get on the right road."

Vinny nods obediently, hoping that means Carlos will be busy honoring his promise to protect Camille.

Carlos offers Vinny a deep sigh and a thoughtful expression, and lays his large hands on Vinny's narrow yet broadening shoulders. "If you work hard, you should be square in a few months. When you get back in town, I want you to look me up. I intend to keep you employed."

Vinny starts to follow Joe to the door.

"Don't forget this!" Peggy's long legs carry her across the room to hand him the envelope he left on the bar accidentally on purpose (having already learned how easy it is to manipulate women). She embraces Vinny, his face buried in her nineteen-year-old bosom.

"Come on, girl, we gotta shake a leg," Old Joe says impatiently, waiting for her to let go of the boy.

Vinny smiles, enjoying her goodbye hug. He nuzzles against her softness, filling his nose with her floral scent.

Joe rolls his eyes and snickers at Vinny's goofy grin as he leads the way into the alley beside the bar. Parked in the alley is a handsome sumac red Chrysler Town & Country sedan. Joe opens the wood-paneled passenger door. Vinny hesitates, looking in at the strange combination of red leather and Scottish-plaid upholstered seats.

"This is your car?" he asks Joe.

"Do what you're told and the boss'll pay *you* good, too," he says, walking around to fire up the eight-cylinder engine. "Get in. She ain't gonna bite."

Vinny's obstreperous mind keeps him busy and silent on the ride to the bus station. The white-walled tires on the car slowly stop their rotation before Joe throws the gear into Park and turns to Vinny.

"What's your real name, kid?"

Vinny shrugs. "I used to know, but now I'm not so sure." He pauses with a heavy sadness. "I don't think it matters anymore." He opens the door, holding the envelope with his bus tickets and new assignment inside.

"Whatever yo name is," Joe says, "if you find yo' self needing a friend, you got one in Ol' Black Joe." He offers the boy his hand, and Vinny accepts it.

"Carlino does have a nice ring to it," Vinny admits. "I think I'll keep it."

Old Joe gives the boy a kindred wink. "Have yo' self a safe trip now, Mista Carlino."

Saturday
May 6, 1950

The operation **Vinny** joins in Arizona is a lucrative traveling magazine scam. The employees are mostly delinquent youths taught to peddle fake magazine subscriptions door to door. They teach each other to not get caught shoplifting, pickpocketing, and stealing cars—just a few of their deceptive side practices. None of them are in school, but all of them receive a top-notch education—on-the-job training in every form of thievery and sleight of hand.

Vinny, being the quick study that he is, has absorbed more than enough knowledge in these long months to know when someone delivers him a smelly load of bullshit. And no one has ever showed Vinny a bigger bullshit shovel than Quinn, the twenty-two-year-old heathen left in charge of this band of miscreants.

Vinny pushes through the door in a huff into Quinn's flea-infested motel room in Palo Verde. "I know how to add and subtract, asshole," Vinny says fearlessly. "Do the math. I've been keeping track and I know I'm paid up." He slams a piece of paper with his numeric estimations against Quinn's chest.

Among the many skills Vinny has acquired, controlling his hot-headed temper is one he has yet to master. His young, flexible body, combined with weaponry, has proven him dangerous to anyone who sets off his short fuse, and made him a reputation that precedes him.

He is amongst the youngest in the bunch; no one of any age has made fun of Vinny twice.

"Have a drink, Sparky," Quinn laughs nervously. He lets the paper fall to the floor and offers the confrontational youth a bottle of whiskey shaped like a fiddle. "I know the real reason you have a thorn in your paw . . . I hear that gorgeous starlet you're so hot for got hitched today."

Vinny takes the bottle and narrows his eyes. "What the hell are you talking about?" he asks, and takes a swig.

"Elizabeth Taylor. Looks like your doll is off the market, pal," Quinn says with a nasty, satisfied grin.

Vinny dribbles, chokes, and coughs. "Is that lie supposed to distract me or somethin?" he asks, handing back the bottle.

"No lie." Quinn pushes his bottom lip out in a fake pout and crosses his heart with a finger.

Vinny waves him off. "I'll get over it. There's other fish in the sea," he says, shrugging off his injured heart. He reaches down to pick up his ticket to freedom. "Quinn, I need you to look at this."

Squinting and with shaky hands, Quinn lights up a Pall Mall cigarette. "I don't need to look at it." He exhales two smoke trails through his nose, his hand quietly searching for the switchblade in his back pocket. "Your debt to the Little Man of New Orleans has been paid up for some time now."

Vinny blinks. "What? Why wasn't I told?"

"Because technically you're still in debt," Quinn explains, his Adam's apple bobbing. "You still owe the company room and board."

To Quinn's dismay, Vinny doesn't take the bait and leave. Instead, the kid backs away, calmly plops on the bed, and sighs, looking up at the water-stained ceiling.

"If that's the case, I'll never be paid up. None of us will."

"I hope you're not too surprised, kid." Quinn breathes out a small sigh of relief. He puts out his cigarette, sits down beside Vinny, and kindly offers the whiskey bottle again. "We're all bought and sold. It's the American way—some of us will die in a war, the rest of us will die paying for it."

Vinny tips the bottle up in the air and takes a long pull. He wipes his chin and swings the bottle at Quinn's head as hard as he can, making a sick, deep *clunk!* on contact.

He empties Quinn's pockets and trashes the room looking for cash, finding only enough green for a meal or three. Vinny realizes that Quinn wasn't much higher on the food chain. In light of that fact, he feels a pang of remorse for bludgeoning a fellow veteran of the streets.

Without enough money for a bus ticket, Vinny finds himself running on the hot desert terrain alongside an open boxcar of a Southern Pacific train set in motion and gaining momentum. Vinny wants on, to put some miles between him and the life of a common street rat.

"Gimme your hand, boy!"

An old vagrant appears and reaches down to pull him up before they reach the trestle bridge. Vinny locks onto the man's forearm and swings his legs like an Olympic athlete onto the platform, with just enough momentum to roll to safety.

The old man slaps his knee and laughs. "Welcome aboard, sonny boy!" He smiles wide, proudly displaying the few teeth that haven't finished rotting out of his head.

"Thanks for the lift," Vinny says, and gags in the back of his throat. By the old man's wafting fragrance, Vinny can tell that he is either allergic to soap or has been riding the rails quite a while. Vinny has seen a few pictures of Einstein in the news, and this man could pass for his long-lost, less hygienic brother.

"Where we headed?" Vinny asks.

The old man scratches the small bald spot on the crown of his dirty head. "Not real sure where this one goes. East is all I know. But it'll be fun getting there." He reaches inside the coat lying on the floor and pulls out a bottle without a label.

"What is it?"

"I dunno, but there was a half dozen of em over in the crate when I got on this ride in Sacramento. Shared em all but this one here."

He places it in Vinny's hands like a gift from a foreign dignitary. The train whistle blows with excitement as the wheels clack faster against the rails. Vinny holds the bottle with apprehension, examines it, and confirms that it is unmolested.

"Go ahead an' open her up," the old man says, rubbing his hands together and licking his lips.

Vinny cracks the seal, takes a whiff of the highly flammable libation, and cocks an eyebrow. "Are you sure this isn't kerosene?"

"It gets the job done, sonny. That's all that matters." He fidgets, waiting for the boy to pass the bottle. "If nothing else, it'll help us sleep most of the way through Texas."

After a few rounds, Vinny soon forgets the heebie-jeebies of sharing the bottle with the old vagrant. The drink also helps him ignore the angry quake of his empty belly.

Neither of them needing the confining structure of social graces, the two roadies become fast friends, enjoying the cool dry breeze, looking calmly out at the scarlet sky, watching the sun sink low into the west.

Vinny opens and closes the silver nickel Zippo he stole out of Quinn's motel room, loving the sound that it makes.

The old man raises his eyebrows. "You got a pack of sticks to go along with that thing, sonny?"

Vinny digs into his pocket and pulls out a slightly crushed pack of Pall Malls.

The old man's leathery face crinkles with anticipation as he exchanges the bottle for a cigarette. As an afterthought, he says, "Aren't you too young to smoke?"

"Aren't you too old?" Vinny scoffs, leaning over to open the Zippo again and give him a light.

The old man takes a satisfying drag on the cylindrical roll of finely cut tobacco. "You from Palo Verde?" He looks back at the small town in the distance, picking a tiny flake of sun-dried tobacco from his tongue.

"No, I've been traveling around for a while, working."

The old man gives a raspy, hollow laugh. "I used to travel the rails all over the country for work when I was a roustabout with the circus," he says, sweeping the open countryside air with the glowing cherry of his cigarette.

Vinny's mouth falls open with surprise and envy. "Oh, yeah? Which circus?"

The old man straightens his shoulders and puffs out his chest. "The big boys—Barnum and Bailey," he announces. He takes another drag of his cigarette and sighs. "But now I can't get anyone to hire these old bones."

"Why'd you quit?" Vinny asks, passing the bottle back to the old man.

He frowns and looks deep into the neck of the bottle. "I didn't," he admits, and chugs down the alcohol, drowning his regrets. "I loved my job. I left because I did a stupid, stupid thing." He pauses and his eyes fill with painful tears. He tosses the cigarette butt out onto the cactus-speckled dirt and pounds his leg with a self-loathing fist.

Vinny's eyebrows knit together. "Couldn't have been all that bad, could it?

"A bunch of people got hurt," the old man says with a quivering chin. "Thousands . . . mostly women and children."

"What happened?!"

He takes another shot of courage and a long, ragged breath. "Back in '44, we put a paraffin wax coating on the big tent to protect it from the rain. In Hartford, I fell asleep during the performance." His hand cups his mouth and he crumples.

"Go on, get it all out," Vinny says, placing a hand on his shoulder.

The old man surrenders the last of the bottle to Vinny.

"The tent caught fire," he says, tugging at the sides of his wild, fuzzy hair. "I was nearly asleep when I tossed that cigarette butt. I woke up to smoke, flames, and screaming. *Thousands* of people screaming . . ." He falls silent.

Vinny's gaze probes the old man's despondent features for more information. "Were you drunk?"

The old man shakes his head. "No, I didn't drink a whole lot back then. I was just tired in the heat. It was July."

"What did you do after?"

"I ran."

"Why didn't you stay and face the music?"

The old man looks up at him and says, "Why didn't you?"

Vinny hangs his head, feeling as if the old man has just reached into his soul and touched all the secrets hidden there.

Sunday
May 7, 1950

Throughout the night, the closed boxcar shakes and rattles down the tracks in the dark. Some of the motion feels like spinning, but it's more likely a result of the alcohol. Two hours before dawn, awakened by several unnerving screeches and the old man sliding the cargo door open, Vinny stirs with a throbbing head, a cotton mouth, and a queasy stomach.

"Well, I'll be damned," the old man says, and shakes Vinny's foot. "Wake up, kid. We gotta get out."

"What's going on?"

"We didn't get too far. They've just been moving us from track to track. Looks like we're stuck in a hump yard in Phoenix."

"What's a hump yard?"

"It's a place where they re-sort and exchange the cars." The old man ties up his bundle. "If the Bulls catch us, they'll clobber us for sure."

Practiced, the old man leads Vinny through the classification yard to artfully dodge the security staff. "Stay close and keep your eyes peeled, kid. You don't want to get cut in half in the knuckles," he says, pointing at the train's coupling mechanism.

They slink along the side of a coasting car. "Step over the tracks, or you could lose a foot," he tells Vinny, and breaks out into a full run for a well-traveled slit in the tall chain-link fence.

Vinny walks through knotted brush and into a clearing, then freezes, hearing the mournful howl of an approaching coyote. "Where are we going?"

"We need a meal, and I know where to get one." The old man points to his ear. "Listen."

Vinny, in his stillness, hears voices and the soft crackle of a fire.

"It's a hobo camp in back of a salvage yard," the old man explains, tapping two sticks together to the tune of "Pop! Goes the Weasel." He grins over his shoulder at Vinny, adding, "And I've been to this particular one before."

Vinny follows him to the hobo camp, where three men stand naked around a trash-can fire topped with a cast iron pot, looking like a trio of witches cooking up a spell.

The tallest of the three looks up and smiles. "Well, if ain't Shadow Sam!" he says, and shakes the old man's hand. "It's Sunday. We're having a boil-up. Want to join?"

"Don't mind if I do, Sycamore Lee." Sam starts to remove his clothes to place them in the hot water.

Vinny shoots them all a look—clearly they're all insane—and backs away. He considers making a run for it.

"It's okay, little feller. It's to keep the lice away," says the second man, nodding at the boiling pot full of clothes. This man has blond hair and a gnarled left foot. Taking a hobbling step toward Vinny, he reaches out a hand. "I'm Switchfoot Larry."

Vinny steps back again with caution.

"I swear we ain't no perverts," Larry says, chuckling, and shrugs. "The sisters said they won't let us in the mission house iffen we don't clean up."

"They call me Rat-face Ronnie," the third man announces, his arms folded over a bare barrel chest. He takes a sniff at himself, lowers his beady eyes over two protruding front teeth, frowns, and says, "Wish we had us some soap."

"Me, too," says Larry, standing in his own pungency, suddenly self-conscious.

Vinny reaches down in his pocket and feels the last token he saved from home. "I have some," he mumbles.

Lee elbows his old friend. "Hey, Sam, I think the greenhorn said somethin."

"He's probably just hungry. We both haven't had a meal in a while," Sam says and scratches his wiry beard.

"What's your name, greenhorn?" Ronnie asks.

Vinny looks to Sam with questioning eyes, scared of being stuck with an embarrassing moniker.

"I haven't named him yet," Sam admits.

Vinny wriggles the soap figurine free from his pocket and hands it to Sam. "My contribution."

All the men gather to see the gift. "It's a little gator," Ronnie says with blank features, like a man who doesn't quite get the punchline of a joke.

With empty bellies and empty pockets, the novelty at first peek has no real value to any of the men. Brief glances are exchanged in the confused silence as they consider the marketable worth of the homemade toy.

Vinny's eyes flick upward. "It's soap."

Ronnie takes the green figurine, brings it to his nose, and inhales. "Mmm . . . pine tar. Thanks for the soap—Gator."

The men look at each other like Ronnie solved the mystery, and they laugh.

Larry holds his hand out again, and this time Vinny shakes it. "So, what's your first name, Gator?"

"Vinny," he replies, rubbing his shoe in the dirt.

Sam wrinkles his nose. "I think we'll just call you Gator."

Lee takes out a blade and shaves the soap's tail into the water with the clothes, then spins them around with a stick. He conservatively chops the rest, giving a slivered portion to each man. "To polish your mugs, gents."

Sam lifts an empty metal pail. "I'll go fetch us some more water." He soon returns after getting a work out at the water pump, whistling an old familiar work tune.

Lee spreads a smile full of nostalgia and shakes his head. He wrings out an article of clothing and throws it on a tired chain-link fence. "Shadow Sam, as I live and breathe," he laughs, hanging the last item to dry on an open-framed crate that once housed a bicycle. "You old boozehound, I ain't seen you since picking season of '47." Lee takes the full pail and claps Sam on the back.

Ronnie dips his hand in the water and lathers up his armpits. "I didn't know you two were a couple of apple-knockers."

"Hell, we musta picked half the apples in Washington that year," Lee boasts, rubbing soap bubbles on his ragged cheeks.

"And whatever happened to Cracker Jack?" asks Sam.

Unexpectedly hearing his old first name, Vinny's face and ears burn red. Nervously, he splashes himself with water and covers them in suds.

At Sam's mention of their old friend, Lee's face melts and he swallows hard, losing his jolly demeanor. "Sorry to be the bearer of bad news, friend, but . . . somebody convinced poor Cracker Jack to go to the clinic this spring, and they fed him the black bottle."

"The black bottle?" Vinny asks.

Lee sniffs. "It's that secret syrup them doctors give us undesirables when no one else is lookin."

"Is that true?"

Larry shrugs, his eyes somber. "We go in, but we never come out."

Sam drops his head and gives a heavy nod. "That's too bad. Jack was a good man." He inhales a long breath and blinks slowly, as if fighting off tears.

Raking each other with brief looks of delayed mourning, the men continue their moments of communal hygiene in an uncomfortable silence, until Larry decides to hum a Baptist hymn he remembers from his youth in Augusta, Georgia.

The sorrowful melody causes Sam to ache, his face twisting in discomfort. He pulls on damp clothes that awkwardly cling to his anemic skin. "I need a drink." He shakes his head and mutters to himself as he walks away.

"But Sam," Ronnie calls out after him, "breakfast service is in an hour!"

Sam waves him off and keeps on walking.

"Let him go, Ronnie," Lee says, looking up at the sunrise. "He just got some real bad news."

"That's why we call him Shadow Sam," Larry explains to Vinny. "He tends to disappear from time to time. But he always comes back eventually."

Vinny pulls out his cigarettes and his Zippo. Lee, Ronnie, and Larry all look at him as if he pulled out a pack of chewing gum in a classroom, hoping Vinny has enough to share. He rolls his eyes, reluctantly handing out the last of the pack, and lights them up.

"Who was Cracker Jack?" Vinny asks, squinting and lighting his own.

"He was a good friend from back in Sam's days with the circus." Larry explains. "Those are Sam's stories to tell . . . iffen he deems you worthy to hear em."

Down at the mission, Vinny learns that on any given Sunday, the price of ham and eggs on toast is to perform duties that help maintain the mission house and adjacent grounds—and, of course, attend a twenty-minute sermon about the healing power of the Lord.

Vinny's comprehensive education in dog-eat-dog crafty street survival makes him feel like a hardened cynic next to these men and their help-and-share community. Lounging on the dusty terrain of their quasi home, the group is laughing, giving Vinny a rundown of the ethics and code that they live by, lessons in hobo civility and communal living, when Sam returns late Sunday evening. He moves around the outside of the circle and touches each man on the shoulder before finding a spot to land by Ronnie.

"So let me get this straight," Vinny says with his hands up. "A tramp, a hobo, and a bum are not all the same animal?"

"Not at all," Lee says, leaning forward. "A bum is a worthless drunk, a tramp is a beggar, and a hobo is a worker with itchy feet. We like work and a fair wage same as the next fellow. We just don't want to be chained to a place too long."

"Itchy feet," Vinny repeats with an understanding nod.

"And Sam has the itchiest feet of us all," Ronnie laughs, tapping Sam's worn boot with his own thin-soled shoe. "What did you end up doing today, you old coot?"

"I found me a widow with a broken fence," he announces. He stretches back and smiles, dancing his fingers on a full belly. "She just so happens to make chicken and cornbread on Sundays."

They all laugh, envious but amused.

"And she wants me to come back tomorrow," Sam adds, "to take a look at her back porch."

"I bet she does!" Lee says, slapping his knee.

They all laugh harder.

For the first time in a long time, Vinny feels at ease, not constantly wondering what the angle is or hovering his hand over the blade in his pocket. His mind still tugs at him to search for Camille, to find out how she's fared this long year without him, but his feet are as itchy as Sam's—itchy for whatever adventures the campestral horizons of North America have to offer.

Monday
November 13, 1950

Several patient hours are spent lying in wait for the next ride to screech and groan to life. Vinny, Sam, and a stray traveler they've acquired along the way jog for nearly eight minutes to board. Out of breath and jelly-legged, Vinny enjoys lying on his back, bouncing on the clumsy junk train to Chicago.

He has spent these past six months apprenticing under Sam, picking up valuable skills in carpentry, plumbing, patching leaky rooftops, and other temporary jobs in exchange for any combination of food, money, or shelter they can receive. He and Sam have avoided many a close call on their travels. They have seen others who are not so lucky, falling prey to workplace hazards; some being severed by the unforgiving old rusty iron or cold hard steel in the yards; others arrested by railway security Bulls; and those unlucky saps who have their throats slashed while in slumber by some sick, penniless, and desperate soul.

Most of the time the thunderous noise of the train drowns out Vinny's thoughts, but in those rare moments of quiet they turn to Camille and whether or not she is safe. He admits to himself that he is avoiding her; even in the privacy of his own mind he doesn't quite know how to look her in the eye.

"Many miles of road can pass by some men and reveal nothing, while some men can stay perfectly still and see the whole universe," recites their unusually talkative and educated fellow traveler, whom Vinny dubs "Professor." The scholarly man adjusts his broad shoulders to scribble furiously across the pages of a small journal with a knife-sharpened pencil. When this day's thoughts are down, his hand grows still. He lifts his head to watch the undulating horizon. The Professor closes the notepad and places it in a discrete chest pocket of his expensive but now slightly tattered coat. He uses his long fingers to sweep a limp swath of light brown hair from the narrow bridge of his wind-chapped nose, drawn to and inspired by the spinning wheels he sees in the depths of Vinny's young eyes.

"What are you thinking about, little Gator?"

Vinny flashes the well-bred man a look as if he has asked for the length of his penis.

The Professor shrinks away in good humor. "I forgot—only *you* can ask the questions. I used to think government operatives were tough," he says with mirth, and glances over at Sam, who is in the middle of his afternoon nap.

Vinny also looks at Sam. The old man shivers, snorts, and smacks his lips, disrupting his usual calm, buzzy concert of snores.

Vinny's face softens and looks back at the Professor's sunken, malnutritioned cheeks. "Don't you ever miss being a big shot? You don't belong in this dusty bone-shaker with the rest of us."

"Don't I?" the Professor replies, looking at the dirt in the creases of his raw hands. "When I started working for the government, I thought I was going to help make the world a better place for you, me, for all of us. It didn't take me long to figure out that any real improvement would never be part of the agenda." The Professor looks deep into Vinny's glassy eyes. "My boss told me to be proud, that I was one of the privileged few. He said, 'You shall know the truth and the truth shall make you free.' "

Vinny raises his eyebrows. "Did it? Did the truth make you free?" he asks with a light veil of sarcasm, passing his eyes pointedly around their current accommodations, and reaches for a cigarette.

The Professor stares out at nothing, his unshaven jaw clenched for a moment, then says, "I was allowed to see all the sides of the megagon we call Earth, and the truth made me want to jump off of it." He suddenly feels claustrophobic.

Vinny studies the sincerity on the Professor's face while casually lighting his cigarette. "I know a few bridges along this route that would do the trick, but is it really all that bad?" he asks, eyes squinted, leaning on one arm, the lit cigarette bobbing from his lip.

"Son, this life . . ." the Professor replies slowly, as if these were some of the most important words he has ever spoken, "the one you're living . . . looking at the beautiful, wide open spaces, unbeholden to anyone, roaming at will . . . *that's* what freedom feels like."

"What about that whole 'pursuit of happiness, land of the free, home of the brave' thing?"

"It's malarkey. A sham. What they have planned is a land of monogrammed prisons to house a nation of permanently indentured servants."

Vinny shakes his head. "Smart people won't allow that to happen."

"I used to think so, too," the Professor says, nodding sagely, "until I met a man named Edward Bernays."

Vinny gives a quick snort of doubt. "One guy?"

"His poisonous ideas will change everything." The Professor's eyes spread wide with fear and turn to the sky. "Literally *everything*," he breathes in defeat.

Vinny takes a long drag from his cigarette. He looks out at the crystal blue November sky littered with white puffy clouds, a sky passing peacefully, unaware and unconcerned about the psychological skullduggery of the world below it.

"You're a dead man," Vinny exhales dryly, and taps the ash from his cigarette into the wind.

The Professor's slack cheeks fill with an anxious breath until he lets them slowly deflate. "Yep. Just a matter of time now." He hangs his head in resignation. "How'd you know?"

Vinny coolly takes another drag on his cigarette. "Clearly, you know too much."

The Professor rises, takes off his coat, revealing a dirty tailored suit, and covers Sam with the full-length wool to stop the old man's shivers. "It won't matter. It will all die with me." He sighs again.

"It doesn't have to," Vinny says, looking up at the Professor and offering him an unlit cigarette. "Tell me what you know."

The Professor shrugs, takes the gift, and sits beside Vinny. Passing the tip through the flame, he quivers—not from the cold, but from fear of putting the boy in added danger. "Ignorance is bliss. Are you sure you want to know?"

Vinny's brow furrows as he looks out at the world. "Denying the truth won't change the facts."

Friday
November 24, 1950

Learning all about the intricate diabolical plans of the professional poisoners of the public mind makes Vinny's heart as heavy as his eyelids, his brain as numb as his ears in the frigid pre-dawn air.

In his exhausted and troubled dreams, Vinny sees the Professor standing in his dirty suit at the edge of the open boxcar, looking back at him with a serene face as he waves goodbye and silently leaps from the Great Northern Line into the fog. The boxcar jerks and jostles, making Vinny realize that this is no dream.

He shoots upright, rubs his disbelieving eyes, and bravely looks out over the edge where the Professor last stood. Through the mist, Vinny can faintly see a steep, perilous drop leading to a certain death in the gully far below.

With the Professor gone, Vinny is alone in his burden of enlightenment when he shakes Sam awake from a drunken stupor to get prepared to exit the train. Sam buttons the sturdy wool coat gifted to him while he slept, quickly fond of the new armor against the harsh winter storm—an incoming blizzard that will disrupt the train schedule and pummel most of North America with high winds and record lows.

As the train slows, Sam and Vinny hop off, once again vigilant trespassers on railroad property, doing their best to not get caught, injured, or killed.

On this gray, bitterly cold morning, trudging through snow and clouds of diesel fumes, Vinny does not expect to see any men on patrol. Yet there they are: two brutes, billy clubs in hand, ready to strike.

Vinny does what Sam taught him to do—run, dodge, and weave through the dangerous and ever-moving city of trains. Heart pounding, Vinny hides behind a flatcar loaded with fresh-cut pine, waiting for Sam. But this time the old man isn't close behind. To Vinny's dismay, Sam is standing unaware with his mouth open, distracted and awed by something on the side of a retired railcar. He doesn't see the dangerous men closing in on him.

When Sam does notice, he turns to run and stumbles over a rusty iron track hidden beneath mounds of slippery white. With the freezing wind burning Vinny's face, he watches in horror as the two yard Bulls viciously beat Sam with their clubs. With every loud *thonk!* he hates himself more for still being too small in this big and nasty world.

"Let's go tell the yard boss we got us one," one of the cruel men laughs, and gives Sam one last kick before they both leave, satisfied with themselves on a job well done.

The snow drift around Sam's head grows red and melts in his warm blood. He raises a hand, reaching for whatever it was that gripped his attention before. Vinny rushes to Sam's broken body to see the damage of his blunt-force injuries, skull sickly dented in on one side, and what might be brain matter poking out of lacerated skin.

Sam chokes and gurgles on his own blood. He turns his gaze on Vinny. Tears of remorse make clean tracks on his unwashed face.

"Take the coat," Sam manages, spraying fine droplets of blood into Vinny's face.

The old man looks at the side of the railcar one last time and expires.

Vinny turns to see what Sam's unblinking dead eyes landed on: a decrepit railcar with a large, faded paint decal advertising *The Greatest Show on Earth*.

Sunday
November 26, 1950

"Storm of the century, they're callin it!" cries the older boy, twice his size, falling into the snow as Vinny dominates and pummels his face. He bellows more sad excuses for trying to steal Vinny's dark, ill-fitting coat right off of his back—and, Vinny notices with a wrenching heart, popping off one of the buttons in the process.

When Vinny has released all of his bottled rage and backs away, the older boy spits two bloody teeth out onto the frozen Chicago pavement and groans, "I'm sorry."

Vinny hears a guy laughing across the street, and turns to give him a "you want some of me?" look.

"Whoa, kid," the man says, raising his hands, still laughing.

Vinny shoves his raw-knuckled hands into his pockets, puts his head down, and begins to walk away from the boy writhing in pain on the cold concrete.

"Hey, kid, you hungry?" the man calls out.

Vinny freezes. His belly won't let him take another step.

The stocky, bandy-legged man jogs across the street and reaches into a pocket of his fancy tan overcoat. He pulls out a card, hands it to Vinny between two sausage fingers, and asks, "You like steak? I'm in town on business and I'm meeting a friend for lunch. Would you like to join us?"

Vinny gives him a suspicious glare, studies the card, and gives a half-hearted shrug. "You buyin, Mr. Palermo, boxing promoter?"

"Only if you call me Blinky." He smiles and claps Vinny on the back. "So what's your name, kid?"

Vinny sniffs. "My friends call me Gator."

"Wait till you meet my friend, Gator. He's a sixteen-year-old powerhouse, destined for the heavyweight championship. We call him 'Two-Man,' on account of he's huge, got the strength of two grown men."

Moving Vinny's empty plate out of the way, Two-Man, a sweet-faced, lion-headed colossus, places a gym's business card in its place. Blinky is doing the majority of the talking, since Two-Man seems to have busied his mouth with half of the menu.

Blinky waves the maître d' over and pulls a shiny pen from his breast pocket. The maître d's face objects, and he frowns for a third time at Vinny's presence in his restaurant.

"You know I'm good for it," Blinky scoffs, and waves his dismissal.

The maître d' snorts his disapproval once more and leaves in a huff.

Blinky opens the pen with his mouth, scribbles on the back of the card. "No pressure, Gator. You can stop in for a visit anytime. There's a room with a cot at each of these gyms if you ever need a place to sleep . . . or train," he says. Blinky replaces the pen cap with a twinkle in his eye, clearly smelling money in Vinny's future, either as a boxer or an enforcer.

"I haven't got the open road out of my system just yet," Vinny admits, looking at the list of gyms—located in six major cities—before placing it in an inner pocket next to a dead man's journal.

Two-Man holds a meaty fist over his napkin-covered chest while he quietly belches. "I love boxing, Gator. I think you'd love it, too. If you're ever ready to make some fairly easy money, just let someone at those places know that we sent you."

"I'll think about it," Vinny says, surrendering his cloth napkin to the table. He can feel the judgmental stares of other irritated guests upon him. "Thanks for the meal, but I need to be on my way."

"I guess I must let you go if you won't be persuaded," Blinky says, shaking Vinny's hand. "I'm not gonna beg."

Two-Man wipes his fingers. When he reaches out for Vinny's hand and sees his post-fight knuckles, he says, "You should save that for inside the ring. Don't do it for free." He smiles, and carefully shakes his new friend's hand. "You should keep in touch."

"I will," Vinny says, and leaves the posh restaurant to continue on his journey.

Sunday

December 3, 1950

After a week of hitchhiking to warmer weather, Vinny finds himself in Florida, chasing down the rumor of a circus set up at the Lake County fairgrounds. He doesn't know why he feels compelled to do this, other than an overwhelming need to experience what it was about the circus life that Sam loved so much that he died for one last glimpse.

It is mid-evening when Vinny finally reaches the large circle of sawdust in the barren field where just a few hours ago a circus tent stood. Remnants of tickets, flyers, popcorn, and candy wrappers dance in the humid air. The temperature has dropped further with the sun's slow departure, but it seems the show went on despite the threat of rain. Just not long enough.

Disappointed, frustrated, and alone, Vinny kicks a discarded tin across to the other side of the field.

"Hey, you!" a voice calls out to him. "Kid!"

Vinny is startled and spins around, instantly prepared to run or fight.

The voice belongs to a man standing by a thick line of Leyland cypress trees. The man cups his hands around his mouth. "You looking for work?" he projects.

Vinny scratches his head. He looks around the empty land and back to this man yelling to him at the edge of the fairground as if he might be a mirage. "Maybe," he calls back, and decides to walk closer.

"Can you drive a truck?" the man asks before he sees that Vinny's face has never seen a razor.

Vinny hears the loud purr of a diesel engine. "Sure, I can drive." Not entirely a lie.

The man nods and disappears into the line of trees. Vinny follows, emerging alone onto the asphalt that leads out of town, where two commercial-size trucks sit with their doors open, idling in the middle of the road.

Aside from stealing a few vehicles for a quick getaway or joyride, Vinny has no driver's license or prolonged experience keeping anything between two parallel lines—and certainly not enough experience to drive a truck that looks to be bigger than the ice-delivery truck he had imagined. Painted on the side of the red truck, in big yellow letters, is:

MILLER BROS. CIRCUS

The man reappears, a shadowed figure in the bright beams of light coming from the second massive truck's blunt nose. He waves Vinny over. "Come on, kid! We're behind schedule."

When Vinny opens the cab door to climb in, his faculties are accosted by the acrid stench of booze, bile, and sweat. The source is an overweight man lying against the passenger door, passed out drunk.

Vinny steps back down to be able to breathe.

"I know it's bad," his recruiter admits, "but we need to move, and as you can see, he can't drive. If you get this truck to our next stop, I'll pay you well for the trouble."

Vinny, listening with the back of his hand over his mouth, nods. "You got a handkerchief?"

Loaded up and on the move, Vinny sits on the seat edge to reach the pedals, his face wrapped in a white handkerchief. The overweight man grunts and farts and moans all the way to Pensacola. He wakes only once to weakly slap at Vinny for trying to steal his truck, sending them swerving all over the road, before dropping back into his fitful slumber.

Vinny drives.

For a few short months, Vinny expands his family to include a large gaggle of eccentric souls who give him the most intensive training that anyone could ever ask for; people ousted by normal society for one reason or another, driven by their artistic passions more so than money, each one with a mastery of their skill set and a willingness—in some cases an *eagerness*—to share, and Vinny an enthusiastic student.

Vinny works hard and fast, building his body and his mind, learning to maneuver big trucks like a pro and to drive stakes deep in the ground. He learns how to ride unicycles and horses, throw knives and shoot like a sniper, breathe fire, balance on a tight wire while spinning plates, walk on stilts and juggle oddly shaped objects, charm and handle snakes, and care for a whole menagerie of other exotic animals. His motivation for each new accomplishment is to honor the memory of Sam and make him proud.

He could never have imagined that some of the most useful skills would come from the clowns: many ways to cleverly apply theater makeup and prosthetics, to put on a smiling face and perform even when your heart is breaking.

Tuesday
January 2, 1951

Darkness is beginning to snuff out the last rays of daylight that once bravely peeked through the tightly woven blinds of James Angleton's office window when a friendly voice breaks his concentration: "You need a drink, pal. Take a break from this purgatory and let's go have a drink."

With anger and despair eroding any want or need for pleasure or company, Angleton rubs his temples, resistant eyes cast down, weighted by the massive wooden desk dripping with the latest mission reports.

"No, I don't want a drink, Allen." His bark is a deep rumble; his stormy eyes flash in brief confrontation of the frozen smirk in his doorway—the sunny, confident face of Allen Dulles. He blinks in harsh study of a fellow patriot, selective minds sworn to collect, analyze, evaluate, and disseminate information for the sake of national security. "I need to keep working on this," he says, and continues where he left off.

Unwilling to let go that easily, Allen tilts his felt hat and opens his mouth for another try.

Without looking up from the paperwork again, Angleton's hand rises to save his colleague's breath. "I *told* you. I've taken hiatus from the booze and I don't need to know the final score of the Rose, the

Orange, or the Sugar . . . the only bowl that concerns me at this point is the rice-bowl shit-show going down over the Yalu. We need better intel . . . if we can't get a better update than a playoff score, then I suggest you let me find one."

Allen sighs and drops his head. "It'll still be there tomorrow. You needn't bury your good humor along with your friend, you know," he says with a minimal dash of empathy.

Angleton launches his tall, gaunt frame from the high-backed executive chair at Dulles. "Do you know something I don't?" he asks, the corners of his sleep-deprived eyes twitching with suspicion behind bottle-thick glasses. "Did they find a body?"

"Well, no . . . but . . ." Dulles trails off.

"That's right! We do not yet know what happened to field agent Thompson. I believe we have a disease in our den, and I'm determined to find a cure."

"Trust that I am just as concerned as you on this matter. I am assigning one of our brightest recruits to assist in the hunt for whatever fate has befallen our dear Gavin."

"Are you suggesting that someone's brighter than me?"

Dulles laughs. "By no means. You just can't be everywhere at all times. I figured you could use the help. Maguire will be an excellent ferret for you . . . he's young, quick, loyal, and tenacious."

"*Ambitious*, you mean," Angleton says, lifting his eyebrows.

"Yes, I suppose he is . . . but who in the world are more ambitious than we?"

A pause, then: "A tenacious ferret, you say?"

"*Loyal* and tenacious."

"Oh, I'll never doubt his loyalty if he delivers the voles I seek. I may require an army of such ferrets," Angleton says, and retreats back into the seat he has kept warm for too many hours since the last time he heard from his friend Gavin Thompson. Myopically, Angleton ignores Dulles, instead hovering over a blank page, then begins to pen a newly prioritized list of objectives.

Dulles sighs and tries once more to lighten the mood. "Now, how about that drink . . . ?"

James glares up at him.

"Fine!" Dulles capitulates, and shoves a hand in his pocket to retrieve a small ring of keys—a ring of brass crowned in black leather, embossed with the crest and shield of the Central Intelligence Agency. "Just trying to raise morale," he says, his thumb caressing the sixteen-pointed compass rose. "It helps."

Impatiently, Angleton taps his fountain pen against an unopened file. "The only way to help is to find answers."

"That depends on who you're helping." Dulles mentions with a glance at his wrist watch. "Haven't you heard?" He playfully bounces the keys in the palm of his hand, turns to leave, and adds, "Some of us have lives beyond the office."

Beneath the lamplight Angleton is confronted by the echo of Allen's words and a colorized photograph of a woman he occasionally sleeps with and children he rarely sees.

"Let me know how that pans out."

He snorts at his own deficiencies and opens the bottom desk

drawer. Succumbing to his addiction, his hand wanders in hopeful pursuit of a long-neglected bottle of gin; instead it discovers a thick document envelope addressed to Jesus—a name he had not been called in years. A middle name, an old curse word reserved for his mother's use.

Wreathed in rings of cigarette smoke, Angleton frowns, staring at pages and pages; the vertical lines at the apex of his ashen brow deepen as he studies an in-house report left discretely in his desk by a man who is now classified as "missing in the line of duty." Conducting his own investigation into Thompson's whereabouts, he stares at inflammatory words meant to engineer consent, to steer and bend democracy at will, the fruit of an experimental tool in social control designed by Nazi war criminals, employed by a deceitful government—*his* government.

His pupils grow large, absorbing the magnitude of Gavin's personal notes crowding the margins of Operation Paperclip as the project expands and evolves into Bloodstone, Mockingbird, CHATTER, and several other project authorizations. Clearly documented evidence of advanced human testing and hypnosis. Pages boasting of many grotesque experiments on unwitting citizens remarked as success, vandalized by a man who once believed in freedom condemning those findings as global failure . . . or at least that is what Gavin must have thought, leaving these black operation reports for Angleton to find.

"Is this why you left?" Angleton says aloud. He runs his finger along his neatly combed hair and leans hard against the back of the chair from exhaustion, staring at the ceiling in deep contemplation. Surely their learned countrymen must feel that this is a necessary evil, projects beyond their noble comprehension, a service meant to somehow protect democracy.

He thinks to himself,

We are patriots sworn to defend our way of life at all cost, without question, without hesitation—without fail.

Angleton knew this, Gavin knew this; *they all* knew this when they pledged their fealty.

He jumps, awakened, startled by a hard knock on the partially opened office door. He looks to his watch, realizing the night is gone and a new work day is already underway, when his secretary says, "Sorry to disturb you, but I just received a call from someone in the archives . . . says it's urgent. You might want to head over there and check it out."

Wednesday
January 3, 1951

The guard on duty hears the *switch-click* and the *clang!* of a heavy metal door that requires selective security clearance and a key, followed by Angleton's long gawky strides across the inner records office.

"Thanks for the call, Angus."

Angus nods. "Good morning, Mr. Angleton. It's my first shift of the new year and I wanted to make sure you knew about this guy snooping around in the vault."

"I'll see that you get a raise for this. Where's the snooper now?"

"He's set up in one of the audio rooms last I checked. Should I have called Mr. Dulles too?"

Angleton unwinds his woolen scarf, removes his gloves, and shoves them into his coat pocket. "No. I'm starting to think this was his awful ploy to get me out of the office." He grumbles as he walks away, unfastening his coat and moving briskly through the restricted area of the building where few have tread.

Angleton charges into the audio room, surprising a young man with hair the color of spicy red earth who scrambles to his feet. "Oh my, where'd we acquire you? Surely not the secret service," he says, gripping his fedora and placing it on a table equipped with a reel-to-reel tape deck recorder.

"Shaun Maguire, Information Analyst, Camp Lejeune, sir."

"At ease. Can you tell me why we're here, Mr. Soldier?"

"I was told that you would appreciate my help looking into a sensitive matter."

"No, that's why *you're* here. Can you tell me why *I'm* here?"

Stunned, Maguire takes a beat of silence, unsure how to answer.

"I was called because this is *my* house, and I don't like anyone lurking about the corridors of my house without talking to me first."

"I–uhh . . ."

"What was your name again?"

"Shaun . . . Shaun Maguire, and it's an honor to meet you, Mr. Angleton," he says with a bright smile, presenting an open hand.

Angleton glances at the young man's hand with cold dismay, as if his offering were dripping in radioactive slime. "Since we're here, what do you have for me?"

Maguire's smile fades; he bristles and clears his throat, handing over a leather-bound dossier. "According to the records I could locate and my sources, it looks like I have uncovered evidence related to an assignment given to Gavin Thompson, prior to his disappearance, sir."

Angleton ruthlessly bends the document corners looking for answers. "What was the assignment?"

"This mission was kept vague . . . most of the papers I've located are out of sequence, mislabeled, or redacted. No one I've asked seems to know for sure."

"Did you find out who he was reporting to?"

"I did not find out who specifically, but I did find out where . . . he was reporting to someone at Camp Detrick."

"Hmmm." Angleton frowns then regards the reel-to-reel tape deck. "Is there some audio for me to hear, Mr. Maguire?"

"Oh, yes! I found a box of audio files. This is the first recording that Thompson tagged in his latest investigation. I just finished setting it up."

"Okay, so . . . ? Don't waste my time and play me the goddamned thing!"

Maguire flips the lever and sets the analog magnetic tape whirring into motion. The tape winds and crinkles from one reel to the other, transmitting the secretly recorded audio from an attached speaker. Suddenly, through the faint static, there is the echoey sound of shuffling footsteps across a floor.

"The way I heard it, that Halloween gig was one for the books," a raspy voice speaks with intoxicated excitement.

"You heard right. Three sets, and the entertainment that night was aces!" a second baritone voice follows with equal slur, then the sound of a zipper pull. "I'll never forget that night, that's for sure."

A second zipper pull is followed by tandem trickling streams of urine. "Is it true . . . about that Voodoo queen who sang and made a zombie dance?"

A third zipper pulls. "A zombie? What's a zombie?"

"It's like when you bring a dead person back to life," the raspy voice answers.

"Nah, this guy wasn't dead, but he sure wasn't under his own influence, neither . . . this was something else."

"Something else?"

"I saw it with my own two eyes—that lady Laveau put some kind of spell over this guy. I swear, she turned him into some kind of puppet."

"Beeeuuulaah Laveau . . ." the third voice says with fondness, followed by a sultry whistle. "You have to admit that woman is a looker . . . for a darkie."

"Someone beat you to the deep end of that hot-chocolate pool, pal," the baritone says, followed by the sound of him raising his fly and a quick slap of the flush handle.

"You don't say?"

"Last time I saw that fine ass-a hers, from sideways her belly was as plump as a ripe summer melon."

"When was that?"

"Hmm . . . must have been May or June."

Angleton reaches over to stop the recording. "Do you know what year this was?"

Maguire turns a tin over, hoping to find a date marking. "Not sure, sir."

"Are there more of these surveillance tapes?"

"Yes, but most of them are marked as sequenced interviews."

"I want the full transcripts of every tape on this case," Angleton commands. His long boney finger circles the room. "All of it and all of this set up in my office ASAP!"

"Yes. Right away, sir!"

"Laveau," Angleton echoes as he storms from the building, his brain raging with interest.

Angleton's heart slugs away in his chest, the blood a rushing soundtrack in his ears as he stomps through the headquarters' labyrinthine halls. "Why wasn't I made aware of these new projects?" he asks, voice loaded with skepticism as he bursts into the office of deputy director Allen Dulles.

"Which ones?"

"The ones arising from Paperclip."

"Oh, those. Close the door." Dulles gives a sullen nod and clears his throat, stalling like a child who is searching for the right excuse for Mother. "Camp Detrick has been keeping close tabs on our little Nazi friends over the years. They've been conducting a few experimental studies, chasing down many scientific leads in our interest. Not much fruit from it, though."

"So, does that mean we've finally secured funding for the mind-control program?"

"Not exactly," Dulles admits, his tone irresolute. "We're still working on that . . . why do you ask?"

"Apparently, there's some dame down in New Orleans rumored to have the extraordinary ability to bend minds at will without the aid of chemicals or apparatus. Have we brought her in?"

Dulles frowns. "Last August I received a report that she bore a son with similar skills. An order was given for their capture."

"What in the hell happened? Isn't this what we've been searching for? Why don't we have her and why didn't you tell me what Thompson was working on?"

Dulles drags his hand over his face and struggles to breathe, as if Angleton's mountain of rapid-fire questions made the air thin. He sighs heavily. "I wanted to tell you. Thompson was in charge of that mission, and now the woman's current whereabouts are unknown. He seemed reluctant when ordered to bring her and the boy in. He had only located the boy and when he didn't return, I assumed it was an aggressive act of rebellion or cowardice. I didn't want you to be burdened with that knowledge."

"Rebellion? *Thompson?*" Angleton shakes the absurd thought loose from his head. "Did it ever occur to you that this boy might be dangerous?"

"We think he could be, yes, and that's why we sent him. Do you really think a *child* overtook one of our most seasoned agents?"

"So what do we think officially happened?"

"One theory is that a highly decorated and well-respected defender of freedom suddenly went rogue."

"A more likely theory is that he was killed in the line of duty," Angleton counters. "Neither of which can be proven."

"Do you really think this boy might be gifted or capable of murder?"

"Thompson is still unaccounted for . . . we must be cautious and vigilant . . . without testing we don't know what this boy is capable of."

Wednesday
March 7, 1951

Two-Man enters the belly of the Detroit arena and spreads his arms wide, beaming at Vinny. "Welcome to Olympia Stadium, my friend!"

Vinny has been lured, temporarily whisked away from the Michigan fairgrounds and the Miller Brothers Circus, by Two-Man's invitation to watch the main heavyweight event—and to help study for the next scheduled bout.

The two fighters bounce around the boxing ring, seemingly an even match, until a left hook from Ezzard Charles floors Jersey Joe Walcott for a nine-count in the ninth round. In the end, a testosterone-laden crowd roars as Charles, the victor, walks away, maintaining his title as heavyweight champion.

Two-Man and Vinny exit the building and head to the car.

"So, you gonna get in the ring with Charles?" Vinny asks.

Two-Man shrugs. "Maybe. I'm training hard and picking my battles wisely."

"For a guy who's undefeated, you sound unsure. What's stopping you from going after him? I think you can take him," Vinny says, playfully shuffling his feet and jabbing into the air at an invisible opponent.

Two-Man laughs. "I think he might be cursed."

Vinny drops his arms, disillusioned. "I didn't take you for the silly, superstitious type," he says.

Two-Man's forehead wrinkles. "I don't believe in nonsense," he says defensively, "but there *is* some boxing lore out there that actually has teeth."

Vinny folds his arms, smirking. "I'm listening. What makes you think Ezzard Charles is cursed?"

"I'll tell you about it after I have a drink in me . . ." Two-Man rubs his grumbling belly. "And a plate of lasagna."

Vinny tilts his head and purses his lips. "But it's late, and you're not old enough for a drink."

"Roma's is less than ten minutes from here," Two-Man says. He tucks Vinny's head under his muscular arm and gives him a hard, brotherly knuckle-rub on the head. "What are you now, my mother?" he asks, surprisingly kissing Vinny's crown and pushing him away before he opens the door to his car. "Get in. I'm gonna show you that it pays to know Blinky. He has friends all over."

Settled and satisfyingly sauced in a booth in the back of Roma's Café, Vinny leans back, away from an empty plate where a pile of pasta used to be, and sighs. "Now tell me about this stupid spell."

Two-Man flashes his eyes at Vinny. "It's a *curse*," he corrects through his teeth. "I think it was given to him through another boxer—a curse I don't want any part of." Two-Man downs the rest of his single malt and waves his empty glass to the waiter for a refill. "In

'47, there was a fighter named Sam Baroudi who killed an opponent named Glenn Newton Smith in Philadelphia. Smith died of a cerebral hemorrhage after the fight." Two-Man pauses as the waiter puts his fresh drink on the red tablecloth and walks away. "Six months later, Baroudi enters the ring with Ezzard Charles and dies the very same way. If I get a match with Charles, one of us could die in a strikingly similar fashion."

"*Pfft*, you big baby!" Vinny waves off his friend's phobia. "Whaddaya so scared of? The killin or the dyin?"

"Aren't you afraid of dying?"

"No. I'm afraid of not living while I'm here. If you seek a reward, you have to take a calculated risk." Vinny nods toward the miserable people crouched at the bar. "Look around you. Half these jokers are already dead."

Two-Man studies Vinny's face while he lights up a cigarette. He exhales, saying, "Who is she?"

"Who's who?" Vinny replies with a wry smile.

"The female you been dipping your wick in."

Vinny raises his eyebrows and grabs a cigarette for himself, remaining tight-lipped.

"Oh, come on. We're friends, aren't we? Who's the dame?"

He takes a drag. "Her name is Margit."

Two-Man's eyes grow. "Are you in love with Maggie the First?"

Vinny's inhale is stifled. "I don't know," he chokes. "Why'd you call her that?"

Two-Man gives the young stud a playful shove. "Because you never forget your first one, kid. All who follow will be Maggie, too."

"What makes you think she's my first?" Vinny winks and steals a gulp of the drink on the table.

Two-Man squints at him with a bemused twinkle and lets out a whine of amusement. "If you say so, kid." He laughs and shakes his head. "If you say so."

Wednesday
August 8, 1951

Guided **by the** words of ghosts, Angleton pours over the transcript of Agent Thompson's interview with Eleanor for the umpteenth time. He squeezes fast-acting droplets of an experimental fluid—a current CIA project said to increase awareness—into a short glass of water and downs most of the contents in one gulp. His lucid eyes resume scanning the assessments of the retired teacher that possibly hold a clue, some vital detail hidden within the background information about her neighbors. Angleton is frustrated and confused about the significance of the insights of this old woman, a neighbor of a subject. The subject is a male child named Jack who Gavin was tracking for a new branch of Project Paperclip—a boy Agent Thompson curiously refers to as "Gator" in his later reports.

I must be missing something,

he thinks, and squeezes a few more droplets into the glass and finishes the water. Reaching over, he flips the playback lever on the tape player and closes his eyes to fully absorb the nuances of the audio recording, trying to recapture the past—an attempt to see through Gavin's eyes. The serum kicks in and Angleton's senses start to tingle, start to *amplify.*

The taped interview proceeds with Eleanor's girlish giggle. "Excuse me while I check the percolator. Cream? Sugar?" she asks, and Angleton can almost *see* her sparkling eyes.

"Black, no sugar, thanks," Thompson replies, and her tapping footfalls become fainter as she takes several paces into what must be an adjacent kitchen.

Angleton can almost *smell* the sweet roasted chicory, almost *taste* it.

"I appreciate you speaking with me."

"Anything to help," she calls out from the not-so-far distance. "I always knew our Jack was smart and dedicated. He sends money for Camille as often as he can . . . but to be considered for a citizenship award? My goodness!"

"Our school only nominates the good ones." Gavin clears his throat and latches on to a thin guise that was already assumed by the over-trusting hostess, one that need not stand up to any intense or long-term scrutiny.

"How long have you been carving soap?" he asks.

Angleton can almost *feel* Gavin lift a green soap carved turtle to his nose and give it an inspecting sniff. "Mmm . . . pine tar," he says, pleased, and sets it back on the crowded shelf with many other carefully crafted pieces of whittled art.

Eleanor's voice becomes louder as she enters closer proximity to the recorder. Angleton imagines her setting two steaming cups of coffee down on tatted doily cloths atop a knee-height table.

"You can choose a few if you'd like. I'm running out of room for the dern things."

"My space could use some cheer. I may take you up on that offer." With his eyes closed, Angleton can almost see the smile full of admiration that Gavin often bestowed on the clever and the artistic.

"Do you happen to recall meeting a biracial woman who Jack may have been fond of?"

"Oh, yes, I remember. Her name was Beulah Laveau!" Eleanor's voice brightens with fond recall. "A woman who used to care for the children when they were young. My word, I haven't thought of her in ages . . . why do you ask?"

You could almost hear Eleanor's lips pull tightly together as Gavin's pencil furiously scribbles her insights across the pages of a notepad he always kept in his pocket.

"I would like to interview a few more people to support his nomination, but I'm having trouble locating her. Do you know where I might find her?"

"No, I wouldn't in the slightest. I haven't seen her since . . . since . . ." Her voice falters.

"Since what?" Gavin asks.

"I'm not exactly sure, and I never asked Maureen outright," Eleanor says, and lowers her voice, as if to keep the words from being recorded. "I believe there was a falling out, and the poor darlings were abandoned by that terrible Adam creature . . . that's when Jack was sent away to a boarding school. Camille stays with me now and again. She is a dear and the apple of her brother's eye."

In his office, Angleton reaches out for a pencil and writes *locate sibling* and underlines it twice on his desk blotter.

"Who's Maureen?" Gavin asks.

"Why, his *mother*, of course. I so dislike using that ridiculous nickname of hers."

"Ah . . . Mouse."

"Have you ever heard a more ridiculous name for a grown woman? Pfft!"

Gavin chuckles. "I can't judge. My mother's name was Tootie."

Brrrrng!

Angleton bolts upright, disturbed, spine prickling from the shrill cry of the phone, and the light of a secure internal line beckons from his desk. He shuts the recording off and picks up the phone.

"This better be important!"

"Sorry, sir," Maguire says on the line. "We have located the female. She's in custody. Gottlieb has her in Maryland."

"Get her primed for me—I'll be there as soon as I can!"

Friday
August 10, 1951

"She's incredibly unique** research material," Sidney Gottlieb says to James Angleton. Together they are watching Beulah's interrogation from behind mirrored glass in a test facility at Camp Detrick. "However did you locate this one?"

"I didn't," he replies, glancing at Agent Maguire standing close by.

Sidney gives him a look of intrigue.

Angleton sways uncomfortably in the gaze of those silent, questioning eyes. "It's a long story that requires inebriation, I'm afraid."

"Ahhh . . . we'll get to that later, then."

The two executives observe Morse Allen—a veteran of Naval Intelligence, a specialist in interrogation techniques, a behavioral research czar with a fondness for electroshock and hypno-therapies—as he looms in evaluation over Beulah. Beulah's hair and clothing look as if she were rescued from a wind storm, her spirit still composed, unlike her disheveled appearance. He walks around the small room centered by a table topped with a few agency files, intel gathered on time-sensitive issues.

"Don't you get it? With your help we can win future wars with fewer American casualties!"

"If I give you what you're asking for, I'd be helping you *start* new wars—and what about *foreign* casualties?"

Morse flinches as if she slapped him. " 'Foreign casualties'?" he mocks. "How can we concern ourselves with *foreign casualties* when our boys are out there on the front lines fighting for freedom?"

"For *whose* freedom?" Beulah asks, her voice bouncing off the walls of the small cell-like room.

He ignores the question. "You should do this for your country . . . don't you love your country?"

"Why should I?" she asks. "When has my country loved me back?"

"Careful, my dear—treason is punishable."

"Tell dat to Mr. and Mrs. Rosenburg," she mumbles.

"What was that you said?"

She inhales with defiance. "Love under threats of violence is not love."

Both of their attention is drawn by a sharp knock on the door.

"Excuse me," Morse says, and steps away to have a muffled conversation outside of the room.

The baton of authority is passed and Angleton's thin stooped frame enters the room carrying a small glass ashtray. He briefly shows his teeth in a semblance of a smile and nods to Beulah as if he received a formal invitation and purchased a housewarming gift for the occasion. He places the ashtray on the table beside the files.

"Would you like a smoke to calm your nerves?"

She blinks warily at him and ignores the friendly offer. "Who are you?"

Angleton doesn't respond right away and pretends to study the high corners of the walls. He finally levels his gaze on her and asks, "Why don't you use your abilities to solve that yourself?"

"I am not a trained monkey who dances to every tune. I am not in the habit of using my gifts on such trivial details," Beulah says, and her skin prickles watching Angleton's excruciatingly slow and calculated movements around the room. She feels as if he is spinning an invisible web all around her.

"Who I am is of no consequence," he says. Angleton leans over the table to peek inside one of the file folders and then pushes it aside. "We know that your gifts are truly special, my dear. There are others like you already in service, helping us to defeat communism."

"Good, den you can let me go. You don't really need me."

"Mmm . . ." he hums, weighing the option of her release side to side in his head. "You happen to have a specific skill set that we're interested in."

"I'm starving. Can we please take a break?" Beulah pleads.

"We have explained how this works . . . you give us information and we provide you with every comfort."

She throws a hard look at Angleton. "Why don't you ask one of your other talents for information?"

"You are each here with different skills to offer and for entirely different reasons. Now, concentrate."

"It's hard to concentrate when my belly is growling."

"I promise to bring the best meal of your life, but not until you give me something more I can work with."

"I already told de other man about de spies next week. There's to be a meeting in a place called Heaven's Point." She shakes her head in dehydrated confusion. "Spirit's point . . . or somethin like dat."

"And you are sure this spy-harboring city is in France?" He snaps his fingers at the glass for Agent Maguire to check into her claim. Maguire runs from his post to find the nearest relevant map.

"Yes! Now can I get a glass of water?"

"Tell me more about the spy we are searching for?" he pushes again.

Beulah closes her eyes and strains to find the answer he seeks. "There will be more than one . . . both friend and foe. Collusion."

"So, we're looking for a breach in counterintelligence. Is that what you're tellin me?"

"I'm tired!" she cries. "I need to rest."

Agent Maguire rushes back into the room with gridded details of the French countryside. He shoves his finger upon the map beside the uneven edges of the Rhone. "Pont-Saint-Esprit!" he exclaims, victorious.

"A meeting of turncoats in Pont-Saint-Esprit, France, in five days. Is that right?" Angleton looks to Beulah.

Hungry, thirsty, and browbeaten, she lowers her head and nods an exhausted affirmation.

"We got it . . . we'll get those sons a bitches this time!" Angleton claps Maguire on the back and follows him into the hall to enjoy the sounds of mechanical applause, the rapid-fire of a telegraph key transmitting new directives to his operatives in France and the Sandoz biochemical company.

He looks back with a conspiratorial grin at Beulah, who isn't as thrilled about the Cold War delirium these transmissions will cause. She is learning that the CIA's favorite way to hide murder and death's emissaries is to surround them with chaos and confusion.

"Order this lady a big steak with all the trimmings, and bring on the wine!" Angleton shouts down the hall to his team. When the congratulatory banquet is delivered, Beulah devours every delicious morsel on her plate except for the bread . . . something's evil in the bread.

Sunday

January 20, 1952

A **thick bowl** of oatmeal and two cups of coffee line Vinny's belly as he walks around the outside of the tent inspecting the setup, making sure that all the tie-downs are tight and secure.

An angel-faced acrobat walks by his side, speaking in her thick Romanian accent. "I am becoming sixteen today. Would you go to pictures with me after big afternoon show?"

"Sure, doll. What picture do you want to see?" He bends down to pick up a coin from the dirt. He dusts it off and drops it in his pocket.

"The one with Mister Charlton Heston," she says with a coquettish smile.

He freezes. "You mean to tell me that you want to leave the circus to see a movie about a . . . *circus?*"

"It is love story, too." She kisses him on the cheek and tumbles away.

Vinny smiles in her direction, watching her lithe body twirl and bend—a joy to watch both in and out of costume. He is beyond excited at the prospect of having her in the back row of a dark theater.

He resumes his inspection, still feeling Margit's damp kiss on his cheek, when her father, Iosef Popescu, darkens his path, towering over him. The Daredevil of the Air's harsh green eyes elucidate to Vinny that his and Margit's secret rendezvous are no longer secret.

Vinny feigns a look of innocence. "Good morning, Mr. Popescu."

"You are wishing to wed my daughter?" Iosef growls menacingly, foregoing any semblance of niceties.

Vinny is unable to speak; he feels the blood pool in his feet and his head begins to swim.

"My Margit is lovely star of show," Iosef says, and cracks his knuckles. "You are mongrel, but I see you are hard worker. She is telling me you have love for her."

Vinny stumbles over his thoughts, trying to explain without putting himself in danger. "I . . . I do have love for Margit, but—"

Iosef rubs his face in frustration. "You say you have love for my Margit, but you have no wishing to marry her?"

Vinny's mind races. "We are too young to marry . . . aren't we?" he replies; his young voice cracks.

"We Romani people have different tradition in the old country." Iosef wraps his strong arm around the boy and gives him a squeeze. "How about we discuss in my office?"

In the close quarters of the updated gypsy wagon, Iosef reveals a number of curses and methods of disfigurement his family will perform if he finds out that his daughter is ruined before marriage, and the "bride price" that Vinny will owe according to the Romani code.

Later that afternoon, hearing the first notes of Iosef's entrance music play under the big top tent, Vinny slips away, escaping with his life and a small duffel of his belongings.

Tuesday
January 29, 1952

Outside a train yard near Mahopac, New York, the sunlight fades from a brandy-colored sky. Teeth chattering, Vinny sits huddled before a small crackling fire he has created in a wayward metal minnow bucket. He rips a page from the Professor's private notebook after absorbing the power of his words, then feeds it to the flames as he did with all the pages before it. The dead man's messages sear indelible in Vinny's memory as he re-reads the last paragraph of the final entry one more time.

My dream of covering myself with glory, to be the first man to gather provable, empirical data on a plague of global corruption is now dissipating. Somehow, I find myself traveling down some backwoods path on some valor-less mission. What kind of government would seek to harm a youth? What kind of man would carry out such an order? I sit here face to face with the ticking time-bomb, the so-called threat to national security, a boy who isn't even aware that he has the

Vinny looks to the back of the page for the rest of a pivotal sentence that was cut off for some unknowable reason, wondering,

Has the what?

Frustrated, he crumples the page and tosses it into the welcoming pyre. If only that crucial thought had been completed before his pen found distraction.

A thought that will scratch at his brain for years to come.

He drops the tattered husk to the ground. The notebook's purpose lost, its blank wordless face stares up at Vinny, wishing it too had the answer.

Wednesday
January 30, 1952

On the next leg of his American odyssey, Vinny travels alone through snow drifts until finally accepting Blinky's open invitation to Gleason's Gym to escape a brutally cold night in the Bronx.

Vinny enters Gleason's and sets down his duffel, which seems to weigh more now than it did a few states ago. The brightly lit gym is bustling with activity, grown men scattered around, skipping rope, shadow boxing, and brutalizing four heavy bags that hang from the ceiling. The owner of the gym, Bobby, is a feisty, well-dressed man who barks commands with enormous energy at the men in the training ring, one of whom is a dancing Two-Man—six-foot-five and 260 pounds of pure muscle—shaking off sweat like a wet cat, waiting for his older opponent to resume their spirited sparring match.

Two-Man sees Vinny and recognizes him immediately. He taps his gloved fists together and smiles, showing off his rubbery mouthguard. Vinny casually nods in the direction of the mean right hook coming his way. Because of Two-Man's practiced skills, the hit is mitigated by a clever last-minute pivot, showing off impressive agility for his size.

Two-Man hops, bobs, and weaves his way around his opponent, wearing him out as he takes swing after swing without landing a solid punch. In an effort to show off, Two-Man lands a left to the jaw followed by a hard right body shot, hitting like a truck.

His opponent stiffens, raising a hand up for Two-Man to stop before leaning over to puke all over the ring.

Refusing to seek medical attention, the stubborn bastard goes home and dies of a ruptured spleen twenty-eight hours later. Word gets out and spreads faster than syphilis in the Tuskegee Experiment. No manager is willing to commit to a matchup with the powerhouse contender known as Two-Man Pizzolatto.

Saturday
February 2, 1952

Bundled up and dripping sweat, Vinny and Two-Man return from a five-mile run to hear Blinky's loud voice booming from the office.

"So? He hits hard—that used to be an *advantage* in this sport!" he yells into the phone, then pauses to listen. "I *did* make the calls. Hell, I called every-damned-body, all the way to Walcott's people!"

Blinky slaps his leg out of frustration. Still moving to ease into a cool-down, Two-Man and Vinny wave in the doorway to let him know that they're back. Blinky holds up a do-not-disturb finger to them.

"What do you mean, there's nothing you can do? You're the goddammed governing board!"

Blinky hangs up and flings his book of contacts against the wall. He stands behind the desk, throwing his exasperated arms in the air.

"I can't fucking believe this shit! You're finally ready for a pro debut and I can't get you a decent fucking fight!"

Vinny and Two-Man enter the office and sit down. "If Walcott won't fight me, can't they threaten to strip him of his title?" Two-Man asks, stretching out his thick leg muscles.

"Without the license, you won't qualify for a fight. We have to work our way up like everybody else." Blinky's face brightens. "Unless . . ."

"Oh, no." Two-Man shakes his head. "I told you—no bribing, and no interfering in any of my fights. I want to win fair and square."

"And you will—but first we have to get your ass in the ring."

The phone rings.

"Gleason's Gym," Blinky barks, and freezes, recognizing the voice on the other end. "Yes," he squeaks, and clears his throat, locking eyes with Two-Man. His back straightens as he listens. "Yes, I know the place," he says, his hand frantically finding a pencil to write down some directives.

Two-Man looks to Vinny and they both shrug, wondering what kind of news this could be.

"And how many *rings* do you see around the *ducks* in this pond?" Blinky asks in code, rubbing the heart that is jumping out of his chest as he listens to the answer. "Yes—oh, yes, I understand. He'll be there. I'll see to it myself."

Cautiously, he settles the phone back on the cradle and anchors his serious eyes on Two-Man's face in the doorway.

"You've been tapped."

Two-Man takes a seat, leans back and plants his feet against the side of the desk. "By who?"

Blinky glances at Vinny in the doorway.

"You want me to leave?" Vinny asks.

"No." Blinky settles back into his seat. "But close that door, Gator. This needs to stay in this room."

Vinny closes the door and turns the lock.

"By *who*?" Two-Man asks impatiently.

"By the *family*. Albert himself. He wants you to freelance as a bodyguard, an intimidator or something. And when I say 'freelance,' I don't mean *for free*." Blinky hoots and reaches for his pack of Luckies. "I'm talking easier zeros than you could ever make boxing, and you won't have to walk around with a crooked nose."

"Just a crooked conscience, big guy," Vinny says, patting Two-Man's huge arm.

"Which hand do you shoot with?" Blinky asks before Two-Man can speak. "They might want you to carry some heat."

"I'm right-handed . . . but I don't know how to shoot."

"It's easy. I'll teach you," Vinny says. "You'll teach me how to box, and I'll teach you how to shoot."

Blinky laces his fingers across his chest and leans back in his chair. "I think that is a fine idea."

Two-Man looks down at his large, strong hands, and back up at the seemingly innocent boy.

Vinny smiles. "Just don't let your left hand know what your right hand is doing."

Friday
March 7, 1952

Just one month later, Albert Anastasia, the long-feared "Lord High Executioner," a prominent member of the five fingers of the Black Hand of New York, is waiting in the back of a candy store on the corner of Saratoga and Livonia to be introduced to a kid known as Gator.

Vinny walks into the ambrosial Midnight Rose candy store exactly on time and passes a brief inspection by Albert's henchmen. A nod of approval is given to the clerk in charge of Rosie Gold's exotically sweet saltwater taffy. Vinny is silently ushered beyond the absurdly cheerful colors and stripes, down a hall and into a dull inner stock room (mostly used for late-night poker), where the men leave Vinny alone with their boss.

As the teen enters, Albert looks up from a ledger and his eyebrows rise almost to where the hairline of his youth used to reside. He tosses a pen atop the card table, internally discounting the meeting as a bust. Then he chuckles. "So . . . *you're* this 'Gator' I've been hearing so much about?"

Vinny steps forward and reaches out to shake the hand of a contract killer who has literally walked away from a murder rap with no worries. "I've been called that once or twice," he replies with a confident smirk, and twirls a chair around to sit on it backward, facing the hazardous man.

Albert's thumb grazes his nose as he leans back in his chair, almost touching the wall behind him. "I thought I had a job for you, Gator . . . but you look like you still got all of your baby teeth."

Vinny sucks on an incisor in protest. "I assure you, my teeth are sharp. I can draw blood."

Albert touches the outside of his mouth, holding back laughter the way a parent does when Junior does something adorable and completely inappropriate. "You're something else," he says. "Is it true that you taught Two-Man how to shoot?"

"Yes." Vinny looks around the room, eyes searching out possible dangers or advantages, taking mental notes as always.

"And with what types of guns are you experienced?"

Vinny shrugs. "Rifles and revolvers, mostly. Look, if you give me a cold gun, I'm a good shot. But if I get some practice time with it, I can hit a squirrel's nut on the move."

"I want you to prove it," Albert says, reaching into his suit jacket.

In a rush of adrenaline and in one fluid movement, Vinny utilizes his circus-acquired acrobatic survival skills to drop his backward chair to the floor and pin Albert's arm to his lapel with his right heel. Albert is now forced against the wall. The man's nostrils flare as his eyes carefully study the inherent skills in the next generation of Murder, Inc.

"Relax, kid. I'm already impressed." He looks down disdainfully at Vinny's embossed leather shoe tarnishing his fine wool.

Feeling silly, Vinny removes his hold and backs off.

"You have the job, Gator. Now, *sit*," Albert says. Not wanting the kid to know how much he likes him, he affects his voice with irritation.

Vinny cautiously lowers himself back into the chair.

Albert dusts off his jacket. "I want you to know that I can't stand a rat. There's a rat in my city that needs to be exterminated as soon as possible." Albert pauses, looking comically at Vinny, before reaching into his jacket again. He places a .38 snub-nosed revolver on the table and slides the wooden handle closer to Vinny for his approval.

Vinny handles the gun with quick precision, barrel safely pointed away as he wraps and adjusts his fingers to the grip, feeling the weight of it, before releasing and spinning the cylinder for a visual inspection. The mechanism cheerfully clicks and rotates long enough for him to see that the revolver is bullet-free, the moving parts are smooth, and everything is properly cleaned and oiled. Vinny holds the weapon up and out to evaluate the sight plate for alignment, pulls the hammer smoothly as he cocks the gun, followed by the sharp *snap!* of a dry-fire. Satisfied with the gun's condition, he sets it back down on the table and asks, "You got bullets?"

Albert grunts. "How many do you need?"

"Only one to kill him," Vinny admits. "But I'm feeling artistic."

Saturday
March 8, 1952

The mentoring, polishing whispers of the cosmos have called, guiding Vinny to this moment. He steps out onto the concrete path of executioner, and the pilot light ignites, the awareness of his providence blazing and vivid like the neon lights of Broadway. Vinny, the Gator, feels an expansion, the sensation of finally filling his fated skin, having unearthed a source of nourishment without the need for conscious reasoning. Never has he felt so calm and so sure as when he slips cold steel into his custom holster. Primal and guiltless, he takes pleasure in completing this circle of progression through trials, through tribulation, an edification that has left him a whetted tool of morbidity, a gifted prophet of death.

On his first paid assignment, Gator slithers through a grid of streets, known to Brooklyn's local residents as Borough Park, and lies in wait to strike his unsuspecting victim coming home from his job on Fifth Avenue.

Arnold Schuster, a twenty-four-year-old clothier, whistles like a bird let free of his work-cage. The young man is riding a wave of public adoration for his role in apprehending a long-sought prison escapee.

A few minutes past nine, when Gator dumps the clean murder weapon in an empty lot five blocks from his victim, he walks away a legend, leaving Arnold dead on the sidewalk just ten doors shy of his home with a bullet in each of his balls and both of his eyes.

Sunday
March 16, 1952

Gator, kid wonder for hire, is a hot underworld-news ripple that quickly spreads from the mouths of the powerful in New York to Sam "Momo" Giancana in the Chicago outfit, Santo Trafficante in Florida, and the ears of the elite in Las Vegas. The ripple trickles down into the Deep Southern consciousness of Dallas and New Orleans—where Carlos Marcello's interest is piqued.

Making good on an avoided promise to Two-Man, Vinny begrudgingly walks beside him in a calm, lush garden area of the Bronx Zoo. They've finally escaped the lingering funk of the monkey house, which was not entirely unlike a gym's locker-room fragrance; the stench is pleasantly replaced by the scent of warm peanuts on the breeze, coming from a pushcart vendor just ahead, moving slowly along the path.

"Why did you finally agree to come with me today?" Two-Man asks, looking with sullen eyes to his young friend. "Does this mean you're really leaving?"

"I have to," Vinny says. "I have a meeting set in New Orleans—and I suppose it's time for me to go home and face Camille."

Two-Man reaches for his wallet to buy a bag of peanuts in which he can drown his sorrows. Vinny touches his arm. "Allow me," he says, and hands the vendor a dollar bill.

After placing a coin in Vinny's hand, the peanut vendor blows a handful of ash into his face and laughs maliciously. The man darts away, leaving Vinny coughing, gagging, and rubbing his temporarily blinded eyes.

In prime shape, Two-Man catches up to the man and tackles him to the ground, landing with a hard thud near the feet of an old woman sitting on a bench, and hits the peanut vendor repeatedly in the face.

Vinny arrives and pushes Two-Man off so that he can get in a few hits of his own—but freezes, drops to his knees, and stares at the man, who is still laughing, gurgling in the blood from his broken nose.

Vinny recognizes the swollen face of Iosef Popescu.

"The killing of this man will only make it worse," the old woman says calmly to Vinny.

"Make what worse?" he asks, blinking with sore, ash-marred eyes.

She nods wisely as she says, "I see this curse before in my old country. It can't be removed, and will be made worse if he dies without his revenge."

Sitting on the cement by the bench, Two-Man shakes his head in confusion. "Revenge for what?"

"My daughter," Iosef spits, his laughter suddenly drowned by his malice.

Vinny lowers his head in shame and falls back next to Two-Man. "Margit," he says solemnly.

"Oh . . . Maggie," Two Man says, up to speed, and rubs his chin. Now finding a respect for the father's rage, he wishes he hadn't hit

Iosef quite so hard.

The short hairs on Vinny's neck bristle, and he experiences a strong wave of fear. "Take it back," he says, lifting Iosef off the ground by his shirt.

"I cannot take this back!" Iosef cries, his body seething with anger as he pulls himself up off the ground and onto the bench beside the old woman. "I cannot take this back any more than you can give back my daughter's virtue! Or her *life*!"

In shock, Vinny looks up at Iosef for mercy. His mouth falls open, but he has no words to convey his sadness.

Iosef fills the silence. "My Margit is *gone*! She hung herself when she found you had abandoned her love." Iosef sniffs and dabs his bloody nose with his shirt cuff. "As payment for these crimes, a woman that loves you will die by your betraying hands. Anyone that dares to love you, now and forever, will be touched by this curse."

"I have money . . ." Vinny scrambles for his wallet.

Iosef violently blocks Vinny's feeble offering. "Keep your money and be filthy rich. Money will not save you now and it won't save me from this pain I carry in my chest." Iosef stands with a conflicted satisfaction. "We will both be forever haunted by the loves we have lost. You will ever be as I am—you are nothing . . . and you will *leave nothing behind*."

Iosef spits and staggers away.

Vinny's guilt-ridden head drowns in a sea of desperate perplexity, imagining how on earth to thwart this invisible evil wish from manifesting.

Back from an untimely bathroom break, the real peanut vendor arrives with his cart. "Anyone want a snack?" he asks the small crowd of three, who are still watching broken-hearted Iosef fade into the distance. Getting no show of money or verbal response, he shrugs and moves on.

Thursday
March 20, 1952

Following a brief late-afternoon shower, a privately owned twin-engine Beechcraft airplane bounces, glides, and ultimately settles on the slick runway at the Lakefront Airport in New Orleans. The air trip was arranged and financed by Meyer Lansky, graciously acting on behalf of his good friend and business associate in the Crescent City.

This marks an end to Vinny's maiden voyage in the sky.

Vinny disembarks, looks out at the south shore, and fills his lungs with the fresh after-rain smell in the Pontchartrain breeze.

Carlos Marcello cranes his stocky bull neck, waiting to meet the mysterious new "kid wonder" in the biz, and poised to persuade him to call New Orleans home. His eyes glow with charmed recognition when they meet Vinny's older but familiar face.

"I knew it was gonna be you," he cackles, shaking his head. He waves an amused finger in Vinny's direction. "I just knew it!" He shakes the growing boy's hand and claps him on the back, which has risen several inches in the nearly three years since they last met.

Vinny grins at Carlos's excitement as he is led to the backseat of a waiting car.

Carlos climbs in after Vinny and looks at his watch. "We're going to have dinner at the Roosevelt, so you have about twenty minutes to explain to me where you've been and why you've been gone so long." He taps the driver on the shoulder.

Leaving out many private details, Vinny, in his deepening manly voice, gives Carlos an abbreviated, fun-filled version of his time away. His recollections keep him talking through the drive to the Roosevelt Hotel, straight through their meal, and into dessert.

"The Prodigal Gator has finally come home," Carlos chortles. He licks his teeth and drains his short glass from the bar. Carlos's glee finally fades—but only a bit—as he sets down his empty glass. "I kept up that promise I made, you know. There's a sweet little girl down the road that's been missing you for a long time now."

Worry, guilt, and dread fill Vinny's thoughts as he lowers his eyes. "Yes . . . I know."

A well-dressed man adjusts his eyeglasses as he glides across the elegant sea of royal-blue carpet that flows throughout the Roosevelt's opulent supper club. He nods politely to several high-browed people stabbing at their artfully crafted entrées, and as he reaches the table where Carlos and Vinny are busy bonding, he smooths his tie and asks, "Is everything to your liking, gentlemen?"

"Everything is better than fine, Seymour," Carlos replies, briefly gripping the kid wonder by the elbow. "Mr. Weiss, I'd like you to meet my friend Vinny."

"Gator," Vinny corrects, and reaches out to shake hands with Mr. Seymour Weiss. "Nice to meet you."

"If you want to stay the night, Gator," Carlos says, "I can get you the exact room Vivien Leigh stayed in when she was here filming dat

Streetcar movie. Isn't that right, Seymour?"

"Yes," Seymour says, nodding stiffly. Vinny notices small beads of sweat popping out on the hotel manager's forehead. "I'm sure that can be arranged."

"Thanks for the offer, but that really won't be necessary," Vinny says, scanning the physical language in the room, aware of discreet under-the-table transactions, a dance of silent conversations that subtly reveal sordid affairs and illegal offerings. "I have a family reunion to attend."

Mr. Weiss's body sighs with relief. "Just let me know about anything that you need in the future. I'll take care of it personally."

Mr. Weiss walks over to greet a table of equal importance across the room.

And so the copious eateries of New Orleans receive and delight, efficiently mixing business and pleasure, high-caloric meals dripping in decadent information—to please either your body or your wallet—serving the sinful needs of many.

The anticipation of visiting his sister causes Vinny's stomach to tighten . . . but instead, the driver detours, snaking through the relics of Storyville and thumping red-light-district haunts, to park in front of the green stucco house—a notorious space of ill repute—at 1026 Conti Street.

He pulls in a breath and turns to Carlos. "I'm not in the mood for a hussy right now. I want to see Camille before I lose my nerve."

Seeing Vinny's distress, Carlos suddenly regrets not having explained the thorny situation before now. "I swore to keep Camille safe and informed, so I did," he explains, defensively raising his hands. You need to know that Norma Wallace is a good woman . . . and it's only been a few weeks," he stammers. "That soap lady, Eleanor, died, and your mother went batty again, so—"

Vinny listens, his hackles up and his face turning more red with every syllable. "So, you're saying that my eleven-year-old sister is in *there*?" he shouts, pointing at the high-class bordello.

Blood rushes furiously through his veins. He leaps from the car and runs up the marble steps, hearing Carlos's fading voice shouting "It's not what you think!" behind him.

Ignoring the front entrance, Vinny uses his powerful physique to climb a structural pole and tosses himself over the filigreed ironwork and onto the balcony, entering the house through an open window.

"Holy *shit*!" Carlos exclaims, watching the kid wonder at work, and scrambles to the front door to ring the buzzer and warn Norma— but it's too late.

Vinny moves stealthily into the heart of the house, smelling an array of exotic fragrances, mixed with sex and sweat, wafting from each room as he opens them. He discovers that Thursday isn't a slow night at Norma's house: bodies upon bodies, twisted in ways that could make a contortionist blush.

"Camille! Camille! *Camille!*" Vinny yells, then again, "CAMILLE!" His young, commanding voice fills all sixteen rooms of the three-story townhouse in an unrelenting search for his sister. The whole house is in a tizzy, wondering if there is a police raid in progress.

Vinny descends the stairway to the vestibule.

"CAMILLE!"

Finally hearing her name, Camille wanders outside the French doors leading to Norma's private quarters and appears at the foot of the stairs wearing a long cotton nightgown, a copy of *Wuthering Heights* in hand.

Norma, who has just let Carlos inside the main entrance, rushes in front of Camille and takes a protective stance against the intruder. "Who the hell are *you* to come into my home and cause such a commotion?"

Camille peers timidly around Norma's feather-trimmed chiffon dressing gown, blinking her doe-like eyes. A curious, murmuring crowd of scantily and partially dressed eavesdroppers gathers along the balustrade.

Is it *Jack*? she wonders, and looks a little deeper. No, not Jack, not anymore.

"Vinny . . . ?"

Her voice is high, shaky, disbelieving.

Norma covers her slack mouth with her hand. Over the last few weeks, she has listened to Camille narrate many colorful, enveloped tales from a large box of letters inscribed by youthful bon viveur—her protective older brother . . . Vinny, *the Gator*, Carlino.

Norma turns her stunned eyes to Carlos. He smiles back apologetically for the loud yet venial disruption.

"I'm home," Vinny says, ignoring Norma and Carlos as he opens his strong arms to Camille.

Her face contorts as she melts into his embrace; she buries her face in his broadened chest and hugs him tight as her frail arms can hold. He kisses the top of her damp head and notes that it smells of Halo shampoo. Camille's arms loosen. She pulls back to look up into her big brother's eyes.

With a sudden, grim twist to her mouth, she slaps Vinny across the face. Her angry outburst is punctuated by a collective gasp from the captivated mishmash audience above.

Hitching with sobs now, she wraps herself around the refuge of Norma's suddenly stiffened frame. Never having had a longing for motherhood, Norma awkwardly tries to comfort Camille. "There, there, my dear," she says, lightly patting the child and looking to big brother for help.

Vinny rubs his sore cheek, forgiving the injury—he deserves that and more.

"I know you're mad at me," he says, "and that's okay. I will make it up to you."

"You *left* me!"

Camille's cry is muffled in Norma's flamboyant garb, tugging hard on the affluent Madam's heartstrings. Norma silently flaps a dismissive hand to the concerned onlookers, sending them back up the stairs to resume their activities, and throws a hard *You'd better do something good and quick* look at Vinny. He shrugs, not knowing how to undo or dispute such a true statement—he *did* leave Camille. A fine choreographer of tricky relationships (other than her own),

Norma motions for him to come forward and to crouch beside his sister.

"I'm here now," he says softly.

"For how long?"

Vinny sighs and glances at the ceiling in both self-loathing and frustration.

"You can't stay here, Camille. Come on, get your things. We're leaving." He stands erect and looks to Carlos. "My mother used to work at the Monteleone. We still have friends who work there. Can you drive us?"

Carlos hesitates before nodding.

As the car rolls up in front of the stately Monteleone Hotel, Camille's face brightens at the sight of a familiar doorman. As soon as the car stops, she squeals his name and jumps out to give the man a hug before helping him and the driver retrieve the luggage from the trunk.

Before Vinny can follow her, Carlos grabs his arm. "Meet me at the 500 Club in the morning. I have a few things that could use your attention."

Vinny steps out. He bends down to peer back into the car at Carlos. "I've made plenty of friends, Carlos. Offers for work all over the world. I came back here out of loyalty to you and to that little girl," he says, pointing after Camille. "I'll stay here and work for you as long as the money is right, but let's get one thing straight right off the bat. You will not own me. Capiche?"

There is a pause, and then Carlos laughs. But there is the slightest edge to his voice still. "Meyer told me you had a full sack. Just don't ever bite the tit that feeds you—and you'd better prove to be worth the fees, kid."

"I'll be there at ten o'clock," Vinny says. He pats the car roof twice and turns to take charge of Camille, ushering her around to the garage entrance.

Carlos smirks. He bears witness to this spunky boy becoming a dangerous man right before his eyes, and he is so proud of Beulah's son.

Friday
March 21, 1952

Vinny arrives on Bourbon Street a few minutes early, walking by an inebriated man talking to his dog about a woman named Sheila. The bored dog looks at Vinny as he passes, opens his mouth, and curls his tongue in a wide yawn. Vinny warily crosses the well-traveled threshold of the 500 Club. His stomach rolls, enduring the sticky noise each footfall makes as he walks across a floor that permanently wears a film of God-knows-what no matter how often it's cleaned.

Sitting at a table, squinting through a pair of tortoiseshell reading glasses, Carlos looks up from a small fan of contracts. He snorts, amused by Vinny's curled lip.

"What's the matter, Gator . . . you don't like the muck?" he laughs. "Like booze and women, this place is more alluring after dark."

Carlos gathers up the papers and taps them into a neat stack on the table, getting right to business. "I'm spreading my interests far and wide, but I've hit a few snags in my plans."

He stands and leads his new freelance employee into the office, conveniently located behind a two-way mirror above the bar.

Vinny touches as few surfaces as possible, but his eyes land on everything as he follows Carlos into the office and asks, "Did you get the gun I asked for?"

Carlos opens his mouth, closes it, bites his bottom lip, and doesn't answer. Instead, he formulates a question of his own. "Are you sure you know what you're getting yourself into? After today, Gator, there's no going back."

Vinny parks comfortably in a wide stance and folds his arms, settling a steady gaze on Carlos. "I learned quite a few things in my time away."

Carlos smirks. "What is it that you think you know?"

"I know the game . . . the twisted domestication of man. I know what power and money can do," Vinny says. He casually opens a pack of Chesterfields and pulls one out.

Carlos's eyebrows pinch together. He digs into his pants pocket for the key to a drawer that currently houses many items in need of safekeeping. "The 'twisted domestication of man'?" he repeats, turning the key and pulling the heavy drawer open.

"Take a wild animal," Vinny starts, and waves a flame in front of his cigarette long enough to light it. "When a wild animal is hungry, it goes out and grabs fruit off a tree, or kills something and eats it. It doesn't ask or beg for it. It doesn't have to." Vinny takes a drag and exhales. "And neither do I."

Carlos nods. "We are . . . *we* are the wild animals," he agrees, slowly lifting a pair of binoculars from the drawer and placing them on the desk. "Go on."

"When you make an animal—or a person—forget that he can fend for himself, and you let him go hungry for a while, he'll do anything for a treat."

"You mean like beg and roll over?"

"Yes," Vinny continues. "He'll beg, roll over, shake hands, and be happy with the shitty scraps he's given—so well-trained that he'll believe all the lies, even the ones he learns to tell himself."

He watches Carlos place the envelope of the agreed-upon advance money on the desk . . . along with a Ruger Red Eagle .22-caliber pistol. Vinny's face brightens at the sight of the gun. He puts his cigarette out in a glass ashtray and wraps his hand around the comfortable textured grip.

Carlos watches him thoroughly examine the gun. "So how do we stop believing the lies?"

Vinny doesn't take his eyes from the Ruger. "The ultimate power is to know that truth and lies don't matter. All that matters is what you *believe*. Manipulation can only happen through emotion. You have a choice whether or not to care. If you decide not to give a damn about anyone or anything, you can't be manipulated."

Carlos raises his eyebrows. "My, aren't we the cynical one," he snarks. "Look, fancy theories you got there, but I just wanted to know that you were sure about all of this. While you still have a soul."

"Who's spreading that rumor?" Vinny grins. "Don't worry. I know exactly what I'm doing and why." He tucks the envelope into his pocket, the gun beneath his belt, and hangs the binoculars on his shoulder from their strap. He's now ready to be briefed on a list of facts to be gathered and a few targets in need of surveillance.

Carlos runs through the assignments, each of which presents Vinny with a unique opportunity to pick up new skills; the one that intrigues him the most is to trace the activities of an alcoholic and local foundry owner named Glen B. Denny.

On Vinny's way out, Carlos calls, "Hey, Gator!"

He stops and turns. Carlos tosses him a box of ammo, adding, "You might need these."

Vinny looks at the box, tosses it back, and winks. "I'm going undercover as a metalworker. I'll learn to make my own."

Friday
September 12, 1952

Full-service metal fabrication at the Gretna foundry requires many stages of alloy manipulation to build strong customized structures. Vinny has been studying the malleability of metal and discovers that it is similar to a man's ability to deform under pressure. There is more than one test to see how tightly bound a metal is likely to be to its ore . . . for men as well. To ensure the best results of any large structural design, a failure analysis can be administered to save time, money, and lives. The collection of data in search of any potential cracks or weakness is a chance to troubleshoot and redeem a well-thought-out project.

Glen B. Denny has chosen to spread his allegiance thinner than Carlos is comfortable with, and is consequently undergoing such an inspection. Vinny's job requires him to sniff past the stinging effluvium of burning ore, to look further than the hypnotic glowing rivers of molten metals, to ferret out the facts beneath the dusty berms of Petrobond sand and along the mercurial Westbank of the Mississippi.

Beneath drifting constellations after a late shift in the parking lot of his current place of employment, Vinny forgoes the stargazing to entertain a passing fancy—a coworker's eighteen-year-old sister—in the backseat of a borrowed car. His training comes in handy as he applies all the rules taught in the basics of welding. With a relaxed hand, Vinny oscillates his rod, holding it at the correct angle with proper travel speed, careful not to overfill the root opening . . . control the puddle.

Two bright beams of light sweep across the dark interior of the car, but that doesn't distract either of the young lovers, rocking with the rhythm of a hammer peening in the distance.

"Hey!" shouts a man's voice.

"Fuck you!" shouts another.

Vinny's head pops up to see a pair of red taillights, a running car parked close to the foundry's office building.

"Don't stop . . ." the girl moans.

"Shhh," Vinny orders, and covers her mouth with his hand. He strains to hear the heated conversation taking place, but the words are blurred into indistinct sounds with ugly inflections. The voices cease their bickering, oyster shells scuffle and crunch beneath angry feet, followed by the loud *wumpth!* of a car door's slam.

When Vinny looks again, the glow of a security light illuminates the running car's government plate. A man staggers away from the car—Glen, visible as he turns to wave his middle finger high in the air, a last drunken act of rebellion before he disappears into the building. The engine revs and the car pulls away, spitting gravel on its way out of the parking lot.

The girl playfully clamps her teeth down on one of Vinny's fingers to jolt him back to her attention. There is no shock in her eyes when his other hand strikes her face. He smiles. She squirms seductively and smiles back, intoxicated by his cologne and the newly discovered mutual perversion that only makes her want him more. She pulls Vinny down and kisses him hard. He gives her hair a tug and her ass a hard smack, getting lost in the lustfully sadistic horseplay.

Thursday
September 18, 1952

Vinny pours a shot of imported vodka for his boss, a man who looks like he is wearing a shirt of hair even though he is sporting only an old baggy pair of boxer shorts. "Have another," he says, encouraging Glen's favorite activity at half past noon, an activity that crossed the threshold of self-medication into full-blown compulsion for fire-water a long time ago. Despite Glen's degree of tolerance, the poor man's alcohol level is surely high enough to be more alcohol than blood by now. Glen licks his chapped lips. Inside a pitifully pickled swaying skull, his dilated liver-sick eyes are bigger than walnuts. Through bloodshot and blur, his goggle eyes appear to relish the anticipation of another mouthful.

The barren walls of Glen's small, joyless Algiers apartment have been closing in on him for weeks. Lying, gambling, drinking—pastimes that were once innocent and fun to this middle-aged bachelor had become a dangerous dependency and the catalyst of his ruination, his pale addicted body unable to get through an entire day without the nauseating quake of withdrawal.

"I didn't do anything," he slurs. His hand shakes on the way to his mouth, spilling some of the clear liquor down his chin. "I told them government spooks to fuck off."

Vinny fills the shot glass again. "Stop talking, Glen. What you did or didn't do is no concern of mine."

Vinny removes his shirt and pants, folds them, and lays them neatly on the seat of a chair. Glen, a dedicated addiction crusader, struggles and ultimately succeeds in dumping the contents of the shot glass into his mouth. While Vinny rummages through the kitchen drawers looking for a sharp knife to slice into a crisp green apple, Glen takes the opportunity to slide out of his chair and begins dragging himself along the floor—a hopeless and clumsy effort. Unconcerned, Vinny doesn't give chase. He watches the pitifully slow attempt at escape, crunching his apple slices. He does so in leisure until he swallows the last tangy bite of his snack, listening to Glen retch his way into the other room. The open faucet squeaks and moans for Vinny to rinse the blade, after which he finds Glen splayed out on the living room floor.

Vinny gets to work with the knife, steady and confident and with a blank expression. Being a conscious housekeeper, he employs a towel to block the vodka-thinned blood that spurts from each artery he severs in the wrists and ankles of the unconscious man.

Moving quickly now, he cleans himself up at the sink with lemon-scented soap and a small dish rag. Once he is fully dressed again, Vinny gathers any incriminating evidence, splashes the last bit of vodka on Glen, and carefully uses his lighter to ignite a mass of flames that immediately engulfs the body.

The haunting, unseasoned scent of Glen's burning fat and vodka-marinated flesh is one that will stay forever in Vinny's memory.

Tuesday
November 4, 1952

A primed informant from the Federal Courthouse nervously touches the tired pin-curled waves of her fine, mousy brown hair before setting down her cup to join Vinny at the café table. He flashes her a *What you got for me?* look, triggering her big blue eyes to survey the area for other naughty spies like herself, her hands distractedly adjusting her modest plaid skirt suit.

"There are signed warrants for state police raids on gambling and hooker houses all over the city," she reveals.

Vinny frowns and stirs his tepid coffee with a hissing cigarette butt. "Do you think this will look like one of Kefauver's politically fueled witch hunts?"

She tugs at her scratchy wool sleeve, wraps her hands around her warm cup of coffee, and leans in closer to Vinny. "Someone mentioned a guy named Aaron Kohn."

Vinny rolls his eyes and leans back in his chair. "That schmuck flapping around, making noise in Chicago?" She touches his arm, and he searches her stern, lackluster features. "It'll be all right, doll. They all have a price."

She shrugs and glances down at her nails, bitten to the quick. "Word is he's an admirer of Senator Kefauver's work—that he's being recruited to come here to rail against police corruption, against

Carlos and have him deported. Like they did to Silver-Dollar Sam."

"He just wants to make a name for himself like all the other wannabes. If he were a real threat, he'd be gone by now."

She nods nervously. "I'll keep my ear to the ground and let you know if I hear about the whens and wheres."

"Good girl," Vinny says. He stands up and pulls some cash out of his pocket to count out her fee.

She fidgets and rubs her brow, unable to hide her disappointment.

Frustrated, Vinny drops his hand. "What, you expected something other than cash? I thought I told you to get off of that shit."

"Old habits die hard, Gator. I cut way back. I'm really trying," she says, bouncing her knee.

"You know I don't deal," Vinny huffs. He studies the desperation radiating from her pleading face, and in the end gives her a sympathetic nod. He counts out five crisp twenties and hands them to the heroin-addicted woman. "Give the Jeweler a visit. He'll have the stuff you're looking for," Vinny says. "Use some of that for food, ya hear?" He places his index finger on the tip of her nose. "Try harder, or you'll get sick and I'll cut you off completely."

Her eyes flare with the threat, her drug-weary pupils floating helplessly inside the delicate blue. She nods feverishly.

Vinny walks with purpose down Decatur Street, leaving Café Du Monde behind. He feels rattled by an overdose of caffeine, combined with the fragments of news given to him by the former peek-a-boo girl.

After completing a secretarial course, she has found purposeful employment at the Federal Courthouse, finding easy access to files, the switchboard, and inter-office communications. Instead of tantalizing the voyeuristic from the stage or behind glass, *she* is now the observer of many men whom she has seen drunk and drooling with their cocks in hand. In the light of day, those same men strut around like sinners on a Sunday morning, nicely dressed and making confessions with their heads held high.

Midstride, a chill washes over Vinny—and it isn't the November wind. He stops dead in his hurried tracks and spins around, only to see a group of tourists gathering to watch a street performer known as Li'l Snooks Eaglin, a blind teenager who amazes the crowd with a twelve-bar sequence of deep, soulful melancholy on his acoustic guitar.

Nothing appears out of the ordinary. Still, as his ears burn red, Vinny looks for something to explain the sudden paranoia that grips him. Finally admitting that there's no apparent evidence, he chuckles at himself, wipes the embarrassment from his face, and continues on his way to report back to Carlos.

There are a pair of dark brown eyes glued to Vinny as he walks away—eyes that have seen him from afar many times before, eyes seeking him out and recording new memories, eyes which know every curve and nuance of his face as it changes from year to year . . . the tender gaze of a mother's eyes.

Vinny disappears around the corner. Beulah takes a large stride forward to follow when two men in the familiar dark-suited fabric of the Bureau of Intelligence and Research suddenly flank her path.

"Ma'am, you need to come with us," the man on her left says, opening his jacket far enough for her to see his holstered sidearm.

She flashes a disinterested glance at the men and takes a brave step forward. Beulah's brief anarchy is quickly neutralized, both arms snagged in the strong grips of the two government men sent to detain and harass her into cooperative submission yet again.

"Your country requires your service, ma'am," one man says, while the other signals the capture.

A car with dark-tinted windows arrives curbside. She struggles to break free of her kidnappers. "What do you need from me now? I'm not one-a your enlisted, and I owe nothing! Lemme go!"

"Ma'am, we have orders, and that's not for us to decide."

"Heaven forbid a soldier wit' a will of dey own. Fools on a fool's errand is what ya are," she says with an irritated shake of her head as she is carefully ushered into the backseat prison. "Don't I have any rights?" she asks the driver, and shifts emphatically, feeling claustrophobic being sandwiched in the close quarters. "Who I gonna save ya from dis time? Mosaddegh? Eisenhower? Or should I save ya from yo' damn idiot selves?"

Before she boards a commuter plane surreptitiously provided by a private nonprofit corporation known as the Civil Air Patrol, Beulah takes slow, cautious steps and looks around beyond the hangers at the open Moisant airfield, knowing it would be useless to run from these armed captors. Her chest hitches with anxiety. She wonders how long it will be before she sees her son again, before she can return to New Orleans . . . or if this is the time that she'll simply disappear without a trace.

She steps into the aircraft's cabin and is greeted by the face of James Angleton—a face that reminds her of a corrupted, lustful character, one who spends his entire life lurking in the dark slimy caverns of a fantasy novel.

We hates it!

she thinks, and is nudged into a seat by her unfriendly escorts.

A little over two hours into the flight, one of the men sent to pluck Beulah from the street exits the cabin and delivers a hushed message into Angleton's ear. He nods and gives a hand gesture that looks like the bored approval of a monarch. The man pulls a long dark cloth from his pocket and heads toward Beulah.

"I'm cooperating," she pleads, and draws away. "Is this really necessary?"

The man in the dark suit is unaffected by her resistance, firmly wrapping the wide cloth around her head, blocking the light, shielding her eyes from recording any of the developing landscape beyond the clouds.

"It's protocol," the man says robotically, and pulls the cloth into a tight uncomfortable knot.

Temporarily blind, Beulah is shuffled off the plane and into the rear of an idling open-air vehicle. She shivers at the temperature that feels several degrees lower than the climate she left. The engine roars behind her, pulling her backward. She tugs her thin coat tight against the accelerated wind on her back.

After a short ride, she is then led through a maze of corridors, some that echo with the sounds of hurried footsteps, some with the hum of equipment, and some which reverberate with the muffled cries of pain and sorrow.

Beulah is deposited in a chair like a sack of groceries. She feels the relief of the blindfold's removal followed by the brisk retreat of the ruffians who left bruises on her arms. The small room designed for eliciting useful information smells of stale tobacco and lies. Peeling paint is the only backdrop to what looks like a table set up for a mean, high-stakes round of gin rummy—or perhaps a higher-stakes game she's in no mood to play.

"Welcome again to our facility, Miss Laveau," Sidney Gottlieb says with a toothy grin. His hands clasped, he stands next to Angleton like a creepy resort's welcome committee. Her body quakes both from the cold and the company. He takes notice of her shiver and asks, "Shall I bring a cup of tea to warm you up?"

She glances at the table, topped with a few confidential files, and then back at the two men. "Why am I here?"

"I'll be right back," Sidney says with a wink, and hobbles out of the room.

Beulah draws her eyebrows together, watching his awkward gait.

"Believe it or not, that clubbed foot doesn't stop him one bit," Angleton says conversationally. "He can out dance the both of us."

"Is dat why I'm here . . . to dance?"

Angleton chuckles and then composes himself. "Your help is still needed."

"Needed for what? If you could just spit it out, maybe we can get dis ova wit' befo de next sock-hop."

"We have a few questions that only you can answer, Miss Laveau. But they can wait until you've had your tea."

Without spilling a drop, Sidney enters the room with a small mint-green cup and saucer set, fine china brimming with herbal tea, chattering away in his hands. "For the lady," he says, and delivers the fresh brew to Beulah. He scampers away on the twisted foot, reminding her to wiggle her toes in recognition and appreciation of small mercies.

She studies the translucent amber liquid as if it contains rat poison. Satisfied with its appearance, she lifts the dainty cup to her nose to inhale the delicate scents of peach, chamomile, and a hint of vanilla. From the first sip, the lightly sweetened brew begins to soothe her throat and her spirit.

Beulah enjoys every languid mouthful. Angleton begins to pace the room with welling impatience, waiting for her to finish. "I told you before . . . I'm no trained monkey. I refuse to perform tricks at your every beck and call."

At hearing her renewed confidence, he lowers himself into a chair across the table and bares his teeth. "Tell me . . . Beulah . . . whatever happened to your child?"

"My child?" she asks, eyes widening with fear.

"We know you had a child in the summer of '38 . . . what happened to that child, Beulah?"

"My . . . my child did not survive," she stammers.

"Does your child have the same gifts as you?"

"I don't know what you're talking about."

He slaps the table and yells, "Stop with the lies!"

Beulah is stunned. She desperately tries not to whimper or show signs of weakness. Angleton sits in silence for a long while and stares at the cracks in her armor until his eyes become softer, and so does his voice.

"I don't want to hurt you, my dear. Don't make me hurt you."

He opens a file in front of him and slides to her a dated black-and-white photograph depicting a troop of performers and their crew posing in front of a circus tent.

"Do you recognize anyone in this photograph?"

She leans in to take a closer look. "No. I don't recognize anyone."

"Are you certain?" he presses.

She leans forward again and squints at the image. "The faces are a bit small and blurry."

He smiles and wags a long boney finger at her. "You know, I had a feeling you'd say that." He pulls another photograph out of the file folder and places it atop the other one. Beulah disguises her horror, looking at a photograph prominently featuring an unmistakable, magnified image of her son. "What about this one? Do you recognize this face?"

"I . . . I . . ."

"You know what? I believe you *do* know who this boy is, and I completely understand that you're trying to protect him. But what do you think will happen if our enemies were to discover this young man's talents and decide to turn him against us?"

At her silence he adds: "How well do you think you know your son?"

"I told you, my son did not survive. He can neither be dangerous nor be in danger."

"And I also told you, Miss Laveau, that there are others with gifts such as yours. In fact, I have someone here that is more cooperative and happens to have a difference of opinion on this subject."

Wearing a satisfied grin, Angleton stands and opens the door to allow another man to enter the room. Beulah expects another pale legacy from some government frat house, but shifts in her seat when her gaze locks with the piercing green eyes of a younger, more muscular man. A man with dark hair, high defined cheekbones, and the grace of a prowling tiger. "I'd like to introduce you to Iosef Popescu."

Transfixed, Beulah responds with a weak, "H-hello."

Iosef's face conveys warm sincerity. "Nice to meet such beauty," he says in a smooth English-Romanian blend.

"Likewise," she says, yet something sharp and inexpressible makes Beulah recoil from his outstretched hand.

Angleton clears his throat. "I know we'll ask a lot of you, but I promise you'll be well compensated for your contributions to protecting this nation's interests."

"You cannot continue to stir up de future and expect it not to spill," Beulah warns Angleton.

He looks back at her in deep contemplation before he leaves the room. The door closes and Beulah watches Iosef, his eyes unblinking and uncomfortably fixed upon her.

"This is wise statement. Sounds like you speak of personal experience," he says, and raises a mesmerizing flame to light a cigarette. "This foretelling of futures."

"I understand people . . . deir longing for a better future," Beulah says, tears welling, the flame reflected in her eyes. "So bad dat you'd move de stars in de sky."

He snaps the lighter closed. "Is that what you wanted for your son, Beulah . . . to move the heavens?"

"M-my son?" she stammers.

"No need to play coy with me. I have met your son and I know what he is."

Beulah moves her head in slow oscillation. "I can't help you."

"Yes, you can. We need to speak with him. Do you know where we can find him?"

"I can't help you," Beulah repeats, filling with the dread that her boy will somehow find out the truth that she has been hiding from him all these years.

Iosef smokes; calmly, he watches the gears pick up speed behind her distraught eyes. "Aww, don't worry, my *drága*, your secret is safe with me . . ."

He stands and smashes the rest of his cigarette into the thick ashtray.

He exhales a cloud of smoke.

"For now."

A few moments later Beulah's chest begins to rise and fall more rapidly and she fans herself as if someone turned up the heat in the room. Iosef sees her pupils expand and tiny beads of sweat gather just above her plump lips.

"Stupid hormones," she says, seeing his face fill with concern.

"Can I get you some water?" he asks, and turns to pour a glass.

Iosef smiles in self-congratulation while his back is turned. Earlier, he used a medicine dropper to administer a healthy dose of a hybrid blend of lysergic acid diethylamide onto the sugar cube that easily dissolved into her tea.

He offers the glass to her.

Suddenly ravenous with thirst, she downs the glass. "Oh, t'ank you," she says with relief, and licks her lips.

"Cooperation—she is a two-way street, no?"

"I guess . . ." she says, unsettled by the lights becoming brighter—too bright—and the walls that warp and sway.

"Haven't you ever been curious about your own future? Your son's?"

"I'm not able to see everyting for everyone. When I am unable, I guess it's not for me to see," Beulah says dreamily, beginning to feel dizzily buoyant with a wave of sensory distortion, seeing colors that were not there before.

"What if I told you that if you take my hands you could see it all, whenever you wanted?"

She blinks at him, eyes fascinated with his face that glows, luminescent, like an angel descended from heaven. Beulah wipes her clammy hands on her clothes and holds out their elongating mystical shapes to steady the swirling air.

"Are we . . . falling?"

"Take my hands," he offers.

She looks at them and slowly shakes her head *no.*

"Go on . . . it's okay, take my hands."

Unable to move, she feels Iosef's powerful hands envelop hers, and the filters of her brain dissolve.

The valve of knowledge opens and the walls fall away.

She is helpless in a flood of incipient time.

A blur of all the horrors yet to come is rushing toward her.

Iosef is visibly shaken and agitated when he exits the interrogation room. James Angleton has been pacing the hall as if he were a father awaiting a new arrival, and now he eagerly charges toward Iosef when the man appears.

"Well?"

Iosef extends his right arm and pushes Angleton aside. "Give me space to breathe," Iosef warns sharply.

Angleton takes a step back, surprised by his aggression. "Her son is an important asset we need to harness. Do you think you convinced her to help us?"

"I have no need to convince . . . I spin her like a top. When we let her go, she will lead us straight to him."

Delirium subsides and Beulah drifts into a fitful sleep, into a dream of being stranded in a dinghy with no engine, no oars. Floating helplessly on a vast lake, she hears splashing and a woman's garbled cry for help.

"I'm ova here!" Beulah calls out, and drags her cupped hands through the water to propel the dinghy forward and rescue the woman in distress.

"He's coming, please help me!" the voice cries more urgently.

Beulah struggles to get closer. "Stay calm and float, child, or you will surely drown!" She leans as far as she can without toppling, arms stretched out, desperately pulling at the water alongside the boat.

Suddenly a swell appears. A swimming wave of spiky armor-plated muscle rushes by like a torpedo.

Beulah gasps and looks around the room: the lamp-lit interior of 1018A of the Hotel Statler in New York City. She doesn't remember how she arrived here—or anything, for that matter, beyond the magnetized grip of Iosef's hands.

Sunday
March 1, 1953

"**Why do you** like coming to this zoo so much, Two-Man?" The young men stop to observe a silly chattering squirrel on their stroll along a curved path at the Bronx Zoo. Vinny is on a two-day visit and has just delivered a personal message to Jimmy Hoffa and Johnny Dio in response to a deportation order issued against Carlos in an ongoing battle of wills.

Two-Man shrugs, the early afternoon sun bathing his face. "It's safe to have a conversation here. Besides, it's easy to pick up a good-lookin' dame or two," he adds, and waggles his eyebrows. "Turns out, girls like animals."

Vinny slaps his forehead in disbelief. "First the subway, next the deli, and now the zoo." He shakes his head, amused. "No woman is safe from your lame flirting routines."

"I'm not lame," Two-Man replies, playing with his shirt collar as they resume their stroll. "If you haven't noticed, the ladies happen to like me." He smooths his shirt and kicks a small rock off the path. "Speaking of safe, how's Camille?"

Vinny abruptly stops walking and gives him a stern look of warning.

"What?" Two-Man asks, leaning away. He throws his hands in the air. "I'm supposed to be your friend, but I'm not supposed to ask about your family?"

Vinny resumes walking and clears his throat, calming down. "Camille's fine. She's making good grades in school. She has nightmares, but they haven't been as bad lately." He lifts his gaze to the broad overhead branches of a rustling tree to keep his shoulders from drooping, and says rigidly, "I think she still hates me."

Two-Man places a hand on Vinny's shoulder. "Don't be silly. She doesn't hate you."

"If you say so." Vinny lightly shrugs away Two-Man's hand.

Two-Man changes the subject, tapping Vinny on the arm with the back of his hand. "Look, check it out—here comes that Oswald kid I told you about."

"Oswald? The kid getting into trouble with the BB gun you gave him?"

"Yeah . . . Lee," Two Man confirms. His brow creases with concern as he watches the little guy's boots hit the concrete at a brisk, erratic pace. The boy's head and shoulders are stiff, his hands shoved deep in his pockets. He takes a short sideways glance, as if something were snapping at his heels.

"Hey, kid, you can relax! It's not a school day," Two-Man jeers. "That truant officer is at home with his feet up."

Lee signals Two-Man with his wild blue-gray eyes and shakes his head, waiting to be close enough to whisper. "Keep it down. You're being followed."

"What?"

Two-Man and Vinny search for any signs of a spy.

"I don't see anyone," Two-Man says, and pats the boy on the back. "I think you're being a little paranoid. You need to go easy on the reefer, pal."

Lee pulls away, exasperated, and runs a hand through his unruly hair. "I told you already, I don't smoke that shit!"

Vinny, projecting nonchalance, pulls out a stick of Doublemint gum to offer the boy. "All right, all right, calm down. What did you see?"

"A . . . a woman," Lee says, and coughs gently into his hand as if embarrassed.

Two-Man starts to make a joke, but Vinny raises a hand to shut him up. Lee smiles uneasily as he takes the stick of gum, locking eyes with Vinny like an obedient snake does with its charmer.

"I'm listening," Vinny says with a deadpan calm. "Tell me about this woman."

Lee blinks, searching his memory for the details. "She was pretty. Alone. Her skin was smooth and colored, but not dark like chocolate cake. More like chocolate milk. I was curious about her . . . the way she moved like a cat . . . so I followed her for a while. Until I realized she was watching *you*," Lee says, fully under Vinny's spell.

Two-Man is still and quiet now. He has seen Vinny do this before, and finds the trick fascinating.

"How do you know she was watching us, Lee?" Vinny asks.

"Because . . . she was careful to stay far enough away to not be noticed, but always within sight of you. And when I tried to talk to her, she seemed startled. Walked away in a hurry. I lost her."

Vinny looks at Two-Man, grins, and snaps his fingers, breaking his spell on Oswald. "Stop scaring the ladies in the zoo, kid. How do you expect Two-Man here to get a date for Saturday night?"

"Hardy, har, har," Two Man says, giving Vinny a playful shove.

Feeling inexplicably lighter, Lee giggles, unwraps the gum, and folds it into his mouth as if nothing strange happened.

Like a good clown, a good illusionist, Vinny entertains the guys with stories of his time in the circus, caring for the animals. His eyes remain serious and alert, searching for a glimpse of the mystery woman. One thought loops in his head, over and over:

I can feel you. I know you're still there.

Monday
June 29, 1953

Puffing on a Lucky, Vinny paces restlessly in front of Carlos's new office building. The one-story gray cinderblock structure is an unadorned afterthought at the rear of the Town & Country Motel compound, hiding in plain sight behind the restaurant, lounge, and rooms for let. It's one of several new investments Carlos has acquired recently, all strategic and inventive streams of revenue—plenty of irons in the fire now, not all of them troublesome or illegal.

Just as Vinny's belly complains loudly about the thick black liquid Carlos's secretary Frances likes to pass off as coffee, he sees the shiny bronze Cadillac ease into one of the slanted parking spaces. Looking up at the darkening clouds, he takes one last hard drag on his cigarette and sends the butt skipping across the cement.

Carlos flings the car door open, clearly aggravated. "More bad news," he grumbles, handing Vinny a cloth sack full of cash—but not full enough. Vinny frowns. Another lighter-than-usual weekend haul.

Carlos covers his vain, neatly combed head with the *Times-Picayune*, attempting to dodge the random raindrops suddenly pelting him from above. Vinny trails coolly behind, letting the drops fall where they may.

"You act like you're going to melt, princess," he teases.

Carlos snorts, opens the door, and heads down the corridor to his large mahogany desk. He slams down the newspaper. "I knew them badge-wearin fools were unprincipled, but now they've drawn too much attention and stirred up a new goddamned SCIC investigation. Everybody's laying low, scared of getting caught up in dis shit," he snarls.

Vinny opens the bag and and glances at its meager contents. "Those idiots are going to be punished, I guarantee it. Morrison will see that it goes away."

"How is the mayor gonna make dis go away with Aaron Kohn shining a big damned media light up our skirt?"

"We just need to wait it out. Eventually they'll all become greedy and pliant once again." Carlos looks up at Vinny dubiously, so he adds, "I have a feeling that Aaron Kohn will move on after he gets some attention. He's looking for a pat on the back from the big boys in D.C." Vinny removes the uneven short stacks of bills from the bag and places them neatly on the desk. "I discussed the raids with Norma last night in the lounge. She said Big Mo has taken a personal interest, sniffing around her brother Elmo's place and the house on Conti like a Blue-tick Coonhound."

"What beef he got wit' Elmo ova at the Moulin Rouge?" Carlos asks, and plops in his chair. "Captain Joseph Guillot," he says with disdain and rubs his chin, watching Vinny silently count a stack of twenties like a seasoned bank teller. "Dat cop has me wondering if he wants to mount Norma on his wall, or just *mount* her."

Vinny rolls his eyes, then picks up a pencil to write the first total down before it slips away. "I told her that she can use a few of our rooms if it gets too hot in the Quarter. He knows better than to pick on someone his own size."

"Sounds like you have something brewing," Carlos says, tapping his chubby fingers expectantly on the desk. "Come on, Gator, I can keep a secret. Fess up."

"You know . . ." Vinny starts, the corners of his mouth curling up. His volume lowers. "I have a philosophy about secrets."

"Go ahead. I'm all ears." Carlos licks his lips.

"Between you, me, and the desk," Vinny whispers, leaning forward, "three can keep a secret if two are dead." He straightens back up, licks his thumb, and begins to count out the next stack of dead presidents.

Carlos's face goes slack. He stares at Vinny with probing eyes that don't blink. "That's it!" His eyes flash as he slaps the desk and bursts into hearty laughter. "I love that!" he squeals between cackles, and wags a relaxed finger in Vinny's direction. "I'm going to put that on a plaque and mount it on my wall!" He laughs, wiping tears of mirth from the corners of his eyes, and presses the intercom button.

"Frances, get your tush in here!"

Sunday
October 18, 1953

"That playful bastard** surprised me again. That's the second time he's had me in cuffs this month!"

Taking a break from being serenaded by the Town & Country's live lounge entertainment, Norma recounts the details of the previous night's personal arrest by Captain Guillot—better known on the street as Big Mo, as the ebony and ivories tinkle.

"I tells him he's not the only fella who wants to wrap my wrists in bracelets," she declares with a haughty toss of her head. "To wanna watch me get my fingers dirty and take pictures-a me after dark."

Her brags carry a sexy arrogance, entertaining the small crowd that gathers around her and the piano. Her face lights up when she sees Carlos walk in.

"Please excuse me while I get myself a drink."

She slinks across the room, every eye drawn to her almost cinematic allure—including Carlos, who nods and winks in her direction. He stands behind the bar, quietly discussing an update with a stocky man named Joseph Poretto, a trusted member of his organization who runs the restaurant and lounge, and whose name Carlos borrows for legal reasons. This clever law-circumventing practice is merely one of the mounting reasons the Kennedy brothers have it in for the immigrant tomato-salesman. Respectful of his privacy, Norma orders a drink from a handsome young bartender who is as generous with his compliments as she is with the gratuity.

"I don't know who's getting more unsolicited attention lately—you or me," Carlos whispers in Norma's ear as she leans on the bar, swirling her Tom Collins with a skinny straw.

"According to Big Mo, I'm *always* soliciting," she cracks. "Bah-dum bum-*tshh*. Wait." She turns and places a concerned hand on his chest. "They're not still trying to deport you, are they?"

He lowers his head and flutters his eyelashes as if he were an innocent girl. "Apparently the Feds think I'm undesirable," he pouts.

Norma takes a noisy drag on her cocktail straw and sets the glass of clinking ice cubes on the bar. "Honey, you may be a lot of things, but undesirable isn't one of them." With one fingertip, she wipes a trace of gin seductively from her bottom lip, careful not to smudge her bright-red lipstick.

Carlos smiles with rosy cheeks. "It's past my bedtime. I'd better go." He taps the bar. "Fix this fine lady another drink. On the house."

When she touches his arm, he looks down at her glossy red nails.

"Where's that good-looking muscular creature you've been keeping from me?"

"Who?" Carlos shrugs. "Gator? He's next door playing cards with Nofio and Old Joe. Besides, that one's too young for you, Norma."

She takes a step back. "Ouch! You really know how to sting a girl."

"Don't get me wrong. I mean no offense . . . but the boy's only fifteen and some change."

She grins unapologetically. "Wow! They grow 'em nice where he comes from. I'll have to keep up my shape a few more years, then." Norma slides her hands down the expensive material draping her still-slender sides.

Suddenly the piano comes back to life, singing out to her in a bouncy rhythm she can't resist. "Go catch your *Z*'s, Paw-Paw," she says with a wink. "I have a hot date with the dance floor."

Carlos and the bartender watch Norma shimmy and bop her way to a small merry crowd that parts easily to envelope her into its center.

"Make sure she gets home safe," Carlos tells the bartender, and tosses some cash on the damp bar surface.

The bartender picks up the bills and mops the condensation rings with a fresh towel. "Gator really only fifteen?"

Carlos snorts. "Does it matter? Age is a useless number. We choose the age we want to be and act accordingly. Take our Norma, for instance. She'll never admit to her real age—and she'll never *look* it either." He pauses to watch her dance. "How old do you think that vixen is?"

As the bartender smiles in her direction, Norma waves at him and blows a kiss.

"I guess you're right—it doesn't matter," he says, enamored.

Carlos laughs. "That woman is old enough to be your mother." He walks away, leaving the bartender staring at her in wide-eyed disbelief.

Meanwhile, in an unrented motel room, three intensely competitive egos sit in silence, staring at each other across a small round table, looking for cracks—any microscopic sign of weakness, some small tell that will give them an edge over the others.

Breaking the spell, Vinny tosses a short stack of blue plastic chips. They land with a loud clatter in a scattered pile, joining the rest of the carefully measured bets of red, white, and blue plastic disks.

Nofio Pecora rubs an eyebrow. "Fold," he says, placing his cards down on the table.

Vinny's eyes land on Old Joe, who narrows his eyes at the boy and snorts. Vinny's smile broadens and he dances his eyebrows in a taunt. Joe tosses his cards across the table, mumbling profanities as he shoves a self-rolled joint in his mouth.

Vinny stretches out his arms to encircle the plastic pile, and pulls the lot to his chest. "Come to Papa," he says, pissing Old Joe off even further.

"Since when are you such a sore loser?" Nofio asks Old Joe.

"Man, I ain't sore." Old Joe takes a long toke on the joint. "I just need a little visit from my girl Mary Jane befo' I kick dis turtle turd's ass," he says with a restricted exhale.

Vinny frowns at him as he gathers up the cards.

Nofio rolls his eyes. "Big talk for someone who hasn't won a single hand tonight, huh, Gator?"

"Yeah, all talk." Vinny is tapping the cards into a neat pile when he gets a faceful of Old Joe's herbal smoke. Vinny coughs, waving the wisps into a vaporous swirl.

Nofio gets up from the table and shakes the blood into his legs.

"I'm going to get a drink. Y'all want somethin?"

"Nah," Vinny says, and Joe just waves him off.

"All right, just don't kill each other while I'm gone."

After Nofio closes the door, Old Joe sneaks over to the window and peels the curtain back just enough to see the Italian light a cigarette and walk across the parking lot. He turns back and rubs his dry hands together.

"So what you got for me, kid?"

Vinny smirks. "He touches his eyebrow when he has a weak hand."

"That's it?" says Old Joe, collapsing with frustration onto the queen-size bed.

Vinny shrugs, cuts the cards, and riffle-shuffles the deck. "He doesn't always bluff with it, either," he says, allowing the card bridge to fall, interleaved, with the soft fluttery noise of a dove's wing. "I don't think this is going to work."

Old Joe wets his fingertips on his tongue to smother the lit end of his anxiety-relief. "It's gotta work. Do you know how much money I've lost to that guy this year? I just want to see his face when I take it all home tonight."

Vinny chuckles at Joe's revenge plot, shaking his head. "He's going to know something's up. You're going to get us both in trouble."

Joe thrusts his chest out. "What, Ol' Joe can't have a damn hot streak once in a while? Some friend you is."

Vinny laughs fully, allowing another card bridge to cascade into his hands.

A devious thought enters Joe's mind. He purses his lips and taps his chin. "You know . . . you could use that hocus-pocus shit on him for me."

"What 'hocus-pocus shit'?" Vinny asks.

"Don't play me, boy. I know who you are . . . and I know what you can do."

"What's *that* supposed to mean?"

Old Joe stiffens, swallows hard, and pinches the loose skin on his throat. "I know yo mama . . ."

"Oh, *please* don't let him start those stupid jokes again! I can't take it."

Nofio stands in the doorway with a tall glass of rum and Coke, armed with a large unopened pack of Oreo cookies.

" 'Yo mama so *this*,' 'Yo mama so *that*.' " His voice is thick with sarcasm as he launches the pack at Old Joe. "Do us all a favor and shove *these* in your mouth."

Joe peels the cardboard box open, removes a cookie from the stack, and looks at it with a newfound curiosity. "You ever wonder why they make these black on the outside and white on the inside?"

"Because the other way around would be kinda weird," Vinny says, dealing out another round of five-card draw.

Joe dusts the cookie crumbs from his hands. "Let's make dis interesting and double the ante, shall we? I'm feeling lucky tonight."

Nofio joins the table and tosses in the doubled amount. "That weed makes him soft in the head," he scoffs, looking at Vinny.

"Soft as swamp mud," Vinny agrees.

Tuesday
October 20, 1953

Beulah awakens freezing, hungover, head throbbing, on an operating table. She gasps at the discovery that the only thing that covers her naked body is a thin white sheet and bolts upright. Brain still in a groggy haze, she draws the sheet up tight around her.

"Here, you need to drink some water." A man startles her, holding out a glass. "It will help to clear your mind."

She winces and blinks, trying to bring the fuzzy world back into focus. She sees the glass in his hand hovering before her. "No!" she shouts, pulling away from him as if he has green skin beneath his stark white lab coat. He sets the glass down and unfolds a dark blue blanket to wrap around her bare shoulders.

"Who are you?!" She fights to bring his middle-aged face into focus. She begins to absorb information about him and wonders if his prematurely receding hairline is from heredity, stress, or exposure to chemicals in the biological weapons laboratory where he spends most of his days. She feels sick, seeing a vision of animals in cages and humans locked in rooms behind him, all pleading for release. She closes her eyelids, but the sad images are reluctant to leave her mind's intuition.

"I'm sorry you don't remember meeting me before. My name is Frank Olson."

"Where are my clothes, Frank Olson?" she asks, and scans the expansive room brimming with equipment she could never have imagined existed outside of a science-fiction movie.

Pre-warned of the dosing's side effects, Frank avoids her direct eye contact. His cheeks go pink and he coughs into his hand. "Um . . . there was an issue," he says, smiling apologetically. "A new outfit is on the way"—he glances at his wristwatch—"here at any moment."

"My head," she groans, her mouth feeling as if her last meal was a jar of kindergarten paste.

"You really should drink some water," he says, and offers the glass again.

She looks at him with sharp mistrust.

"It's only water. I promise."

"And why should I trust you?"

"I'm not evil. I'm just a family man trying to earn a decent living."

"Are you deaf to it, man? Blind? Haven't you ever wondered what all dis research will lead to?" Beulah asks, her voice weak and raspy from thirst.

His face floods with shame. "Please, drink."

She studies the creases of his worry lines and hears the sound of children, his children's laughter, the joyful noise of two boys and a girl at play.

"For the sake of our children," she says, and takes the glass, gulps down the water, and wipes her dripping chin with the sheet.

He takes the empty glass and presents her with a clipboard and a pen. "They said you can be transported as soon as you sign this document."

" 'They' who?"

"Mr. Gottlieb and Mr. Angleton."

"What's this for?" Beulah asks, skimming the paperwork.

"It's standard. Merely precautionary, really. Everyone working within our programs has signed it . . . including me. It gives Camp Detrick the authority and permission to make any and all arrangements in the event of your death."

"My death?!"

Whoosh! the loud vacuum wind shouts in the pipeline of a pneumatic tube delivery system, followed by a *thunk!*

Frank moves toward the receiving station and waits for the tube to depressurize. A thin door opens to reveal the new arrival. *Beep! beep! beep!* an alarm announces the large canister before it drops into a resting slot. He twists the canister lid open to retrieve the garment conveniently packed inside. He hurries to Beulah, unrolling the navy gingham, all the while smiling. He proudly presents the lightweight, out-of-season frock draped across his arms.

"All better."

"If you say so," she says, hopping off the table in the loose temporary toga. She inspects the knee-length wrap. She frowns at having no brassiere, no underwear, nor a slip, and sighs. "I need you to turn around, please."

"Oh, of course," he says, spins around, and touches his nose as if she bopped him with a rolled-up newsprint. "It looks like a sensible fabric. It should fit nicely."

Despite having doubts about coverage, Beulah lets her makeshift toga fall in a puddle at her feet and quickly shrugs the dress on. Frank hums a tune with the round-eyed innocence of a boy; not once did a peek ever cross his mind. With nimble fingers, she feeds the tie through the eye-hole in the right bodice seam and, once firmly swaddled within, fastens the panels shut with a snug bow in front. She nervously smooths the skirt. Without a mirror she imagines looking like the town harlot at a springtime lawn party, one simple string holding all modesty in place. Beulah's attention is drawn back to the clipboard and she touches Frank's shoulder.

"Can you tell me what's really going on here?" she asks, and points to the fine print.

"It's a release form. You won't be allowed to leave the facility until you sign, and I'm really not at liberty to discuss the inner workings of our programs."

"What do I care what happens after I'm gone?" She scrawls her name next to the X and places it on the bed. "Tell me. Is dis how you wish to spend your time on dis Earth?"

Frank looks lovingly around the room filled with expensive diagnostic equipment. "Science is all I know, and I have mouths to feed."

"In de end, we must all own our choices," she says, and grabs both of his wrists.

Locked in her electric field, Frank Olson's back arches in distress as Beulah channels a myriad of disturbing images. A reality Frank never wanted to believe existed beyond the sterile cavities of the lab: visions of serums injected, of scalps penetrated by industrial needles, sleeves drilled into craniums, electrodes grazing gelatinous brain tissue as they are violently slid into place; pathways of human and animal minds altered, split, and primed for reprograming with volts of electricity, ridding them of all conscience and destroying natural will; images of victims—past, present, and future, undergoing brutal psychiatric, biochemical, neurophysiological, and sociological testing—flash with the velocity of atoms smashing before their eyes.

Tears of intense misery flood both faces.

"Why? *Why?* Why?!" Beulah cries out as blood starts to trickle from their noses. An anguished prayer forms in Frank's heart and she releases his wrists; both fall to the floor in exhaustion and agony.

Gasping in panic, Frank wipes the blood from his upper lip. "You've seen what they're capable of," he says. Helplessness overwhelms him and he begins to sob. "What are we going to do?"

Beulah stands and dusts herself off. "All I know for sure is that I can't let them find me again." She walks around frantically. "I had a purse, and it's still here—I can feel it."

"What about me? What am I supposed to do now?" he cries, still traumatized by the graphic horrors she's shown him, the places he never intended his research to go, a truth that cannot be unseen.

She turns to him and squeezes his shoulders in brief solidarity. "I'm not going to lie—we bot' have some hard choices to make."

"How will I keep my family from knowing about these hideous things?" Frank sobs harder, his upturned face slick with tears.

"I don' know what's best for your children, Frank, I really don't, but I didn't choose to be in dis position and I'm gettin the fuck outta here."

Beulah helps Frank rise to his feet. "As far as they know, everyting went fine . . . I signed the paperwork, see?" She lifts the clipboard. "Do whatever you need to do to keep dem safe. We don't have much time, Frank. My purse! Where's my purse?"

He sniffs, weakly nods in agreement, and uses a key to unlock a metal cabinet door to return her belongings. He presents the black leather kiss-lock handbag she repeatedly asked for, along with a one-way bus ticket—courtesy of appropriated tax dollars—to New York.

"Is this exchangeable?" she asks, and takes the items.

"Maybe, why?"

"Didn't you see? Don't you get it?" she asks, frantically searching the ticket for details. "This is a trap and I'm expendable. They don't need me anymore—dey're after my *son!*"

Harold Abramson, a doctor with security clearance and credentials at Mount Sinai, arrives to an urgent meeting at 81 Bedford Street. If Gottlieb and Angleton had taken a car to the musty-smelling apartment, it would have taken three hours and forty-nine minutes with no impediments to roll up I-95 and arrive in New York City ahead of Beulah's departure time. That simply would not do, not when taking a plane gave them a thickly cushioned head start—plenty time to cover their tracks.

"All you'll have to do is sign the damn commitment papers, Harold," Gottlieb says, and turns to look out the window through privacy panels at the pedestrian-lined streets of Greenwich Village.

Angleton opens and closes cabinets in search of libation. "We need this woman on ice indefinitely . . . at least until we have everything we need from her. It should only be for nine months, less if the insemination didn't take."

Harold considers options—other than putting his license at risk. "If that's the case, can't we just keep her under wraps here? I thought that's what safe houses were for."

Angleton's face brightens, finding a nearly empty bottle of Cointreau. "It's more than just keeping her. We could have monitored her in Maryland. It's about *discrediting* her," he says, pouring the last ounce or two into a short glass. "If her story ever leaks, I want her to not only sound insane . . . I want a clear diagnosis on record to prove it."

Harold frowns at the empty bottle. "Where is she now?"

Gottlieb looks at his watch. "On public transit."

Harold tilts his balding head. "No escort?"

"Olson is one of us, upstanding and respectable as they come," Gottlieb says with an irritated *don't-question-my-logic* growl. "I trust him not to deviate from protocol. If there is ever any scrutiny, she will be recorded leaving our custody unharmed and of her own free will."

The phrase *free will* is enough to fill everyone in the room with concern and give pause to think.

Angleton stares pensively for a moment at a cloud of dust particles dancing in a ray of light from outside, then says, "Go back to your sessions, Harold. Do your rounds, flirt with the nurses, or whatever it is you do at the hospital. Our plan is to dose her in public and let the sparks fly. There won't be any doubt to her mental state when she arrives on your doorstep in cuffs."

"Is this official?" Abramson asks, drawing a head snap from Gottlieb.

"Unofficially, yes," James Angleton says, followed by a soft grunt of amusement.

Gottlieb approaches Harold and places a stern hand of warning on his broad shoulder. "I agree with Angleton—Dulles needs plausible deniability on this one."

All three spines in the room go erect at the sound of a knock at the door. Agent Maguire uses a patterned knock before he enters the apartment so as to avoid getting shot. He delivers a large paper bag of deli sandwiches onto an oval dining table, along with enough bar provisions to survive the afternoon.

Maguire disperses the sandwiches, handing Abramson a tuna on rye. "Is this woman the one who took out Thompson?" Abramson asks.

"We think it was her son. He's our target now," Maguire answers, and unwraps a thick Reuben.

Sidney opens up a file and places it in the center of the table—a thin paper trail and scattered pictorial timeline of a young man's life, the new horizon of hope for Project MKUltra.

"Our boy, Jack, goes by Vinny Carlino—and Vinny Carlino happens to be a freelance killer they call the Gator. He's currently employed by the Marcello crime syndicate."

"He's with *our* tomato salesman?" Angleton says, eyebrows lifted, strutting across the room like a banty rooster toward the new bottle of Cointreau. "Could there be any doubt to what happened to Agent Thompson now?" Glass replenished, he becomes immediately distracted by one of the more recent surveillance photos, one with the smiling faces of Maureen and Camille.

"Do we have him in hooks?" Harold asks.

Angleton doesn't answer, the wheels of his mind turning.

"Not yet," Gottlieb says, and rubs his chin. "I want him recruited. I believe we have an assignment for our little reptile friend."

Friday
October 23, 1953

Adhering to the restrictive covenants of segregated society, Beulah rides in the back of the bus, nursing her many aches. Whatever sinister cocktail the government goons administered to heighten her gifts has completely worn off; all her senses are raw from overuse, as if every nerve ending were left singed.

The bus makes a turn and a fellow passenger, a man in a privileged row wearing five-and-dime biballs over long sleeves of faded plaid, slips off his hand and wakes from a slack-jawed nap. The white man quickly wipes the drool from his chin with his sleeve and looks around to see if anyone noticed. Beulah tries to hide her weak smile but can't hide the distress still on her face. He watches her a moment with a pinched look and decides to move closer. Not wanting to draw attention and worried that she may have offended this man somehow, she turns her attention out the window. Beulah gasps when she feels his presence in the seat beside her.

"Here," he says quietly. She swallows hard and jumps when he says it again with more insistence. "Here ya go."

Beulah is surprised to see that his cupped hand holds a clean unfolded handkerchief with two small tablets at the center. She smiles uneasily and picks up the tablets.

"It's aspirin," he says, and takes the handkerchief to wipe the edge of his canteen and hands it to her.

Beulah sniffs the opening and looks into the man's face. She sees nothing but genuine concern and kindness there.

He shrugs. "Just some water to warsh it down."

A little round woman with thin tufts of white hair poking out from beneath a scarf cranes her neck and utters disgust in protest.

"You best go back to your place before she has us thrown off, mista."

"Norman," he says, waving at the little woman to ease the tension. Humorless, the woman writhes in her seat at his impertinence, frowns at the exchange, and continues to monitor them.

Beulah decides to give a show. She tosses both tablets into her mouth and turns the canteen up for a swig. The woman's jaw drops and turns away in a huff.

Beulah and Norman share a giggle which unfortunately draws the attention of more frowns, whispers, and sneers from both sections of the bus.

Norman feels the pressure to return to his seat. "Will you be all right?"

"Better now. Thank you, Norman."

The aspirin Beulah swallowed to ease her pain was like pouring a glass of water on a two-alarm fire; it was the stranger's effort that made the ride more bearable.

On top of her physical ailings, she continues to wrestle with swirling thoughts of what she knows, what she can't remember, and a future she can only mitigate but not completely escape. Beulah feels her date with death coming, but she refuses to go down by government hands or to let hate win.

She finds herself at a bus stop in Natchitoches Parish when she climbs into Old Joe's car after a heated exchange over the phone. He arrives almost five hours after she slammed the payphone down on him, and she is still boiling hot.

"Have you lost your ever-lovin *mind*?" Beulah shrieks, hitting Old Joe with her purse.

"For the third time, I didn't tell him about you!" Old Joe explains again. "I said I *almost* told him."

Beulah shoves a furious finger in his face. "I will strike you blind if I ever find out you led him to the trut'!"

Old Joe looks into her eyes, too distracted by his aching love for her to pay more than an ounce of attention to her words.

"Do you hear me?" No response. She sighs. "*Do* you?" she repeats, still angry.

"Strike me blind." Old Joe swallows hard. "I hear you," he says, and closes his eyes to imagine what that darkness might be like. Beulah pinches his upper arm and his eyes fly back open. "Ouch, woman!" he yelps, rubbing the sore spot. "Why you gotta be so damn rough?"

"You gettin off lucky, Joe. You ain't even *seen* rough yet," Beulah warns. "Don't you ever scare me like dat again."

"I said I was sorry. What more do you want?"

"I want my son to be successful and happy, Joe. That's what I *want*. What I've *always* wanted."

Joe raises an eyebrow at her. "And you think him pretending he's white will make him happy?"

"But don't you see? He ain't pretending, Joe. Not as long as he don't remember."

Old Joe rubs his face in tormented frustration.

"I see Carlos been keepin him close," she says. "I don't like him hanging around wit' dose ruffians he calls an 'inner circle.' "

Joe lets out a loud bark of a laugh, realizing that Beulah doesn't know what Vinny does for Carlos.

Beulah folds her arms across her chest and snaps, "What?"

Old Joe shrugs. "You pretty when you mad, is all."

She narrows her eyes at him and swats the air at his nonsensical and diversionary comment. "You know my gift don't work on me and mine, or I wouldn't need your dumb ass to keep me in de know. So what is it dat you know? And don' make me ask you again."

"People on edge," Old Joe explains. "Everybody been gettin pinched left and right these days."

"Oh, you scared?" Beulah says with an edge of sarcasm. "Somebody gonna tell on you hoodlums?"

"They're all the talking type if you twist em just right. Sing like a bird."

"Don't tell me Carlos is still peddling smoke?" Beulah opens her purse and searches inside.

Joe shrugs. "Been going steady with Mary Jane a long time. He's lookin to score something bigger now."

"Is he smugglin? Is dat what he's doing with all dat marshland all along Barataria and de Gulf of Mexico?" She slowly shakes her head in disapproval. "Gambling, whores, booze, drugs, bribes—exploiting de weakness o' de ordinary," she says in sad observation, and wipes at her nose with a handkerchief she's rescued from her purse.

Old Joe jerks back. "You didn't get all that from *me*!"

"You used to tell me you were gon' get away from all dis . . ." She fixes him with a hard stare. ". . . and take my son wit' you."

"I will," Joe says, and lowers his eyes. "I want to."

Beulah lets out a long breath, closes her eyes, and wearily massages her temples. "You just keep runnin around in circles expecting de scenery to change. He needs a way out—does my son have a way out?" she asks in an impatient huff.

"I've been planning and saving, but these things take time."

"Time? Time's no friend o' mine." She scoffs and looks out the window.

Joe bites his lip and stares out at the empty sky, knowing the safe place she wants him to find doesn't exist. He's a proud man, and it isn't easy to admit that this long stint of feet-dragging has no bigger reason than fear.

"Drive," she says, feeling death's hot breath on her neck.

"Where to?" he asks, turning on the ignition.

"I don't know yet. Just drive until I do."

Beulah is struck into silent awe at seeing Norman, her aspirin-gifting stranger, walk hand-in-hand with a child along the roadside.

As the car passes, the gorgeous ten-year-old skips and lifts her smiling face to bask in the light of Norman's own. She glows with happiness, wearing a homemade flour-sack dress as if it were a ball gown.

"Mary," Beulah whispers, straining for a vision that won't completely manifest. Her brain fills with blurry, disjointed pictures that make no sense.

Joe sees Beulah's fascination, her face pressed against the glass. "Who was that?" he asks.

"Angels," she whispers.

Monday
November 2, 1953

Back when the Gator was still nameless, floating in amniotic bliss, geologists from the California Arabian Standard Oil Company were vindicated in locating and securing the rights for a drill site known as Dammam No. 7. It was not just another Middle Eastern oil discovery, but more like a world-shaping event, seeing that it soon proved to be the largest tap in history.

It wasn't the CIA's wining and dining that won him over. It wasn't the sentimental talk of patriotism, the incessant droning on about the need for loyalty and allegiance, rights and wrongs, friends and foes, or even the pleas for the protection of power and false dichotomies, that secured Vinny's participation; it was the large wire transfer that eventually sealed the deal. His personal brand of stimulant makes him no less dutiful, nor any less meticulous.

Before being briefed in the darkest arts of war, entrusted with a travel packet of maps, intel, and falsified travel documents, Sidney Gottlieb bestowed the last of his pep-talk wisdom to Vinny, saying, "Sometimes we can't rely on history to do the right thing for our future, and so we must intervene."

Today, amidst continued economic growth, he moves through the bustling streets of Riyadh. The dry desert air billows in the long white ankle-length cotton thobe Vinny wears to make himself inconspicuous. His mind whirs beneath the cord-bound headdress, launching into an audacious undertaking: a covert plan that has little chance of completion in a deeply religious land where strict criminal punishments include public lashings, hangings, stonings, amputations, and beheadings.

He's reasonably sure that the crime of forcing the life from a man revered by an entire nation would be made to endure a fate far worse.

No wonder the line of volunteers for this job was non-existent . . . no surprise that this risky business ended up in my lap.

Outside of United States jurisdiction and beyond its help, armed with silent acrobatic stealth and a modified weapon, Vinny must complete his mission to destabilize the local regime and secure new backchannels for trade negotiations.

He must also make it back alive without initiating the next World War.

Thursday
November 12, 1953

The phone rings three times, unanswered.

"Frances!" Carlos hollers out of frustration—until he remembers she's gone to a doctor's appointment. "Oh, for Christ's sake," he mutters, and picks up the phone on the fourth ring. "Hello?"

"Hello."

The voice on the other end is familiar. Carlos's mouth falls open; he stops breathing, and drops back in his chair.

"I know you been looking for me," Beulah says when he doesn't respond.

Carlos finally finds his voice, and he sputters, "How have you been?"

"Don't pretend you care 'bout my health when I know you want me dead for something I didn't do."

"Look, I never planned to hurt you. I just wanted you to explain to me what happened. I'm a reasonable man."

Beulah utters one syllable of laughter. "You—reasonable? No need for me to explain after you killed Adam."

"You think *I* killed Adam?" he asked, high with amusement.

"He *was* the one who took your money. What's done is done, it does not matter now."

His eyebrows draw together. "Isn't that for me to decide?"

"I called because I don't want my son to work wit' you anymore. Can you please find him something else, somewhere else?"

Carlos's spine stiffens with agitation. "And who are you to make that decision?"

"His mama, dat's who."

Carlos laughs cruelly. "He doesn't even remember you—and I plan to keep it that way." He imagines the pain on her face in the hush that follows.

Beulah clears her throat. "I'm willing to meet wit' you and talk about a truce."

"Why? So you can work your magic on me? No way, no how."

"Magic or no magic, I will not rest until my son is safe. He is not safe working wit' you."

"Safe?" Carlos snickers. "Trust me, there's no one safer than your boy. He can take care of himself."

"I'm not laughing. I want your word dat you will steer him in a better direction."

Carlos jabs his finger against the desktop. "Look, lady," he shouts, the veins in his neck bulging, "just because we have history together don't mean a hill o' beans when it comes to how I run my business!"

"Don't go forgettin dat I know tings about you. Perhaps I should have me a long conversation wit' Mr. Kohn."

Carlos goes quiet. "I would kill you."

"Haven't you figured out by now dat you can't?" Beulah says, and slams the phone down.

Carlos hears the sound of the phone reverberate from Frances's desk in the front office. He runs to the entrance door and sees it closing.

He flings the door aside and steps into the sunlight, where nothing moves other than cars whooshing by on Airline Highway—but he can smell Beulah's spicy scent in the air.

Frantic, he runs through the parking lot looking for any sign of the direction Beulah has taken, just as Frances pulls in. She slams on the brakes and cranks her window down. "What's going on?"

"Did you see her?" Carlos yells.

"See who?" Frances asks, watching him hop into her passenger seat as if this were a getaway.

"Just drive!" he shouts, still looking. "Someone took off without paying their bill."

"Oh."

Frances throws her car in Reverse, pops her bubblegum, and tears down the road. It takes over a quarter-tank of gas before he is willing to give up the chase and go back to his desk empty-handed.

Sealed in a droning metal tube full of smoke for hours, stuffed to the gills from an in-flight meal, Vinny chooses sleep over the mind-numbing boredom of small talk or staring at the back of the passenger seat in front of him, en route to the United States.

The ride home after pulling off the most stealthy and successful government plot to date is not entirely safe nor uneventful. His rest is disturbed several times by bone-shaking turbulence—not unlike the violent quake of unrest his brief trip triggers in the Middle East. For a person to die of natural causes is the best diagnosis possible; it means no need for any ass-covering bureaucratic diversion of blame.

Sometimes history doesn't just happen.

Often, we have to create it.

Thursday
November 19, 1953

After a hearty dinner on the second evening of a mandatory three-day work retreat, Sidney Gottlieb smiles, setting two seemingly identical open bottles of Cointreau on the living-room table in clear view of the small gathering.

Frank Olson takes a spot on the couch next to his division chief and friend, Vincent Ruwet. Another CIA employee, Robert Lashbrook, takes the liberty of pouring and serving drinks to the twenty or so esteemed attendees. Frank welcomes the after-dinner refreshment, finding it increasingly difficult to relax in the secluded cabin at Deep Creek Lake. Surrounded by agents and scientists with whom he has worked for years, he bravely pretends that everything related to the joint project with the Special Operations Division is going along without a hitch. When pointedly asked about the bioweapons research and mind-control initiatives, he answers, "Just fine and dandy."

Unbeknownst to Frank, his own mouth—his own thoughts—may soon betray him, his judgment conquered by a tasty liqueur with an undetected chemical chisel, enough micrograms of LSD to pry loose what remains of his highbrow ethics and dislodge the enduring plates of his psychological armor.

Twenty-five minutes pass. Frank's lower lip trembles. He slides off the couch and attempts to cross the room, but his knees come unhinged and he falls heavily onto them.

"What's happening?" he cries.

Gottlieb, schooled in many interrogation techniques, uses calm calculation when confronting Olson in his disorientation.

"*Shhh* . . . it's okay. There's no trouble. You're going to be fine," Gottlieb quells. "All we want is for you to tell us again how our Miss Laveau left your custody."

"It's just like I said before," Frank explains, his heart thumping, the room leaning, and the color fading from his face. "She took the ticket and got on the bus."

Gottlieb stands over him and looks down disapprovingly. "She never arrived in New York, Frank. Tell us where she is and this can all be over."

Frenetic, Olson tries to hide from Gottlieb's multiple angry eyes. "I don't know . . . please make it stop," he pleads with gasping sobs, then calls out: "Help me, Ruwet!"

When Vincent Ruwet comes into Frank's view, there's a unique expression of both concern and pity on his friend's ghastly inverted face, and he urges, "Come on, just tell us all the truth, pal."

Olson slams his eyes shut. "But . . . I don't know where she is," he cries, gripping the thick carpet.

"Tell us what you remember, Frank," Gottlieb demands. "What did she do? What did she say?"

Frank opens his eyes and screams. He continues to wail, his fingers clawing at his own face. He's surrounded by grotesque forms and cabin walls that begin to melt and drip like hot wax into a void.

"I really don't know! *Pleeeeassse* make it stop!"

Gottlieb ignores the thrashing theatrics, mentally spits on his hands, and continues the interrogation, allowing the LSD to strip Frank's reality away like a banana peel. "You should know by now that our projects are too interconnected, too vital, to allow any threat to take root . . . to *invade* what we have built, what we are still building."

"I think you may have given him too much," says Ruwet, rushing to check Frank's pulse.

Frank retreats, screams again, and slips into the void.

Friday
November 20, 1953

James Angleton is deep in conversation on the telephone, his weary head propped up on his hand, when a young man with a fresh buzz cut rushes into his office with an armload of envelopes containing sensitive data—the type of scandalous evidence that can topple an administration.

Angleton lifts his eyes and they pop wide with interest. "Look, I'm gonna have to call you back with the details," he says abruptly, and stands, placing the handset back into its cradle. "What you got for me?"

The young man dumps the haul on the desk. "Sir, we've been inspecting press releases that were sent out to major TV and radio networks, just as you commanded, and we intercepted these."

The handwriting on each incendiary package resembles Beulah's signature. "That bitch!" Angleton shouts. He shrugs off his crumpled tweed suit jacket and loosens his tie. Beads of sweat pop out on his brow as he frantically opens one of the golden envelopes stocked thick with facts and figures—enough documentation to have precipitated his organization's undoing. The damning information slides out onto the desk and is crowned with a smaller envelope bearing his middle name, scrawled in that clairvoyant's flowery script.

Angleton snorts at her audacity and lifts the envelope for closer inspection. "You think you can disarm me?" he asks, and stabs a letter knife under the fold to slice it open. "What game are you playing?" he whispers.

Awkward witness to his superior's bouts of soliloquy—a phenomenon which is rumored to be just one symptom of Angleton's escalating paranoia—the young man sways on his feet. "Shall I leave, sir?"

Focused on stratagem, Angleton raises a finger, barely glancing at the young man. "No, no, stay here a moment," he says distractedly as he begins to read, not wanting to be alone with Beulah's words, as if they might cast a spell on him.

> *I knew this package would never make it into the proper hands, but I needed to try anyway. I needed to tell someone, anyone, how deeply sickened and disturbed I am by what you've done, by what you're still doing, Mr. Angleton. I can see that you and your agenda won't be dissuaded by me or anyone else. I'm going to call your office today at 2:00 p.m. EST on the dime to extend an olive branch of sorts. The catch is that you don't trace the call and I want Iosef to answer the phone or I'll hang up.*
>
> *—B.L.*

His head snaps up to consult the clock on the wall: 11:53 a.m.

"Son, you have two hours to track down Popescu and get him here, or our gooses are cooked!"

"On it, sir!" Buzz Cut says, running out of the room.

Angleton picks up the phone and presses the buzzer to alert his secretary. "Perdita, route all calls to me," he says, then lifts his eyebrows and adds, "Better yet, bring me your phone and take the rest of the day off."

Angleton insures that both phones are set up and ready to entertain Beulah's demands, then stomps out a bald path across the office floor with his anxious energy, his blood pressure rising with every tic of the clock . . . that now reads 12:18 p.m.

Back in 1944, if the British were to capture a German spy, they would attempt to manipulate the battlefield by sending a judicious mixture of false and accurate data to send German troops shuffling to and fro, needlessly, across the countryside. In this battle, Beulah is the code breaker; she is one step ahead and has them all tap-dancing to her tune.

At 1:55 p.m., Iosef bursts into the room, breathless.

"Oh, thank heavens," Angleton says, pushing an office chair over to receive him, and pours him a glass of water.

Iosef is gulping on a second glass when the phone comes to life. He burps and wipes his mouth on his sleeve before lifting the handset to his ear. "Hello?"

"I know you're both on de line and I don't have very long, so listen close."

"We are listening." Iosef turns to nod at Angleton.

Angleton holds the receiver with clenched white knuckles. He nods back to Iosef in the beat of silence, and perches himself on the ledge of his enormous desk.

"I don't care about 'we' . . . I want to speak with *you*, Iosef."

"I'm here."

"Poor, poor Frank," she laments, and sniffs. "Did you know about all de experiments? Dat *we* were an experiment?"

"This was meant to preserve both of your talents," Angleton blurts, wondering if the insemination process has proven successful.

" 'Preserve'?" she scoffs. "Don't you really mean to *extract* and *combine* our talents? Isn't dat closer to de trut'?" she says, her voice unusually icy and calm. "I know all about de little pieces of tissue dat you steal from us, t'inking you can create an elite army of gifted servants."

Iosef turns to Angleton, who is looking back at him in slack-jawed dismay, and mutters, "What is she talking about?"

Angleton feels the pressure of Iosef's gaze, lowers his eyes, and clears his throat. "Beulah, we don't want to hurt you. In fact, it's the opposite. We desire to keep you both safe."

"Both?" Iosef asks in confusion.

"Yes, Mr. Angleton, tell us more about who is included in dis warm embrace. What about Mista Olson—will he be safe, too?"

Angleton licks his lips, searching for the best answer. "These decisions aren't entirely up to me, but I can promise that if you return to us right now, no harm will come to you."

"If I agree to come in, you'll have to let go of my child."

"Which one?" Angleton asks, unable to meet Iosef's glare.

The question hangs in the air—the stunning revelation that there may be another life that hangs in the balance, an innocent soul caught in the maddening crossfire of their impulsive politics.

"No need to think up your lies, Mr. Angleton," Beulah scolds. "I know how greedy you are. It's Iosef dat I plead to now. Iosef . . . I know why you hate my boy, and I feel your pain. I can sense it . . . de rage crawling just beneath your skin like a maggot. But, Iosef, please swear to me dat when he's paid da price you seek, you'll leave him be."

"Hey! *Psst!*" Angleton pivots the mouthpiece and snaps his fingers at Iosef.

Unresponsive to the background antics, Iosef listens to her breath and closes his eyes, mind racing.

"Iosef, I need your vow," she says, and hums a few bars of a soft, soothing lullaby.

He can feel his thick wall of revenge fracture beneath the force of her love, and his voice cracks when he says, "There is another way for us . . . we both saw it."

And she did see it. She yearned to explore where that love could go. But the difference between conceptualizing an alternative and going forward with a future that would betray her son was too inconceivably vast. "I can't give you what you want," Beulah admits.

Angleton covers the mouthpiece with his hand and steps toward Iosef. "Don't let the niggress cunt dazzle you!" he says through his tightly gripped teeth. "She'll have you chasing your own tail!"

Wrestling with his pride, Iosef releases the handset and steps to Angleton, his eyes bulging with hurt and anger. "Shut up!" he shouts, raising his right fist.

Phone still tightly in hand, Angleton instinctively flinches, yet he proudly wears an *I triple-dog-dare you* expression on his face.

Iosef lets loose a deep, sorrowful growl of frustration and retreats, tugging at the sides of his hair—a pawn with no good moves to make. He lifts the handset to his ear. "Then I can't give you what *you* want," he says as a bitter tear drips onto his upper lip. He licks it away, resigning himself to her choice, and hangs up the phone.

"Iosef?" She sniffs. "Iosef?"

"I'm still here," Angleton says, watching Iosef leave the room.

"In dat case, Mr. Angleton, I'm going to provide you with one last prediction," Beulah says with sour indignation. "I'll have me and my son lobotomized before I'll stand by and let you run your tissue tests on him."

"You wouldn't!"

"Wouldn't I? I'd rather see him docile than to spend his life as your obedient dog or locked up in the belly of your lab."

"You know what happened to Rosemary Kennedy . . . no one wants that repeated."

"My boy keeps his emotions in check and still does not know what he's capable of. What do you think will happen when he figures it out? Do you really think you're prepared for that?"

Buzz Cut rushes into the room. "She's in Texas!"

The line falls dead.

Angleton throws the handset down. "Fuck, fuck, FUUUCK!"

Refreshed, regrouped, and with a cooler head, Angleton dials the phone number of the owner of the Pelican Tomato Company, the man who singlehandedly keeps Louisiana Naval bases in fresh marinara and ketchup.

"Hello again, Mr. Marcello," he says, followed by a heavy sigh. "Sorry about the interruption earlier. I was sincerely hoping it would not come down to this . . . but I think your problem just became *our* problem."

"You need to be careful," Carlos says. "She's a mama bear. You know what mama bears do when they're cornered? They fight. They kill."

"That's why I'm calling you. I think she's a bad poker player, my friend, and I'd bet the roof that in the end, she won't."

Sunday
November 22, 1953

Entering Mosca's just in time for lunch, Vinny finds Carlos talking to property lawyer Philip Smith, one of several legal advisors at his beck and call.

"Bring me his head on a goddamned plate," Carlos tells Philip as he stabs his fork deep into a large mound of al dente spaghetti.

Without a word, Philip turns to leave. On his way out, he gives Vinny the benefit of a *yikes* expression as they pass each other.

"What was that about?" Vinny asks Carlos.

Flashing angry eyes, Carlos takes a bite out of a large spicy meatball.

Vinny settles in front of his own steaming plate of garlicky goodness. "Never mind. I don't really want to know," Vinny says, and tucks a cloth napkin inside his collar. "If I have to hear about Kohn or that newlywed pain-in-the-ass Senator one more time, I'm not going to be able to enjoy my food."

Carlos gives Vinny another dirty look as he grunts and chews. He swallows and wipes a drop of tomato gravy from his chin. "I got a call from Bethesda. Looks like someone is pleased with the work you did in Saudi Arabia. I'd ask, but I know you won't tell me."

"A magician never reveals his secrets," Vinny smiles, wielding his fork as a weapon of pasta destruction.

"Are you and Camille coming to the house for Thanksgiving?" Carlos asks.

Vinny makes a *hmmm* sound in the back of his throat as he chews, followed by a noncommittal shrug. His spirit shrinks, knowing no limo or state-department official is going to swoop in to save him from this invitation.

"Gonna have a ton of food. And you know my Jackie loves Camille."

"Will Nofio be stopping by?" Vinny asks. "You know he doesn't like me very much, and he's been making a big stink about it for a while now."

"He just thinks you haven't earned your stripes because you never served any jail time. He has trust issues. He'll get over it," Carlos explains. "Besides, I didn't invite him. So? Will you come?"

Vinny rocks his head from side to side in contemplation. "Will you have pie?"

"I'll make sure of it."

"All right—but let's not make a habit of it. You know I'm not looking to start any kind of tradition."

"That's my boy." Carlos chuckles and shakes his head, knowing by now Vinny's disdain for daylight socializing.

His merriment is cut short by a painfully thin man walking into Mosca's with timid steps. He lays an envelope on the table in front of Carlos. Without taking his intimidating eyes off the man, Carlos drops his fork and pushes the envelope to Vinny. Vinny opens it, licks his thumb, and counts out the contents. The thin man shakes like a wet puppy, tugs at his ear, and clears his throat, watching the greenbacks stack up, his conscience gnawing at him for the things he had to do for every last one.

"It's all here this time," Vinny smacks with indifference, returning to his meal.

Carlos sucks his teeth and waves the man away. The starving man smiles and dips as if he were leaving the presence of sovereignty. In the brief silence that follows, Carlos recovers his fork, hovers over his plate, and releases a deep, agitated sigh.

"Heavy is the head that wears the crown," Vinny says, and shovels in another mouthful of spaghetti.

"Lemme guess—one of Camille's fancy English papers?"

Vinny launches a noodle from his fork and misses his target.

Carlos checks his sleeve for sauce splatter. "Son, you'd better stick to guns."

"It was a warning shot," Vinny says, and scrapes his teeth along the fork as he takes another bite.

Carlos pushes his food around on his plate. "I have a mark I can't seem to locate," he says uneasily.

"No problem." Vinny shrugs. "Just give me what you know."

"I'm sorry to say that I don't know too much."

"Well, then I suppose it might take me a while"—he grins—"but you know I love a challenge."

"You are not to use a gun," Carlos commands. "I need you to do whatever you did for the government. Spotless. Untraceable."

Vinny's eyebrows pull together, perplexed by the unusual request.

"All right."

Carlos puts his fork down and rubs his chest. "It won't hurt though, will it?"

"Do you care?" Vinny asks.

Carlos presses his lips into a fine line and doesn't answer.

Vinny lays his fork down and pushes his almost empty plate away. "You want me to kill someone, but you don't want it to hurt. What's up with you?"

"This target is going to be different from the others."

"They're all dead after I walk away. How will this one be any different?"

"This one has curves."

Vinny briefly averts his gaze and shifts in his chair. "What did she do?" he asks.

"Will that make it any easier?"

"It might."

"Trust me, it won't."

Saturday
November 28, 1953

The hallucinogenic effects of the drug-induced mania are over. All of Frank Olson's nightmares of cryptic psychiatric agendas have ended, all the fear gone.

It took nine days for him to succumb, to crumble, for his mind and his reputation to be permanently bent. His skull was already fractured before the drop from the thirteenth-story window, before the concrete shattered his legs, before his body lay lifeless at 2:30 a.m., on the dewy Seventh Avenue sidewalk.

Thirteen stories up, in room 1018A of New York's Hotel Statler, Robert Lashbrook calls a Long Island number and announces, "Well, he's gone," and a voice on the other end simply responds, "That's too bad," a short exchange that is more confirmation than conversation.

The updated CIA assassination manual providing the suggestion to drug, bludgeon, and drop a person seventy-five feet or more onto a hard surface proves effective. A standard-issue contract signed by Frank, to bequeath his employer complete rights over his body in the event of his demise, ensures a swift burial without encumbrance. In the days following Olson's "suicide," reports are made, statements are given. The open investigation is promptly slammed shut—regardless of conflicting accounts—a warped frame that surrounds behaviors and events that occurred in the days and hours before his death.

No meaningful resolution for his distraught family is found.

Gottlieb raises his chin with confidence. "Don't worry. I can handle the Olsons," he says glibly to Angleton's pensive stare.

A student of proper crisis management, Agent Shaun Maguire sits silently trying to absorb the calm and infinite wisdom of his mentors.

Suffering the ill effects of long-term insomnia, Angleton closes his eyes and pinches the bridge of his nose. "What about the Laveau woman? She's still a loose end. How do we handle that?"

"Hmm . . . that one's going to be tricky," Gottlieb admits.

"We're running a huge risk if we don't silence her now," Angleton says, and sees Gottlieb's head snap in his direction, ready to spew another tirade about protecting lucrative assets. Angleton raises his hand. "Look, I know you don't want to risk losing your new golden boy."

"Our—*our* new golden boy," Gottlieb says. "He's ambidextrous, for Christ's sake!"

Angleton rolls his eyes. "Yes. I know this new prodigy is everything you've been hoping for. He's the killing machine we've been unsuccessful in developing on our own. How can we hope to recreate this phenomenon if we don't know what makes him tick? His *creativity.* His *adaptation.*"

Gottlieb brightens. "I would like to observe him, his decision-making, to test his weaknesses and hone his capabilities in real-world situations."

"What are you proposing here?" asks Angleton. "That type of testing facility doesn't even exist, and this mouse is already too smart for any of our mazes."

Gottlieb takes an excited breath and looks to Agent Maguire. "Tell me . . . what's been our most successful counterintelligence modality thus far?"

At first Maguire's head jerks back in surprise at his inclusion; then he leans forward to answer. "Dynamically warping perception to disguise the real threat. To subvert, sabotage, and destroy the enemy."

"What else?" asks Angleton.

"Critical enabling and risk-management on the fly."

"Yes, that too." Gottlieb raises his eyebrows and looks to Angleton.

Agent Maguire impresses both seasoned men by standing with determination. "Send me to New Orleans . . . I have a plan."

Thursday
March 18, 1954

Holding his hat down and his collar up against a cold gust of wind, Vinny crosses the street. He is looking for any witnesses to the six holes he just placed in John Di Trapani's body, leaving the capo of a Milwaukee family slumped behind the wheel of his black Cadillac on a West Side street corner, the kill sanctioned and underwritten by the Outfit of Chicago.

Within the warm walls of Chico's BBQ, Vinny dials a phone number and impatiently strums his fingers on the window, watching a car outside spit white puffs of warm exhaust out of the tailpipe, waiting for the other end of the line to be occupied.

"Hey, yeah, it's me," he says sharply into the receiver. "I called to tell you that all will be silent in Wisconsin tomorrow." He kills the line without waiting for a response.

He steps outside and cups his hand to light a cigarette before climbing into the backseat of the car paid to drive him to Mitchell Airport. There he will board a chartered plane and do the chore he has been dreading all day: proofreading Camille's chilling report on Edgar Allan Poe that is due in the morning.

Friday
June 18, 1954

Vinny slaps and decimates a mosquito that dared to bite his neck. That won't be the only kill he plans to make on this balmy evening in Phenix City, Alabama. His body is pressed against the red brick of the Coulter Building, eyes trained on a car parked in the wide alley off Fifth Avenue next to the Elite Cafe. He barely blinks.

The dark figure of his target approaches the car around 9:00 p.m. Vinny recognizes the awkward gait from the man's war-wounded leg. Rushing at him, quiet as a cat, Vinny knocks off his eyeglasses, presses a .38-caliber pistol to the man's lips, and fires three times.

Instructed to "send a strong message," Vinny places a spent cartridge into the soon-to-be-dead man's mouth where his front teeth used to be, careful to move his expensive shoe away from the blood leaking onto the pavement.

"So much for driving out political corruption and organized crime," he says to Alabama's Democratic nominee for State Attorney General.

Patterson's eyeglasses crunch under Vinny's shoe as he walks away.

The former state senator manages to get up and stagger thirty feet before he collapses onto a nearby street and expires.

Albert Patterson may not have cleaned up the city, but martial law is declared following his death, and the National Guard is sent in for six months to take Phenix City back from the hoodlums Patterson so fervently spoke of defeating in his final speech. A high-profile investigation develops. A rabid grand jury issues six hundred indictments, including town officials, and reaps the conviction of a deputy sheriff.

Still, the real killer is never revealed.

Saturday
January 1, 1955

Two minutes after midnight and fireworks are still screaming, cracking, and popping into the black sky when he sees her lovely upturned face, showered in brilliant lights from the dazzling display above.

Before she can respond to the pinch of the hypodermic needle finding an exposed vein in her neck, she is already overcome by the large dose of succinylcholine invading her body. In seconds, she is frozen by the ill effects of the neuromuscular paralytic drug. She is unable to cry out or speak, but completely and agonizingly aware of what is happening as her muscles give way. She falls helplessly back into his strong arms. She desperately wants to explain to him that she is the only thing standing between him and the awful curse now unfurling its evil wings.

Vinny cradles Beulah gently, not unlike the time so long ago when her arms held him. She stares at his handsome features as he drapes her body across a padding of soft grass in Audubon Park. The distracted crowd, faces all turned to the sky, is unaware of her distress.

Although it delivers a quiet death, Vinny has been informed that this drug is not painless, nor does it in any way dull the senses.

"*Shhh*, now . . . it's almost over," he says with a carefully measured amount of empathy. He lays her head in his lap and wipes a tear from her cheek.

The muscles in her heart and lungs begin to quiver and disobey their auto-rhythmic functions. During her last excruciating breath, she gazes into her son's handsome face, surrounded by a vast and colorful heaven.

Vinny looks deep into the woman's pleading eyes. In her struggled silence there is still something . . . something like a sound, a low and primitive hum like a stridulation . . . a message, a pulse in the air that only people with a special ability could sense or recognize. The night air is thick with urgency, a warning, a reminder that destiny seeks us all, that death will eventually find us. It isn't the act of death that scares him; death is way too easy. He knows that fate doesn't want him to die—it wants him to *suffer*.

She slips away, leaving him confused and desperate with questions of what those mystical powers are and how to properly wield such a gift. A power to control that worries him, perhaps the only thing that truly does: he has seen what power can do in the world.

Where you find power, madness is not far behind.

These thoughts leave him numb; there is an annoying thrumming in his head, and an overwhelming need to escape those dead eyes that look like his own. Vinny wants to hide from the ghost of those frozen, haunting eyes, and a much larger danger he knows he cannot see.

Where is there to hide from yourself? To hide from the things you've done? The things you will do? Is there a place where life stands still and fate can't find you?

Monday
January 3, 1955

"It's done," **Vinny** says with grim nonchalance.

Carlos gives Vinny a puzzled, half-intelligent look, sensing that he has retreated into that untouchable place where he often walls himself in. An inner protective place where no key, no password, and no secret handshake will gain you entry.

"The woman—it's done," Vinny says, applying pressure on his knuckles until they pop.

Carlos shivers and a solemn hush befalls the office. Racked, pale and sickened by the news, his insides are suddenly too heavy, the violent gravity yanking him closer to the ground. His hands fly to his face to hide the sorrow.

Vinny watches this odd reaction to his report. "How did you *think* it would end? Isn't this what you wanted?"

Unable to meet Vinny's eyes, Carlos says, "I thought it was," in a voice rusty with regret. "There's something I need to . . ." He pauses, his lower lip quivers, and he clears his throat. "Something I should have—"

The sound of a loud argument travels down the hall and disturbs his confession.

"What the hell?" Vinny puts a hand on his gun and positions himself at an advantage in case of an unwanted visit from police or the disgruntled.

Instead, Nofio bursts through the doorway, shoving his young cousin, who happens to be an employee as well, into the room.

Carlos instantly recognizes Stefano. "What did this one do now?"

"Armed fucking robbery, that's what!" Nofio yells, flapping his arms threateningly at the kid, who shies away.

Carlos rubs his face and sits down to think.

"Goddamn it!" Nofio smacks Stefano's head. "I taught this numbskull how to *not* get caught—but of course he doesn't listen! Now it's just a matter of time before they find his dumb ass."

"He still on probation?" Carlos asks.

"Yes," Nofio says, shaking his head in utter disbelief. "Twenty-three years old and already a felon . . . and he's gonna get *years* on the Farm for this!"

Stefano sits down and hangs his head.

Vinny presses his lips tight together to keep from smiling, his eyes suddenly lit with a twinkle of mischief. He now shares an inside joke with the mystics; he asked the universe an outlandish question, and in turn the universe provided an outlandish answer.

A place where life stands still and fate can't find you,

he thinks to himself, then, lighting a cigarette, says in the lull, "I can help."

Nofio whips around. "And how you plan to do that, big shot?"

Vinny shrugs. "We all know most cops are lazy. Only concerned with their image, right? If I tell them *I* did it, they'll wrap their case up with a pretty bow and I'll negotiate with the DA for no trial and a fairly short sentence."

"I don't like that idea one bit," Carlos growls.

"Think about it. I'm a juvenile with no priors. You follow me?"

The worried felon looks up at Vinny and says, "But it'll be on your record." Stefano receives another pop from Nofio for interrupting the smart people.

Vinny shrugs again. "I'm sure I can have it expunged or something. I won't let them pin *me* with a felony or anything," he says with a wink.

Stefano flinches at his poor choices being rehashed, yet again.

Vinny brightens with an optimistic thought. "Or I could just pretend to be him, if that's easier."

Nofio scratches his jaw. "You know, that might just work."

"What's the story—what weapon did I use?" Vinny asks in preparation, smashing the rest of his cigarette into a large green marble ashtray.

The young felon looks at the seasoned criminals and hesitates to answer. At a glare from Nofio, he finally mumbles, ". . . a bat."

Nofio pops him over the head anyway. "Dumbass!"

"Are you seriously wanting me to put one of my best guys on ice for you two ass-clowns? No way!" Carlos shouts. To Vinny, he says, "And what about Camille?"

"She'll be fine," he says, keeping any hint of worry from his expression. "Mouse is much better now."

Carlos snorts, rolls his eyes at Vinny, and shakes his head in fatherly disapproval.

"Besides, I never said that I would do this for free," Vinny adds. He picks up a pen, scribbles a number on a piece of paper, and hands it to Nofio.

Nofio looks at it and raises his eyebrows. "Are you fuckin kiddin me?"

Carlos charges over and takes the paper from his hand. "It's not enough, if you ask me." He takes a lighter to it and lays it in the ashtray to disintegrate.

Before the number increases, Nofio blurts, "I'll get the money!" He rubs his eyebrow.

Seeing Nofio's tell, Vinny circles him and chuckles. "Oh no . . . I want the payment in full and in cash before I set foot inside the station. You'd better save that bluffing shit for the poker table."

Nofio looks to Carlos.

Carlos shrugs. No mercy from him. "You heard the kid."

Vinny flashes a cocky smile and turns his arm to see the face of his new Rolex wristwatch. "I need some time to get a few things in order," he says, grabs his jacket, and heads for the door. "Let me know what you decide. I wouldn't wait too long, though—the cops just might come a-knocking."

Thursday
January 6, 1955

"**D**on't ever speak to me—*ever*—*again!* I *hate* you!" Camille shouts at Vinny. She runs away, crying, cut off by the loud *slam!* of her bedroom door. Too immature to consider his motives or his safety, she squanders the moment, choosing to land on her bed in a fit of rage, to stew in a brutal recipe of teenaged angst and self-pity. Camille will process this news the way she does most of life's challenges these days—by releasing toxic teenaged hormones from her eyes until she sleeps like a stone.

"She doesn't mean it," Mouse says, stroking Vinny's forearm before she leans in for another hug goodbye. He notices that her hair has a few new glinting strands of silver and her skin is not quite as smooth or taught as it used to be. Her arms, as warm and loving as they are, remind him that caring can be dangerous—it can make a person weak—that love can *kill.*

How old are you now? How old will you be when I see you again?

Vinny steps back and clears his throat. "I wouldn't blame her if she did," he admits, and pats himself down for any personal items that should stay behind. He sighs, looking at the naked bone of a well-seasoned ribeye—the last room-service meal he will enjoy for a while—and takes another sweeping look across the Monteleone suite he's called home on and off for the last three years.

"I arranged everything," he says as he looks around. "You have Carlos's number if anything comes up, and there's plenty of cash for you in the safe." He unclasps his expensive watch, slides it off, and lays it gently on the entryway table.

Vinny turns to Mouse, "Are you going to be all right?"

She musters a weak smile that falls away. "Are you?" Her brow furrows, eyes drawn to the discarded watch. She sees the lollypop hand tick off the seconds and looks back at him, her eyes fill with nightmarish flashes of loss from her past. The sacrifice of a beloved husband, one not so dear, a mother figure, a precious friendship, and the dreams of youth all tucked inside folds of memory, lest she forget the love and the lessons, pockets so deeply full of yearning and pain that Mouse admits she lacks the elasticity to hold any more. "Tell me you'll be back."

Vinny takes Mouse by the shoulders and looks into her large glassy eyes. "Don't worry about me. I will find my way back and shouldn't need a watch for this stretch. Where I'm going, there's nothing but time."

Carlos, reluctantly carting Vinny to turn himself in for a crime he didn't commit, is upset, distracted, and so he sees the light turn red at the last second and slams hard on the brakes. The inertia leaves the shiny nose of the bronze Cadillac poking halfway into the intersection.

"I hope you know what the hell you're doin," he says.

Vinny sets his forged ID and paperwork aside to reach out and pinch Carlos's cheek. "Aw . . . you almost sound like you're gonna miss me or somethin."

Carlos swats the hand away. "Stop it! This is serious."

Vinny cranks down the window. "Relax. We all know I've done much worse than what I'm going away for."

The light turns green and the car resumes its path down the road.

Carlos watches Vinny pick up a lighter and shove a cigarette into his mouth. He asks, "Is this about . . . ?"

"No!" Vinny barks through his teeth. He tosses the used lighter onto the seat.

Carlos frowns and shakes his head. "I just don't see any reason for you to take a ride to the parish clink. You don't have anything to prove to Nofio."

"Wow!" Vinny chokes on the smoke. "You really think I'm bothered by a few jealous assholes talking about me behind my back?" He laughs. "You think *that's* why I'm doing this?"

"Well, isn't it?"

Vinny cuts a harsh look at Carlos and takes another drag on his cigarette. He lets out a cloud of smoke in irritation. "For the last time, I'm doing this for *me*. I don't give a shit what you or anyone else thinks."

"Help me to understand it, then."

"Don't you see? I don't *need* for you to understand. I'm looking at this stint as an educational retreat. I want the time to train hard, like I did back when I was with the circus."

Carlos pulls alongside the police station, where his lawyer George Wray Gill waits with briefcase in hand. He throws the shifter into Park and turns to Vinny.

"And you think you're going to have that in some juvie jail?"

Vinny doesn't reply. Instead he gathers up his fake identification information and steps out of the car. After a moment he leans back in. "No one said I was going to juvie," he says. He closes the door and struts away.

Open-mouthed, Carlos squeezes the steering wheel and stares at him, his knuckles turning white as Vinny rounds the corner. Flooded with anguish, shaking violently, Carlos takes it out on the innocent steering wheel. He scrubs his hands over his face and through his hair, knowing it's too late.

The only person who could fix this now is dead.

Monday
January 10, 1955

The anomalous deal is struck, one that a prison-for-profit system and an eager prosecutor's office could not pass up, a signed conviction swiftly pushed through the channels. The assistant from the DA's office wears a triumphant smile—another case slam-dunked—as he watches Vinny and several other doomed souls load up for the three-hour bus ride northwest.

Eerily, the bus driver sings, *"The wheels of Justice go 'round and 'round, 'round and 'round, 'round and 'round!"* as they leave the paved roads of St. Francisville behind.

Vinny awakens from a long nap. His stomach gurgles with acid, bouncing along on the muddy and winding dead-end path of Louisiana Highway 66.

"Welcome to the front gates of hell, fellas," says the foreboding inmate in the seat in front of him.

The bus rolls on and Vinny sees a lighthouse-like watchtower. A red brick sign below it reads:

LOUISIANA STATE PENITENTIARY

The bus rocks onto a dirt-and-shell path which leads to a stark white guardhouse, where they stop under a metal roof extending over the driveway. A uniformed officer hops onto the bus with a clipboard full of paperwork. He counts the heads, mumbles something to the driver, and disembarks. Manually, the officer raises the wooden barrier arm, allowing the bus to roll into the maximum-security compound, surrounded by high double-thick fences wrapped in twisted coils of razor wire.

The bus driver smiles and looks into the large mirror above his head. "You are now on the Farm—our very own Alcatraz of the South," he crows, a cheerful tour guide of evil places. "Yes, sah, Angola be surrounded by the mighty Mississip' on three sides, and Tunica Hill snakes down the other."

Inside the main gate, the prisoners are removed from the bus and forcibly ushered to an enormous yellow reception center for processing. Vinny looks down at his shackled feet and wishes he had purchased some cheaper shoes for the occasion.

The correctional officers (sometimes referred to as "freemen") announce parish- and state-mandated directions and warnings. Intake forms are filed and all body cavities are searched for contraband.

In a pair of cheap cotton boxer shorts, Vinny numbly follows the steady flow of new prisoners toward an older man—a trustee—who is distributing blue denim uniforms, small toiletry sets, and thick-soled work boots to the newcomers.

The trustee locks eyes with Vinny, aggressively grabs his arm, and pulls him closer. Vinny flinches at the man's stinking tobacco breath. He watches the man tuck an extra comb and a shank inside his laceless boot. The trustee looks from side to side.

"You got some friends that don't want you in the long line. You gonna be in the plumber's shop wit' Tony."

"What's the long line?"

"Keep it moving!" a guard yells.

"You don't eva want to find out," the trustee warns.

He is no longer a name, but a number, issued to him by the Louisiana Department of Corrections. This makes Vinny's transition into the lie an easy one.

As his body presses against the hard steel beneath a one-and-a-half-inch cotton-batting mattress in the dormitory, the choice he has made sinks in. Surrounded by newly hooked fish—unsupervised perpetrators of rape, botched robberies, drug dealings, and many other misdeeds—he hears the unsettling *clink* of a steel door being closed and locked . . . followed by the muffled sounds of grown men crying in their bunks.

The moonlight calls to Vinny's nocturnal nature, and his feet find the cool and sweaty concrete floor. Feeling sleep impossible, Vinny seeks out the extra comb, snaps off a few teeth, and scrapes the hard rubber with purpose against the sharp edge of the bed frame. His head aches as it searches for the reasons for this rash decision—only an itch at the back of his brain right now, a foggy purpose that eludes him; yet, like a worn path he might stumble upon in the woods, he must see where it will lead.

"Boy," whispers the large man in the next bunk, "what is you doin?"

Vinny looks over, surprised to see a white man attached to the thick-tongued dialect of a much darker man. He chooses not to answer, blows the shavings away, and continues to work at whittling the comb.

Seemingly desperate for conversation, the man blurts, "My auntie fount me in a trash bin, so she calls me 'Ben' . . . well, she did befo she died, anyways. I calls her my auntie, but her skin's not like mine. See—" He holds out his arm as proof. "What's yo name?"

Vinny winces at the man's child-like intellect. But if he doesn't answer, the man surely will never leave him alone. "I don't have a name," he grumbles.

"What do people calls you, then?"

"Gator."

The man develops a broad smile and props his head up on his hand. "Oooh-*wee* . . . my auntie used to love her some gator sauce piquante."

Vinny flashes his deadpan eyes at him. "You'd better get some rest there, Big Ben," he says, and sharply blows on his whittling project.

"Yeah, retard," a voice barks from the roomful of shadowy figures, "shut the fuck up and go to sleep!"

Ben cries out, "My auntie say that's not a nice thing to tell nobody."

"You got thirty-two teeth, buster. Want to try for none?" the voice challenges.

Vinny hears Ben let out a hurt squeak, and wants to feel something for him. Empathy . . . pity . . . disgust. Something. Anything. But killing that woman beneath a curtain of fireworks has torn something loose deep inside him, like a tendon ripped from the bone, leaving him completely numb and disconnected from the world—and everyone in it. So instead, he imagines that if he were to snap Ben's neck, it would be a form of mercy, considering the atmosphere; the man's weakness will surely draw a far crueler end than what Vinny can provide.

Ben sniffles.

"Why are you in here, Ben?" Vinny asks quietly.

"My auntie's dead and don't nobody want me no mo'."

"No, I mean what did they charge you with?"

"They's not gonna charge me, is they? I thought prison was free."

Vinny wipes an irritated hand down his face and shakes his head. "Get some sleep, Big Ben."

The morning brings one less pile of flesh to rise for the chow line. Several perplexed men gather around the stiffening corpse of a prisoner who somehow dislocated his neck during the night.

A forty-ish man pans the room with wild, paranoid eyes. "We got ourselves a ghost, y'all. This place is haunted by those meat sticks the warden fried up in dat Gruesome Gertie!"

A violent jangle of steel keys precedes several correctional officers rushing the open space for the morning head count.

One officer holds a baton ready for battle and shouts, "Rise and shine, ladies!"

Ben bolts upright in his bunk, rubs his eyes, and frowns as he watches the commotion.

"Looks like we got us a new resident for Point Lookout," complains a tall officer with a thick scar splitting his lower lip. He blows a whistle to alert other guards of the predicament.

Ben winces and covers his ears from the piercing sound. Then he notices the body. "What happened to that man, Gator?"

"I don't know, Big Ben. Maybe he forgot to mind his own business," Vinny says. He inserts a toothbrush into his mouth and heads for a sink.

Ben sits, wringing his hands.

Another guard—an ex-military sergeant with pale skin and ginger-colored hair—enters with a canvas stretcher and approaches the body.

The tall, scarred officer shouts, "Grab the feet, Maguire!"

Maguire meets Vinny's gaze and shivers, somehow sensing this prisoner's unflinching willingness to kill. The guard's leery eyes follow Vinny as he goes about his morning ritual like nothing's amiss.

"Come on, Maguire. Get the lead out!"

Thursday
January 13, 1955

Leaving his new residence at Camp H, Vinny hops aboard the ventilated stake bed of a green Ford truck for an expedition across the 18,000-acre prison property. On the side of the road, a long line of the discarded and damned are bound on foot for fertile plots of Angola soil, long-handled equipment riding heavy on their shoulders. On the bumpy ride, Vinny surveys guards with shotguns, patrolling on horseback as they monitor horse-drawn plows tilling rows in enormous fields. In late August, some fields will be peppered seventeen hours a day, rain or shine, with mostly black inmates, their bare, bleeding hands picking ripe tufts of cotton. Other fields of toil will produce mountains of cabbage, corn, strawberries, okra, onions, peppers, soybeans, squash, tomatoes, or wheat.

Vinny loses his breath at the sprawling beauty of cattle grazing on rolling hills in the distance—and again later by the sight of broken men who have cut their own Achilles' tendon to avoid labor under threat of torture in the oppressive Louisiana heat.

Vinny settles into his coveted position as a plumber's helper, though he is occasionally disappointed to have been spared the muscle-building hard labor of the fields. He learns the lay of the land with chores that take him on a unique tour of every building and outpost of the nation's largest correctional institution.

Prisoner lingo is a challenge to him at first. He learns that "flying a kite" and "catching a ride" have whole new meanings to men serving time on the river. Once the devious females in the women's dormitory over at Camp D discover the handsome newcomer named Gator, the plumbing issues in their area increase, developing sudden and often. During each tryst with a less-than-ideal mistress, Vinny observes that he performs best with his eyes closed, imagining the enticing features of Elizabeth Taylor, his perfect girl, presented to him in dreamy Technicolor.

February, 1955

"**T**hat's my friend Gator!"

Each time Vinny walks away from a defeated challenger in the yard, Ben proudly announces this to the crowd.

Establishing himself as a brutal fighter, able to overpower any opponent barehanded and with ease, Vinny quickly gains the respect of other prisoners, and the word spreads through the camps. Since he adheres to a subtle, chess-like strategy, and only engages the mouthiest of troublemakers, the guards turn a blind eye.

Occasionally a guard falls prey to Vinny's sneaky subliminal persuasion techniques when he is feeling mischievous, which earns him a wide berth by many who see that he possesses an uncanny ability to move freely around the campus and evade punishment. For the weakest or the most targeted of inmates—the ones that strap Montgomery Ward catalogs to their chest, thick enough to protect from any sharp objects, to survive the night—Vinny becomes a source of hope. Some seek out his sage advice . . . while other cocksure men—men like Doug, an ill-tempered man with a skunkish stripe in the front of his hair—plan to put him in check the first chance they get.

Thursday
February 24, 1955

Unbridled emotional outbursts or any other ornery and disruptive infractions rarely go without consequence. Rowdy inmates—like Ben—land in the squalid isolation of Camp E, a cell block of thirty medieval cement dungeons with no glass covering the small ventilation openings in the walls, only thick pipes.

Ben drops the mop he's been carrying, frustrated with the endless hours of drudgery. He looks at his blistered hands. Teeth bared, he charges past a guard, foolishly choosing the destination of the distant, scrubby, overgrown woods and ravines of Tunica Hills.

"That was a dumb move, you half-wit," the freeman says, cracking Ben across the back of the head with a club and knocking him unconscious.

When Ben regains consciousness, he finds himself on the floor of his new hovel. A red pair of overalls is folded on a mattress-less platform beside him. With little protection from the elements, he is soon covered in bites from insects and vermin. Once he is allowed to work the fields again, Ben is forced to wear not only the red overalls, but also a straw hat dipped in red paint—a bright target for the guards to shoot at if the need arises.

A slice of bread, a cup of water, and a bowl of cabbage broth—minus the cabbage, with a tiny morsel of fatback floating in it—is delivered to Ben's temporary three-by-six-foot nightmare. He holds up the thin, almost translucent slice of bread and, just when he thinks he might starve to death, a chunk of "loaf" (a nondescript lump of ground-up scraps baked into a brick) lands at his bare feet. He eagerly picks it up, thankful that it didn't land in the urine-filled bucket a few inches to the left.

"That's my friend Gator," Ben says aloud, holding his gift.

Gator, the clever rogue, moves throughout the expansive compound with impunity and his secret tool . . . a handy comb key.

Returning from an emergency over in Camp D, Vinny whistles a tune and casually swings a tool box at his side until he spies red-headed Maguire patrolling the tiers, weapon in hand.

"Hey, you there!" Maguire calls. "Been looking for you! Where the hell you been?"

Vinny jerks his head back and turns to see if the man is addressing someone else, but no one is there.

"Yeah, I'm talking to you, shitbird," Maguire says gruffly, and waves him over to the raised aluminum-covered walkway. "Come with me. You have a visitor."

Vinny's pupils dilate, unsettled by the surprise.

"You know the way, don't you, son?" Maguire nudges Vinny forward, waving the short barrel of his Remington 870 shotgun. "Walk on to the vehicle, nice and slow."

Vinny's eyes slant to the side and he swallows hard, his keen ears hearing the *click* of the gun's safety catch release behind him. He wets his lips.

"It's not visitors' day today, is it, boss?" he asks cautiously.

Maguire grips his gun. "Don't give me that 'boss' crap," he snaps. "Just walk."

On the way to the truck, the two men encounter some harsh discipline being administered by a sadistic guard, who is raging with a three-foot leather strap on the bare black skin of a man knelt down in the grass, each lash landing with a sharp *pop!* like a pistol shot, echoing through the outdoor corridors.

Vinny has heard many stories about what happens in the Negro camps, under the rule of white officers. Living a mostly segregated existence, however, he had not witnessed such unnecessary brutality in broad daylight. Not knowing what is to transpire on this hike with Maguire, he imagines being lined up next to the black man.

His muscles tense up further as he recalls the disturbing groans of both consensual and nonconsensual sex emanating from the corners of the dormitories at night. For the first time in a long while, Vinny's edges tingle with fear. This makes him feel awake and alive—which means his prison experiment is beginning to work.

To up the ante, Vinny stops. He feels the cold, hard muzzle press against his occipital bone.

"Move it," Maguire barks.

The Earth's pull tugs at the corners of Vinny's mouth; it isn't until the main office administration building is in sight that he starts to believe the journey will be uneventful. If not torture, then Maguire wasn't lying, and someone *is* here to visit. Puzzled, he racks his brain as to who could be wishing to see him right now.

Vinny stops in front of a large metal door and waits for Maguire to knock for entry. The door slams shut behind him. His eyes take a few seconds to adjust to the lower light of the visitation room's interior.

"I'll escort you back to your work detail when you're finished," Maguire says, and he takes a post on a stool behind the counter and pops open broadsheets of stale newsprint.

Behind a small round table, decorated with an expensive briefcase and a large legal envelope, George Wray Gill throws his hand up. "Finally!" Gill says, relieved to see his client. He stands briefly and smooths his tie. "Are they treating you all right, son?"

Vinny looks around the empty visiting room. "What are you doing here?" he asks with a pinched expression, and lowers himself into the chair opposite the lawyer.

George pats the envelope. "A friend of yours brought me some sensitive information that he wanted you to have."

"And which friend was this?"

"Joe."

Vinny cocks his head to the side. "Old Black Joe?"

George pushes the envelope to Vinny, nodding. "He insisted that you have this as soon as possible."

That prickly hint of fear returns. Vinny knows that a malnourished man should start slow, one bite-size portion at a time, so as not to go into shock. He stares at the envelope; it makes his stomach roll. "If it's so important, why didn't he bring it to me himself?"

"He might have, but he had some sort of attack, a stroke or something, right there in my office. We had to call an ambulance. It scared the piss out of me."

Vinny rubs his face. "Is he going to be all right?"

"Yeah, I think so. His doctor said he's likely to go home soon."

"Put him on my visitation list and have him come see me when he gets out."

George takes a stern tone. "Why don't you just let me fix this, son? Hell, I could have you cleared and out of here in a week. Charade over."

"Because that wasn't the deal I made," Vinny replies, slamming his hand down on the table, releasing his inner Carlos. A language that George understands more clearly.

At the ready, Maguire asks, "Everything all right ova there?"

George nods and waves him down.

Vinny stands. "I think we're done here."

George stares at him, nonplussed. "Don't you care enough to open this thing?"

Vinny considers the envelope and what secrets it may hold. He figures it can wait awhile longer. "Have them put it with my personal belongings. I'll read it when I'm good and ready."

Saturday
June 4, 1955

A **gangly seventeen-year-old**, fresh out of processing, stumbles through an exercise yard full of thugs preparing for a sanctioned boxing match on the following weekend. The outside gym is as rowdy as a crowded juke joint on a payday weekend. The rail-thin teenager scurries along the edge of the yard, looking for a place to stay safe and have a smoke, when he finds himself pinned against the fence by a guy with a white streak in his hair.

"New kid in the kitchen, eh?"

"Y-yes," Clarence says with alarm, his heart pumping hard and fast.

"What's that you say? Cha-Cha-Chicken?"

Clarence is too stunned to reply.

Doug gives him a slight shake; the metal chain links rattle and the diamond weave presses deeper into Clarence's soft skin. Clarence can feel Doug's body lean against him, his hot stinking breath in his ear.

"Isn't that what they call you, baby killer? 'Chicken'? Not so tough without a car, now, are you, Chicken?" he taunts, aroused by the sweaty scent of fear in the air.

"Hey, break it up over there," yells one of the guards on duty. "Unless you fellas'd rather dance your way over to the red hats?" he suggests blithely. Considering a stint as a *red hat* was a solitary vacation in the most inhumane accommodations on the property, it was a sadistic offer no prisoner in their right mind would go out of their way to accept.

Doug cracks his neck from side to side, watching the boy quiver beneath his arm. "Awww, you're not worth it," he says, releases him, and raises both hands in the air to show the approaching guard cooperation. "Just playin, Your Heinous, just playin around."

Clarence rubs his fluttering chest in relief.

The guard gives the two prisoners the same look of warning that mothers give to siblings when they are misbehaving.

"We was just horsin around," Doug says to the guard, then he flashes a quick *don't-you-dare-tell-Mom* glance at Clarence.

The guard takes a long look at each of them, eyes narrowed with doubt. "Just playing, huh?"

Doug's lips spread in a wide, yellow-toothed grin, and he gives Clarence a gentle jab with an elbow. "Well, then, Chicken? Didn't you say you had a smoke for me, buddy ol' pal?"

Clarence slowly reaches into his pack of generics and raises up a cigarette like a white flag.

"Hey, my friend needs a light over here," Doug says to the guard.

The guard walks over and obliges the request.

Grinning, Doug widens his stance and asks the guard, "So, who do you have your money on?"

The guard points and ignites a short flame for both inmates. "You see that kid waiting to use the heavy bag, the one shadow-boxing? That one is the top stud if you're looking to knock someone down next week."

Doug takes a drag, turns to look, and his smile dissipates.

Clarence looks over to see Vinny's destructive fists slicing through the air, 170 pounds of muscle drenched in sweat.

"They call him Gator," the guard continues. "That boy is the most dangerous kind of people."

"What kind is that?" Clarence asks. He takes a long drag on his cigarette. Doug curls his lip and walks away.

"The kind that doesn't give a damn about anything or anyone," says the guard. "That one doesn't care if the sun comes up tomorrow. Nothing more dangerous than a man who has no burden of caring."

"You think he's the kind of guy you can trust?"

"Hmmm." The guard contemplates, scratching his neck. "Possibly . . . but only if you kept your end real shiny."

Clarence watches Vinny's calculated contact with the heavy bag. "Thanks for the light," he says, and walks across the yard, gathering the courage to ask for help.

Pfft!–pfft!–pfft! is uttered with every strategic hit Vinny makes with his wrapped hands. He delivers powerful left-right combinations, stepping in and away from the swaying bag. He pauses when he sees a lanky giraffe of a boy arrive in his periphery.

For several minutes, Clarence nervously crosses and uncrosses his arms. "I hear you're the one to beat next weekend," he blurts, and chews at his bottom lip.

Vinny doesn't engage, just shoots the dimwitted delinquent a few cautionary glances between punches.

Clarence rubs the back of his head and looks around the yard at all the unfriendly faces. "You think you could teach me a few moves?"

"What's in it for me?"

Clarence shrugs. "What do you want?"

Vinny lifts his fists and shrugs back. "I don't want anything."

Clarence grabs the punching bag from behind, holds it steady for Vinny's jabs. "I need to be more like you. I need your help!" he cries, hugging the hard cylinder tighter. "Help me. *Please!*"

Pfft!–pfft!–pfft!

Vinny punches while looking at the disheveled teenager's large, round, imploring eyes; then he inhales deeply and straightens his back. "Listen, kid . . . I feel the days ticking by, racing toward my own mortality. I long for the universe to swallow me back up into an eternal sleep. You don't want to be like me." He crouches and begins to punch again.

"I don't want any trouble," Clarence admits. "I just need to do my time and get out in one piece."

"Shoulda thought of that before you decided to be a rebel," Vinny says, bouncing on his toes. He peers over Clarence's shoulder to see Doug hanging on the fence, glaring in his direction. "Is that your trouble over there?"

Clarence turns to look. "No, that's just some shmoe from Kokomo. We mostly re-label packages and cans of expired food in the kitchen."

Vinny's eyebrows furrow and release. He rubs the stubble on his chin with the tips of his fingers. "So you work in the kitchen?"

"That's where they put me."

"What are you wanting to learn?" Vinny asks. "Boxing isn't going to help you in a real fight."

"I just want to protect myself if someone comes after me."

"Do you have a shank?"

Clarence furrows his brow. "A what?"

"Oh, boy." Vinny offers up a deep sigh and glances around. "Can you get your hands on some can keys?"

"Like on the corned beef?"

"Yeah, that'll work. Bring me those and a metal spoon as soon as you can."

Clarence's eyes are wide and glowing, but he doesn't dare smile just yet. "Does this mean you'll help me?"

A devilish grin grows on Vinny's face; he knows this Clarence may present the ultimate challenge. "This means when we're done, no one will want to be on your bad side, and your name will strike fear in the hearts of the opposition . . ." He trails off and tilts his head. "What's your name, anyway?"

Clarence thinks, then says, "Just call me Chick."

Vinny wrinkles his nose with a condescending smile. "Wow, kid, with that name you're a walking bull's-eye."

Friday
August 12, 1955

Agent Shaun Maguire continues to take a special interest in Gator, keeping his discerning eyes on the movements of the slippery inmate. Maguire doesn't know why he's so magnetically drawn to Vinny, but he volunteers to fetch him every time the need arises. Today, this undertaking brings him to the mess hall during the distribution of the first meal of the day.

Doug and Clarence stand side by side, serving breakfast to the line of peckish inmates. Doug's prying eyes catch Chick plopping an extra chunk of loaf on Vinny's plate while giving him a shallow nod.

Vinny lethargically carries his well-stocked tray to the tables until Maguire obstructs his path.

"Eat fast. You have a visitor."

Vinny looks down at the nasty leftovers—meant for Ben. Out of curiosity, Maguire picks up the loaf and sniffs. He gags, pulls back in disgust, and lets the quasi-food fall from his fingers into a large trashcan. Vinny clenches his jaw; he's tempted to lash out, but he knows where that would lead.

"You won't need that today," Maguire says with a grimace, and wipes his hand on his uniform. "I heard your puppy's getting out of the pound today."

Vinny takes a sidestep and slides his tray onto the nearest table.

"Have at it, boys. Seems I got me a visitor waiting."

Fully expecting to walk in and see George's overpaid hog-jowls, Vinny bows his head to hide his smiling eyes at the sight of Two-Man's large frame bouncing from foot to foot with excitement in the visitation room.

"How the hell are you, man?" Two-Man beams, reaching out to clap Vinny's shoulder.

Maguire settles on a stool and barks at the so-called legal assistant: "No contact with the prisoner!"

Two-Man raises his hands and takes a step back. "Whoa, you got it, chief." He looks at Vinny with a twinkle in his eye and leans in. "Geez, your new girlfriend's the jealous type, huh?"

Vinny falls into a chair, amazement still on his face. "What are you doing here?"

"That's funny—I was going to ask you the same damn question."

Vinny shifts in his seat and shakes his head. "Don't start."

"All right, all right"—Two-Man taps the table—"don't get your panties in a twist. I didn't come here to piss you off."

"Why *did* you come?"

"I wanted to see this crazy bullshit for myself."

Vinny pokes his tongue lightly into his cheek and inhales a long breath.

Two-Man looks down at Vinny's hands and raises his eyebrows. "I see you still refuse to double-wrap," he says. Lowering his voice, he continues, "I've seen you fire a gun and hit the target every time—even the moving ones. Don't you think your hands are much too valuable to be fighting anymore?" He bounces a knee in frustration at Vinny's silence. "You gonna tell me what's going on with you, or what?"

Vinny yawns and stretches, ignoring the question. "So . . . what have you been up to?"

Two-Man massages his temples, tilts his head to the ceiling, and lets out a heavy sigh. "Do you remember that kid you dazzled at the zoo?"

Vinny scratches his cheek. "You mean that little Oswald kid?"

"Yep. Lee's not so little anymore, and he's been stayin down here a while with his uncle. His uncle Dutz."

"Dutz?" Vinny pauses to think where he's heard that name before, and then his jaw falls slack and he takes in a breath of recognition. "You don't mean Dutz Murret? Our numbers guy? The bookie?"

"That's the one!" Two-Man says, slapping his knee.

"No kidding," Vinny says with a brief twinkle of amusement in his eyes. "What a small world."

Two-Man nods. "Well, I just saw the kid . . . and he says he spent the summer sniffing out the Civil Air Patrol."

"Really?" Vinny taps his fingers on the table. "You'd better tell him to stay away from Ferrie then."

"Why's that?"

Vinny raises one eyebrow. "Because I've heard that dear old David has a fondness for new recruits."

In denial, Two-Man leans back and makes the time-out sign with his hands. "Clown Face is a . . ." He covers his mouth and starts laughing quietly.

Vinny smirks and rolls his eyes. "Yes. Ferrie is a *fairy*."

Two-Man hits the table and whoops with laughter.

When Maguire looks over at the commotion and points at his watch in warning, Vinny shrugs back defensively, then says to Two-Man, "I have to go soon."

Two-Man wipes the corners of his eyes. "I sure do miss you on the circuit, man. When do you think you'll be out of this mess?"

"When I stop wanting to kill."

Two-Man draws in a sharp breath.

Vinny stares back at him with dark, formidable eyes. "I'll be done when I say I'm done."

Monday
November 7, 1955

When he's not training Chick to fight and fetch, Vinny is under careful watch, surrounded by raucous construction noises; zestful preparations are underway for a concrete foundation of the new addition to the main building.

With a sharp No. 2 pencil in hand, he pretends to study the drawings for the plumbing rough-in work. Instead of watching Tony to learn how to verify the correct placement of drain and vent pipes, Vinny's eyes wander across a treasure trove of discarded construction supplies he could use to his advantage. He waits patiently for an opportune moment to add an ample segment of durable steel tie-wire to the roll of vinyl electrical tape already tucked inside his sock.

"Hey, Gator," says a troublesome inmate, pushing a cart on trash detail. "I heard your dimwitted chump is gonna get a visit from the Booty Bandit."

Vinny's face tightens and he rubs the tip of his nose. "Oh yeah, Pete the Pest? And which one would that be?"

"Oh, that's right," Pete says, and comes closer, flashing a mettlesome smile. "I forgot you have more than one pet these days."

Vinny refrains from harpooning Pete's neck with the pencil's sharp end in broad daylight, and instead clasps his chin in a deceivingly harmless, ponderous pose. "I meant which *bandit*. There are so many of you chicken-shit punks, I lost count."

"You'd better watch your back, champ." Pete sneers and begins to walk away, pushing the trash-cart and muttering under his breath.

Appearing out of nowhere, Maguire grips Pete by the scruff and pulls him away from the cart and into a corridor.

"Do you have a death wish or somethin?" Maguire snarls, pressing Pete against the wall. "Gator isn't someone you want to be threatening—his kind will dial your number eyes open, no blinking. I don't want to be cleaning up any of your greasy carcasses in the morning. It makes for a ton of paperwork and ruins my day." Maguire releases his grip on the pest and dusts his shoulders off apologetically. "Now go tell your friends to behave."

Pete backs away from Maguire with burning cheeks. "Never took you for no thug-hugger," he says, loud enough to attract plenty of onlookers, before he spits and walks away.

A small group of inmates is shooting craps just inside the dorm when Ben returns from a meal of boiled mystery-meat and mustard greens served in the dining hall. He attempts to sneak by them without being noticed.

Pete ambles confidently in front of him. "Are you here to learn the dice, Benny boy?" he asks with a sly smile.

"I'm n-n-not supposed to talk to you," Ben says, avoiding Pete's hard hazel eyes.

Forcing a wicked bark of laughter, Pete asks, "Oh, why n-n-not?" with a superficial charm that makes Ben's stomach roll. "We could have so much fun together."

Ben takes a side-step to get away—but Pete matches his step, taunting, "Uh-uh-uhhh," and his looming intimidation steers Ben against the wall. As Pete's small group of cronies encircle the pair, snarling like a pack of rabid wolves and egging Pete on, he says, "But me and the b-b-boys want to play—don't we, boys?"

"I wouldn't do that to him if I was you," a wizened voice warns from somewhere inside the dormitory.

"Why don't you mind your own business, old man?" Pete says, caressing Ben's soft and frightened cheek. His touch triggers a gush of pungent urine that darkens the right side of Ben's pant leg. Pete snickers. "Looks like someone could use a shower." He steps away to allow the others to take Ben roughly by both arms and hustle him away to the shower room.

"Somebody need to go tell Gator," the old man says from his cot, too scared to get involved. He covers his head with a pillow to block out the muffled thumps, followed by screams, echoing from the shower room.

Teeth bared and swaying sure-footed inside a circle of men lusting for violence, in the bowels of the kitchen as evening shift ends, Chick breathes in short, stilted huffs, his fingers clenched around the thickly taped handle of his laboriously honed spoon-knife.

"Come on, let's dance," he growls at Doug, crouching like a wild animal ready to pounce; Chick is sick of being constantly harassed by Pete's crew, and is ready to rumble.

"Stop pretending you're some badass. You don't have it in ya," Doug mocks, and turns to his friends for support.

Chick sees the opening, lunges out, and grazes Doug, liberating a button from his shirt. The kitchen prep-room goes silent except for the light *tap-tap-tap* of a plastic button skipping across the concrete floor.

Doug's eyes bulge with rage, and the fight ensues. Chick employs every skill Vinny drilled into him for fighting in close quarters, relying on footwork, deception, balance, and a lightning responsiveness to his opponent's every move. With a forward grip on his makeshift dagger, Chick blocks, sidesteps, spins, and counterstrikes, slashing Doug's face across his eyebrow.

Warm blood cascades from the gash into Doug's eye. "Well, well, well . . ." he says, taking a small step back. He blinks hard in an attempt to see. "Looks like the Chicken found his teeth."

Chick takes an aggressive step toward him.

"Enough," Doug concedes. He raises his hands and backs away, out of reach.

The rest of the men groan in disappointment, losing a diversion from their mundane existence.

"What, we done?" Chick asks, eyes wild, his veins pumping adrenaline, swaying warily on his feet, still on guard, his weapon wet with Doug's blood. "Will you guys leave me alone now?

Doug smears the blood through his white-streaked hair. "We'll see."

Chick stands his ground, watching the audience recede from the room.

Doug smiles as he leaves, saying, "I wonder if your friend enjoyed his shower."

Chick's face drains, ashen with fear, as he listens to the vicious cackles trailing behind them.

When Chick reaches the shower room, his eyes flood with horror, and he drops the shank. Ben lies on the tiled floor, crumpled, naked, shivering, and moaning in pain under a pounding spray of steaming water. A trail of blood runs from his savagely violated body into the drain, his eyes swollen shut.

At the sound of Chick's footsteps, Ben flinches, reaching out and crying, "No more! Please!"

"It's just me," Chick manages, choking back tears of empathy.

Ben's chest hitches. "They hurt me, Chick . . . they hurt me real bad."

Chick turns off the water and wraps a towel around his friend. "*Shh* . . . it's over now."

"Is it?" Dissolving into sobs, Ben folds himself into a corner.

"Course it is," Chick reassures him.

"Nuh-uh-uhhh, Chickadee." Pete is walking slowly toward them, spanking his hand with a section of pipe. "Don't go tellin the boy lies, now. It's over when I say it's over." Moving closer, he scrapes a jagged path along the tiled wall with the pipe, a ghoulish and unnerving screech of metal. "I'd say we can squeeze in a bit more fun before the next head count, don't you think?"

Chick presses himself against the wall and slides down to join Ben on the floor of the shower room. "What did you do to Gator?"

Ben raises his injured face. "Gator?"

"Aww . . . so sweet," Pete coos, and looms over Chick to pet his cheek with the smooth part of the pipe.

Chick turns his face away and shivers with fear.

Pete puts a hand to his chest in insincere earnestness. "I didn't do anything to your precious Gator. Didn't have to."

He lifts Chick's chin with the pipe, enjoying the terror shining in the young man's eyes. Pete positions himself like he's up to bat. Gripping the pipe with both hands, he touches it gently down on each of Chick's shoulders, as if to line up the first shot.

"Face it, your 'Gator' is just another yellow-belly," Pete sneers, cocking back for a hard blow.

Chick winces, bracing for an impact sure to break bone.

Instead, he hears the hollow pipe hit the floor.

His eyes fly back open and Ben screams, "What's happening?!"

Chick sees Pete clawing at his own throat, his face flushed and distended. He drops to his knees—revealing Vinny standing behind him. Vinny's teeth are bared. Wearing plumber's gloves, he holds firm to the taped can-key handles of a homemade garrote wire, which he has looped around Pete's neck.

Vinny places his foot on Pete's back and slowly lowers him to the floor near the drain. With eerie calm, he says, "I fear nothing. I *am* nothing. I have nothing to lose," pulling ever tighter at the thin, durable steel wire as it sinks deeper and deeper into Pete's sinewy neck. In shock, Chick covers his mouth and blinks furiously as the blood from Pete's severed artery sprays across the room.

"Gator . . . ?" Ben's swollen and frightened face searches for information. "What's happening?!" he repeats.

"Be quiet, Ben," Vinny says. He squats, both boots atop Pete's body, and yanks until the wire snaps free. "Turn all of the spigots on," he orders Chick, who is still staring open-mouthed at Pete's disembodied head.

Vinny snaps his fingers in front of Chick then lightly slaps the kid's cheek. "Snap out of it. We have to hurry. Clean yourselves up and get the hell out of here," he demands.

Chick tries to shake his head loose of the grim reality so that he can function enough to stand Ben under the nearest shower head, as if this were a quick rinse after gym class instead of washing the dripping gore of rape and murder from their shivering bodies. He looks up and yells, "Behind you!"

Vinny turns to see his plumbing mentor Tony approaching, a roll of cotton insulation under his arm.

"He's here to help," Vinny says, nodding at the embittered work-mate who once served ten months in isolation because of Pete.

"The trash-cart is outside," Tony says, nodding back, and proceeds to wrap the head in the absorbent material.

Tuesday
November 8, 1955

Maguire salivates, watching an eager team of confused search hounds bark and bay in the misty distance, attempting to track a scent that doesn't go any farther than the fence line.

Chick can hear the hounds as he is escorted to the warden's office for questioning. Ben can hear them through the open window near his bed in the medic's office. Tony can hear the dogs, too, as his weary lids blink in protest of the morning sun poking through the mist; he and Vinny are outside, watching a contracted laborer pull and push the cement truck's discharge chute into place, hovering over a patch of recently turned soil.

"Hey, fellas," the laborer says. "Lemme ask you somethin. What's the word on that escapee—did either of you know him?"

Vinny ignores the dogs and the question.

Tony brushes a drip of sweat away from his chin and shrugs. "Not really."

"Pete is just a dumbass gone AWOL. He won't get far," Maguire answers sharply, his bottom lip protruding from a wad of Skoal. The laborer cuts his eyes over to the guard, who projects a brown stream of tobacco through his teeth. Legs spread wide with confidence, Maguire adds, "We'll have his head on a stick in no time."

Vinny and Tony share a knowing glance that goes unnoticed.

"Now, get back to work!" Maguire snaps.

Tony lifts his sore arms to direct the Diamond T cement-mixing truck back into pouring position. He coughs in a cloud of diesel fuel, shouts, "Whoa!" and steps out of the way so the contracted laborers can take over.

He glances over again to see Vinny's sleep-deprived features fixed in the direction of a hog pen recently filled with a cacophony of ghastly munching and beastly execrations, destroyers of flesh and bone—too far away to see, but he knows it's there.

Sunday
September 2, 1956

On the outside—as prisoners often refer to the world on the other side of Angola's caged walls—roads are being expanded for the ever-growing motorist population. The Federal Highway Act sends rolling explorers traveling farther from home, to wander across miles of wide-open spaces listening to Elvis croon on the radio. Networks of interstate highways begin to change the meandering landscape and give birth to a blur of gas pumps, retail, drive-ins, drive-thrus, motor courts, fast food, and lodging. American tourists are falling in love with the smooth trail of asphalt as it emerges, connecting sea to shining sea.

On the *inside*, however, it is harsh prison business as usual, stagnant moments that tick by without reverence as inmates live life by a broken clock. Acres of doomed, incarcerated workers—or, in more apt terms, *slaves*—wasting away the days, the months, the years of their convicted lives hoping for clemency, commutation, or the pitiless death that they were promised.

How can such different worlds exist under the same sky?

Chick wonders, his eyes lackluster and far away.

He is chewing at the jagged edge of his thumbnail when the church bell bravely calls out for sinners on this quiet morning, but its voice goes unheeded by the busy heathens in the exercise yard.

Another year of prison behind him, his mind and body vastly older and wiser, Chick is prepared to follow his mentor's directions without question. He stands guard while Vinny exhales on the bench, slowly pressing a heavy barbell away from his chest with a close grip.

"They're gonna let me out of here in a couple of days," Chick says, absently scratching the side of his nose.

"Good," Vinny grunts with another exhale. He places the weighted bar securely in the bench rack, sits up, and wipes the sweat from his brow.

Chick turns and laces his fingers through the cyclone fence, waiting in vain for more words to come. He frowns in frustration, looking over his shoulder at Vinny stretching and shaking out his arm muscles. "Do you think we could meet up when you get out?"

"I guess so," Vinny answers with a noncommittal shrug.

Chick lowers his eyes. "It isn't true, ya know." He brushes his shoe against the fence.

Vinny looks skyward. "What the hell are you talking about now?"

"When you said you don't have anything."

Vinny shakes his head in disgust. "Don't go trying to get all pansy with me." He wipes sweat away from his snarled lip. "I'll have you put into a protection cell next to Ben for the rest of your sentence."

But Chick doesn't relent. "I know you don't want anybody to see that deep down you're a good person. But I've seen it."

Vinny growls, drowning out Chick's sentiment, and storms off to the shower room to wash away the sweat and the ridiculous.

Saturday
December 8, 1956

The lambent sun, smug in the winter sky, taunts Vinny on the third day of a rare extended lockdown after five thick-headed men tunneled out and plunged into the churning, muddy, unforgiving waters of the sinuous Mississippi.

"They got a limp one!" a betting inmate reports happily, listening to a guard outside speak of a single lifeless body fished from the river. As the inmate collects the money, contraband, and cigarettes wagered on the fate of the escapees, he adds, "So, that's one down and three still a-loose."

"Man, I thought there was five of 'em," a sore loser with buck teeth says, questioning the pool runner's math.

"Nah, they only fount three sets of tracks on the river bank."

"Still technically four on the loose, though," he says, with his palm out for a small refund and his buck teeth exposed in all their glory. "Five escaped, one dead, three tracks, one missing . . . that be four."

Listless and agitated by the unusual in-house restrictions, the prisoners buzz about like a jostled hornet's nest. Annoyed by too much noise and movement, Vinny lies still in his meticulously kept bunk, staring at tattered clouds as they race across the sky, his view impeded by bars, transcending his urge to add a few more cold bodies to the tally.

A head of wild salt-and-pepper hair and two large sable eyes transgress Vinny's peaceful scenery. With no change in his slow, even breaths, he blinks back at the familiar man, waiting for him to either state his business or move from view.

"Crazy Eights?" the man says. He pulls out a pack of playing cards and pats the box against his hand. "Feel like burnin some time with me?"

At first Vinny wrinkles his nose at the suggestion, but then makes a *hand-them-over* gesture and slides the deck free from its thick paper sheath. Sitting up, he begins to fluff the cards.

"If you're waiting for a written invitation to sit, you should know that I'm all out of stamps," Vinny says, tossing ten cards into two messy piles.

The man happily sits, lifts his half of the cards, and organizes them by suit.

Vinny places a starter card—the five of clubs—face up in the center of the bed, then the remainder of the pack face down in a neat stack beside it. He lifts his own fan of cards up for inspection.

With no fives, no clubs, and no eight, the man draws several cards from the pile. "I've been meaning to ask you something," he says, playing the five of hearts.

"Oh yeah?" Vinny says, disinterested, laying down a two of hearts.

"Is it true that you know Carlos Marcello?"

Vinny makes eye contact and the man shrinks a bit.

"What's it to you?"

"The last time I was in the joint, I met a guy, I think his name was

Johnson, worked with Carlos until he pulled a job for his wife, is all," the man explains, rubbing the back of his head.

Vinny pulls back in dismay. "For Jacqueline?"

"Is that her name? Yeah, I guess." The man shrugs and lays down a card.

"I don't believe that for a minute," Vinny scoffs, and tosses a card on top.

"He sure sounded pretty convincing at the time."

"Did this Johnson guy ever mention what the job was?"

"He was supposed to damage a woman who was getting too friendly with Carlos, to scare her off, but the job didn't go as planned."

Mildly intrigued, Vinny asks, "Do you know what went wrong?"

The guy laughs. "*Love* went wrong."

"Love?"

The man gives him a strange look, as if Vinny were a flying disc man from Mars. "Did you ever fall in love with someone that didn't love you back?"

"Nope," Vinny says with a high chin. "I don't ever want to fall in love."

The man blinks and cocks his head to the side. "I didn't either . . . but sometimes it happens whether we want it to or not. It sure does muck things up."

"Love is a weakness I plan to avoid."

The man nods, absorbing this edification. "The guy I was telling you about could've used that kind of wisdom, all right—because what he called 'love,' she called *rape.*"

Vinny's throat tightens. "That's too bad," he says with a cough.

"Damn fool should have known better than to dip his spoon into some hot-chocolate dame," the man says, and plays a card.

A vision of a beautiful Creole woman's last tear glistening under a pyrotechnic sky moves across the screen of Vinny's mind.

"It's your turn," the man says, interrupting his haunted thoughts.

Vinny plays an eight.

"What suit?"

"As it lays."

The man plays a four of diamonds. "I guess that means you're all out of hearts?" he snickers.

"Don't pretend to know how many hearts a man holds," Vinny says mystically, and leaves the card game behind, to his partner's dismay. His attention turns to the whisper of raindrops against the barred windows as a storm pulls a cold gray blanket overhead to douse the afternoon sun. With every prisoner and guard on high alert during the lockdown, Vinny feels someone creep up close behind him as he moves toward the window. Unshaken by the presence, he turns only his head.

"Do you know who I really am?" he asks. "Because I know who you are."

"If you've got me all figured out, then I suppose your training is over and it's time for you to get out of this god-forsaken place," Shaun Maguire says triumphantly.

"Silly Mr. Agent. I was just being observed . . . *you* were the one they were training," he says, and turns his attention back to the gathering storm.

Out of the dimness, Vinny sees the elegant milky figure of a great egret steady itself and float, the large bird confidently riding the turbulent winds. He feels a subtle shift in his spine, like a subluxation that spontaneously heals, a realignment that relieves the constant itch in his head, his mind suddenly flooding with a new sense of purpose. For the first time, he senses there might be something out in the world to look forward to. The hallowed call of destiny beckons to him on the wind, and that sacred voice utters,

Time to fly.

Sunday
March 3, 1957

After two years of monitoring, observing Vinny navigate and neutralize institutionalized routines at will, periodically reaching into the minds of those around him as casually as slipping his hand into a leather glove, the CIA programs are thrilled—they now have enough positive data to present for an extension of funding and resources to devote to developing subtle methods of behavior modification for use on the masses.

This is not the only win they are celebrating. New ideas and technologies have been generated from monitoring many subjects in secret programs around the world. One of these on-going programs involves a race for space exploration, and another a special plane that requires the utmost in protection, to be kept under wraps and away from prying communist eyes.

Thousands of miles away, in the far east, a boy Vinny once met is now grown and nearly a year into his military service. Lee Harvey Oswald is now a proud Marine and a protector of the U-2 spy plane, posted—with high security clearance—to the Naval Air Facility in Atsugi, Japan.

For the time being, as long as Vinny is assumed miserable and on ice in prison, Iosef spends his days traveling with a circus troupe. At the behest of James Angleton, he performs high-flying drama with triple somersaults as a trapeze artist whilst extracting valuable intel from loquacious aristocrats relative to nations of interest. On March 1st, those directives are modified, considering both men have latent scores to settle.

Vinny's release from prison thrusts him back into prominent circulation both professionally and socially; his skin has sorely missed the decadent feel of private showers, tailored Italian silk, and deep pockets full of cash.

"Progress" is usually a positive word to describe the passage of time, a measurement to quantify a rate of change. Vinny does not have to consult the sun's rotation, a calendar, a clock, or repeated cycles of the moon to know how much time has passed. He simply looks out the window at businesses that have changed hands, at houses and buildings that have sprouted in once-wooded lots . . . and, finally, he looks to what two years can do to change a little sister.

Camille's legs have extended and her face is less round, but the rest of her isn't. Vinny is bothered to see her curves sway when she crosses the room on princess heels, disappointed that his sister's sixteen-year-old body has continued to mature beyond his memory—as if there might have been a way to stunt her growth. Watching her flit about, he makes a mental note to purchase a brand-new Louisville Slugger.

Mouse shares in the experience with a wistful smile, in the frustration of losing your station in life, of having everything you hold dear outgrow the need of your tending—a humbling demotion, realizing that *progress* has reduced you to a glorified bystander.

Carlos playfully grips Vinny's shoulder. "Out on good behavior," he chuckles in Vinny's ear as guests arrive, "who'd-a thunk?"

Wholly reluctant to be fussed over or gawked at, Vinny forces himself to attend a homecoming soirée arranged by Carlos. At the Beverly Country Club he is accosted by a boisterous parade of colors, smells, handshakes, and smiling faces. Overstuffed with food and overstimulated by activity, Vinny longs to escape, to be quiet and alone with his thoughts. He closes his eyes and feels a warm hand wrap around his.

"Let's blow this crowd," Camille whispers, and pulls him away from the noise. "Don't open your eyes," she says, leading Vinny into a meeting room that smells of bourbon, cigars, old leather, and new money.

"What are we doing?" he says, stepping forward with caution.

"I want you to see something."

Vinny bumps against the arm of a tufted wingback chair. "Just tell me what it is," he says with irritation.

"Keep them *closed*." She giggles, guiding him over to a table. "Be patient."

"Fine."

"Your friend Joe sent a gift . . . it arrived earlier this afternoon," Camille explains, and places his hands on the table. She takes a step away. "Okay, now. Open."

When he takes a look around, the room is mostly dark, but Vinny can still manage to see the shape of a large globe that sits on the table before him. Just when Vinny is about to feign interest in the impractical gift, Camille turns on a light that illuminates the miniature Earth from the inside. Vinny's wonder is captured by the glow, as if he were transported back in time, to a boyhood before learning of cruelty or rules of survival. His eyes delight in whimsical awe at its simple radiance.

"Isn't it just *gorgeous?*" she says.

The shock to his senses has abated; the party seems far away, the room is serene, and Camille's eyes twinkle at Vinny. They smile and gaze together, and it is as if nothing bad has ever happened. The complete freedom of choice is suddenly exciting and edgy again, to do *anything*, to go *anywhere*, to create something new. He spins the globe on its brass wire axis and spreads his hands, hovering over the passing of dark and light, of distorted borders, of oceans and continents.

A gift of the world.

Tuesday
March 12, 1957

Vinny walks slowly and carefully as he holds a shiny black Labrador on a leash, guiding it on the sidewalk that runs alongside the Brown Bomber Bar. He peeks around the corner of the building and spies on Old Black Joe at the entrance.

Staring out with unseeing eyes, Joe is sitting sentry on the same relic of a stool that was next to the door on the day Vinny first met him.

Vinny moves forward on tiptoes, and winces when his silence is followed by the light *click-clack* of the four paws behind him.

"Don't you know you can't sneak up on me, Vinny?"

Vinny's shoulders slump with disappointment. "How did you know it was me?"

"Because everybody has a smell that arrives before they do."

Vinny sniffs at his forearm tentatively. "I don't have a smell."

"Course you do. Everybody has a smell."

Vinny passes a splayed hand in front of Joe's face, in persistent denial of his retinal occlusions.

"Yep, still blind. Are you gonna do that every time you visit me? Shoot, last time I felt like some spoiled Egyptian pharaoh with your hand fanning me all day."

Vinny drops his hand and frowns. "I guess I don't want it to be true."

"Who's your furry friend?" Old Joe asks, reaching down to make contact with the cool wet nose of the friendly pooch.

"Happy birthday," Vinny says with less excitement than he planned. "I was trying to surprise you."

Old Joe scrubs his fingers in the dog's silky fur. "Who said I'm not surprised?"

"She's a guide dog, trained to help you get around."

Joe pulls a long white mobility cane away from its resting place against the exterior wall. "I got this thing. What makes you think I need a dog?"

"She can help you avoid unsafe situations."

Joe snorts. "Look around dis neighborhood. My whole life is an unsafe situation."

Vinny ignores Joe's cynicism. "I'll be back tomorrow with the fella who trained her. I just wanted you to have a day to get to know each other first."

Joe removes her lead strap. "It's a sad state of things when even a dog got to earn hisself a living. Why can't a dog just be a dog?"

Joe can't see Vinny's red face, but he can hear his frustrated breathing.

"So, you're not going to cooperate with me?" Vinny replies.

"Oh, like *you* 'cooperate'?" Joe says. His long-held resentment comes forth like water out of a busted pipe. "Tell me about that, huh? Go and leave everybody, come back like nothing ever happened."

Vinny takes a moment, his hand squeezing his own Adam's apple to halt angry words he knows he wouldn't be able to take back. "I don't have to stand here and listen to this. I'll come back when—"

"When? When you feel like it? When I decide to fart rainbows and sunshine for ya?"

Vinny draws a long breath, closes his hands into tight fists and releases. "I know you're angry about being blind—"

"At least I ain't as blind as you!" Joe seethes. He listens to Vinny's footsteps carry him away. "What am I supposed to call this damn dog?"

"You can call her Christmas for all I care!" Vinny yells back.

Thursday
April 4, 1957

The Nevada air is electric, in the center of Las Vegas opulence, tonight at the Tropicana. Eddie Fisher mingles with guests of the grand opening, charming a full house, pressing the flesh of wealthy influential hands before he takes the stage alongside other members of the entertainment world.

Not easily impressed by celebrities, Vinny has grumbled for days about having to witness this spectacle on his boss's behalf—but he's not grumbling now. Eddie's wife, Debbie Reynolds, sits at a VIP table only steps away from Vinny's, talking and laughing with her good friend Elizabeth Taylor. His eyes are riveted on Elizabeth's legendary features as she takes notice of him, too; neither is a stranger to the occasional dalliance.

When he was younger, he dreamt many times of meeting this goddess in the flesh. Now here she is . . . yet something about her is not what he expected.

But what?

Vinny is fully aware that Elizabeth is newly wed to a third husband, Mike Todd—but marital status is not something that would normally deter him from pursuit. In the study of her face, her body, she is not missing a single thing that he desires most in the female form—yet still there seems to be a flaw.

Back in prison, talking in depth with an old jewel thief, Vinny learned how to study fine gems. The gemologist explained that once you know what impurities to look for, it becomes harder and harder to find a gem worth claiming. No matter how perfectly a diamond is cut, you have to evaluate it closely and deeply. If a cloudiness is detected with the naked eye, it's not worth sticking your neck out. The old jewel thief also mentioned a tale of youth and inexperience, when he was fooled by a synthetic stone that left him heartbroken and penniless.

At the conclusion of the Tropicana Revue's premiere performance, the audience rises from their seats and gives a tremendous ovation. Vinny stands, disillusioned by the woman he has always held up as the ultimate gem . . . the only one worth stealing. He is still able to see Elizabeth's extraordinary worth and beauty as the brilliant diamond that she is. Most men have their eye out for a well-cut diamond. The Gator is not like most men. He is looking for something even more rare: a pure and natural Alexandrite. A magical woman, an emerald by day and a ruby at night, to be the private specimen of his crystallography.

Friday

May 3, 1957

"When was this?" Carlos asks, and swallows hard to keep sour stomach acids from invading his esophagus.

"Late last night," Vinny says with an unavoidable yawn.

Carlos paces around his Town & Country office and drags his hands slowly down his reddened face. "A wound?" he asks in disbelief, looking at Vinny between his fingers for answers.

Vinny massages the corners of his bloodshot eyes and nods. "The bullet grazed the side of his head."

Carlos flings his hands skyward. "Only a fucking flesh wound!" he yells, and grabs his desk for support, tensing as if he might vomit. "A botched assassination on a boss! This is a fucking disaster!" He shakes his head.

"Costello went down . . . he thought it was done," Vinny says in Two-Man's defense. Carlos glares at him, but Vinny leans forward and continues. "Two-Man was in the middle of the goddamned lobby of the Majestic. What was he supposed to do? He took the shot and walked away." Still lethargic from fighting a wicked weeklong case of the flu, Vinny moves his heavy arm to reach for a silver-plated lighter on the desk. "I could have done it," he adds, his voice thick with smoke. "I *shoulda* done it—I told you I was feeling better."

Carlos studies Vinny's pallid, clammy skin. "That must be the fever talking."

"The fever broke days ago. I'm just tired." Vinny waves Carlos's concern away. "Besides, I bet I can aim a gun with more accuracy when I'm sick than most can on their best day."

The office door swings open and Nofio appears. His face is covered in the same rough sun-damaged hide that Vinny remembers, with the addition of a white battle-scar across his left cheek bone. With an uneven smile, Nofio claps his hands once and rubs them together. "So, here's the deal. The Chin agreed to fall on this sword. He's turning himself in as we speak."

"And how in the hell is that supposed to help?" Carlos asks.

"Vincent Gigante and Two-Man"—Nofio displays his palms and shrugs—"people are always getting those two confused."

"So we're hanging our hat on the hope that Frank Costello needs *glasses*? Is that what I'm hearing?" Carlos asks, sounding facetious, yet slightly fascinated by Nofio's quirky logic.

"We really didn't need to do that, Nofio," Vinny says. "I'm telling you, Frank Costello isn't gonna be giving *anyone* up to the cops. He's going to handle this in-house."

Carlos rolls his eyes. "Yeah, okay, like *that* shit-storm's better."

The phone rings on Carlos's desk. Startled, all three men look at the kettle desk phone as if it were a hissing snake.

Carlos finally reaches for the receiver. "Hello?"

"Hold, please," an operator says, followed by a loud *click*, and then an informer's voice says, "There's a package safely on its way to Italy."

"We appreciate the update," Carlos says, with a crisp nod to Vinny and Nofio before he hangs up the phone. "Just like we thought. The lights of Manhattan got too bright and he had to take off."

Vinny's body sags with relief. "Now we have to wait and see how Frank handles this. We don't want to show him our hand when he doesn't even know we were at the table."

"Agreed," Carlos says.

Carlos and Vinny look to Nofio and his tightly folded arms.

Nofio groans theatrically and makes the sign of the cross. "How can the two of you be so calm? This situation could get so much worse. I got two words for you guys: David Hennessy." Nofio presses his lips together and rubs his neck at the thought of being lynched.

"Stop being so dramatic and go make the call to New York," Carlos orders.

"Fine. I'll go make the call, all right," Nofio grumbles, and turns to leave, adding over his shoulder, "from a payphone."

Before exiting the building, Nofio lets out a shrill wolf whistle, after which Carlos and Vinny hear the angry skittering of high heels coming down the hall. A dazzling blonde enters the doorway, wearing a red dress that features her shapely calves.

"The banquet starts at five thirty!" she complains, hand on hip.

Vinny looks down at his watch. "We still have plenty of time, Camille."

"Wow . . . *Camille!*" Carlos blinks in disbelief. "Look at you, all grown up."

"Hello, Mr. Marcello," Camille says, giving him a tight smile and a curtsy.

Vinny frowns at her flamboyant dress. "Go have a Coke. Give me a few more minutes. I promise you'll be the belle of the beauty-school ball."

"I've already had two." Camille stomps her foot. "When are you going to see that it's a big deal that someone asked me to do their hair and makeup for this Miss New Orleans pageant?"

Vinny narrows his eyes at her. "You know what?"

Camille folds her arms and shakes her bouncy waves. "What?"

"You should calm down before you mess up all that war paint on your face."

"You'll see! Donna Douglas is going to win and I'm going to be the most sought-after beautician in all of New Orleans."

"If you say so."

Vinny and Camille exchange strained smiles of condescension, neither one relenting to the other.

"Mr. Marcello, could you please explain to Vinny that if I'm old enough to study for my cosmetology license, then I'm old enough to drive there by myself?"

Amused by the sibling rivalry, Carlos raises his eyebrows and looks to Vinny. Too tired to argue any further, Vinny shoves his tongue inside his cheek and rolls his eyes.

"Go on, don't keep the pretty lady waiting." Carlos grins. "There isn't anything we can do for him right now. We'll catch up on this tomorrow."

Vinny rises to confront Camille's pout, but instead turns back to Carlos. "They grow up so fast, don't they?"

Camille vocalizes her displeasure through gritted teeth and glossed lips, then pivots on her heel and stomps out to the car.

"Why do you press her buttons like that?"

Vinny smiles. "Because I can."

Monday
June 17, 1957

Two-Man Pizzolatto's poor marksmanship is soon overshadowed by bold maneuvers and grave messages traded between several powerful faction leaders in the pursuit of ascendancy. Now back in good standing, he returns from an unexpected detour through the vineyards of Italy, stepping off a private aircraft into the stifling Nevada heat. Carrying a small, hastily packed suitcase, Two-Man coughs, his lungs rejecting the dry desert air.

A man wearing a chauffeur's cap and a crisp uniform waits on the tarmac just beyond the bottom of the steps. Taking the suitcase, he says, "Welcome to Las Vegas, Mr. Pizzolatto," and ushers him into the back of a limousine stocked with a bottle of champagne on ice—royal transport for such a short ride north of the airport on Los Angeles Highway.

Not bothering with a glass, Two-Man takes several swigs straight from the bottle, sighing loudly, finally relieved of the fine grit of sand between his teeth. His sky-weary eyes glimmer with anticipation at the wide, sweeping approach of the palatial Tropicana Resort.

Two-Man steps out of the limo, awestruck by the sixty-foot tulip fountain, greeted by the sound of cascading water splashing down into a large brilliant pool at the sculpture's base. Standing beside him, the chauffeur removes his cap and places it in the crook of his arm.

His short ginger hair is afire beneath the sun.

"Your suite is ready if you would like to see it," he says, motioning to a bellhop for luggage transport.

Two-Man's nose wrinkles as he presses his memory. "Have we met before?" he asks the chauffeur.

Shaun Maguire blinks with an air of innocence. "Have we?" he asks over his shoulder, and continues to lead Two-Man through the mosaic-tiled entrance into a tremendous lobby, passing by rich mahogany panels of the front desk and the gift shops.

Two-Man, distracted by a fantastical upsweeping canopy of colorfully leaded stained glass overhead, almost loses his speedy escorts. When he enters the spacious suite, he is immediately drawn to amazing views of the sparsely populated Strip and lush, private tropical garden below.

The bellhop places the key on the dresser and the suitcase on the luggage rack. Just as Two-Man reaches into his pocket for a tip, Shaun smiles, raises a hand, and retreats toward the door.

"No need for that, Mr. Pizzolatto. You should get some rest. I'll let Gator know you're here."

Two-Man's large, fully clothed frame causes the deluxe mattress springs to groan beneath his weight, and he melts into the first sound sleep he has had in over a month.

Two-Man stops breathing mid-snore and his eyes fly open at a sharp knock on the outer door to his suite. Disoriented, he runs a hand over his face and moves to peer outside the darkened window at a few bright punches of neon in the distance.

The knock comes again.

"Room service," says a muffled voice on the other side of the door.

Paranoid, Two-Man presses himself along the wall, sneaking over to the door, and warily places his eyeball in front of the peephole. A young porter stands behind a cloth-covered trolley topped by a silver-domed platter. Two-Man opens the door and looks to either end of the hallway to make sure there are no surprises.

"Good evening, Mr. Pizzolatto. I have your dinner, courtesy of the house," the porter says, rolling the cart into the suite, careful not to tread on the large man's toes.

Two-Man lifts the silver dome to discover a steamy plate starring a thick pan-seared strip of steak flanked by lovely mounds of seasoned potatoes and early June peas. When the porter bends to the cart's lower shelf, Two-Man's nervous hand finds the handle of the gun secretly holstered beneath his suit jacket. The porter rises, holding a silver bucket filled with a goblet on ice and a decanter of wine.

Two-Man looks beneath the cloth to see a remaining tray of condiments.

"Is there anything else I can get for you?" asks the porter, pouring a deep red, succulent pool of Cabernet Sauvignon.

Feeling silly, Two-Man lets out a breath of relief and plops himself on the bed. He grins apologetically at the porter and raises up a ten-dollar bill. "Everything looks wonderful. Thank you."

The porter smiles back at the guest's disheveled appearance with understanding. "It is my pleasure, sir. I'm sorry to have disturbed your rest," he says with a bow and a graceful exit—without accepting the tip—and closes the door softly behind him.

Two-Man shrugs and puts the bill aside to enjoy his meal while it is still warm.

Smelling of coconut soap and with a renewed spring in his step, Two-Man wanders through the Tropicana's gaming area to an elongated, serpentine bar.

Responding to his approach, the bartender sets out a napkin and an ashtray. "What'll you have?"

"Make it a Mai Tai, kind sir," he says with a wink to a beautiful blonde taking notice of his broad shoulders from her seat at a nearby blackjack table.

As he waits for the festive libation he leans against the bar, smooths the side of his hair, and lights a cigarette, his eyes all the while on the sexy blonde. She smiles, deliberately uncrossing and recrossing her long legs, the slit in the side of her gold dress affording him a peek at an inch or two of her smooth, sun-kissed thigh. His mouth falls slack, but luckily his cigarette stays attached to his lip via the drool. She giggles, and asks the dealer for a hit.

The bartender smirks, entertained by their flirtations as he decorates Two-Man's Mai Tai with a wheel of lime and gives the sprig of mint a slap before delivering it to his napkin.

Two-Man sets his cigarette down and glances at the bartender.

"Can you make her one of these real quick?"

"Sure, boss," he says, and jumps into action, juicing another lime.

"Thanks. I was supposed to meet someone here, but I'm not sure what time."

"Time doesn't matter here," the bartender says, pouring the premium aged rum. "Besides, it looks like you're doing just fine."

Two-Man smiles, listening to the vigorous shake of ice as he watches the woman cash out and reach for her purse.

"Are you familiar with a guy called Gator?" he asks the bartender. He pulls the lime wheel off his glass and sips the drink.

"You mean the guy coming up behind you?" the bartender replies, then moves to greet the sexy blonde with a freshly garnished Mai Tai. "Compliments of the gentleman," the bartender tells the blonde, who smiles apprehensively and lifts the glass to its benefactor.

"Up to the old tricks, I see," Vinny says, clapping Two-Man on the back. As Vinny grips his shoulders, Two-Man lowers his head and squeezes his eyes shut as if he's been caught with his hand in the cookie jar. Vinny turns to the blonde and tells her, "Sorry, honey. You'll have to catch the next one."

Her face sours. She rolls her eyes, opens her purse to pull out a small mirror, and teasingly applies a fresh coat of lipstick.

"Oh, come on," Two-Man complains to Vinny, watching her work her magic.

Vinny places a generous tip on the bar and gives his friend a playful shove in the direction of the inner offices. "The showgirls get off in an hour. They're younger and free. That one would have cost you the whole wallet."

"Ever thought she might be worth it?" Two-Man bites a knuckle and turns back for one last look.

Seeking privacy, Vinny leads Two-Man into a cozy office and closes the door, blocking out all the sensory assaults of the guests and games. Vinny sighs. He meets his friend's eyes with a grimace and a slightly disappointed shake of the head. On edge, Two-Man rolls his shoulders, crosses his arms, and bounces a curled knuckle against his mouth in the new silence, waiting for Vinny to speak.

"It took some dancing, but Costello got the message," Vinny says soberly. "He sent word that he'll agree to step down as boss and retire . . . with continued compensation, of course."

Two-Man places a thankful hand on his chest and looks to the heavens with a breath of relief.

"That's not all. I got a call from New York. It seems that someone *talked* to the other Frank today."

"Which Frank?"

"Scalice. He was out buying some fruit, and"—Vinny snaps his fingers—"*boom*."

"Fuck." Two-Man rubs the back of his neck. "There's a dangerous game of musical chairs going on here, and it's making me as nervous as a long-tailed cat in a room full of rocking chairs."

"Maybe you should stay low a little while longer. We can always use some extra muscle around here."

Two-Man jerks his chin up in question. "How'd you end up with this cushy gig?"

"Carlos is a silent partner. He asked me to stay here to protect the skim until things settle down."

Both men suddenly become wary at a knock on the door. Two-Man draws his weapon and holds it poised to shoot.

Vinny throws out a cautious hand. "Cool it! I'm sure it's just a delivery."

Still, Two-Man holds his rigid posture until Vinny opens the door to retrieve a leather-handled bag from a clerk, shuts the door, and turns the deadbolt.

"You need to relax," Vinny says. "If I had known you were this tense, I would have sent a girl up with that steak." He opens the bag and removes stacks of cash. "Have you ever seen one of these bad boys in action?" Vinny loads a stack of hundred-dollar bills into the hopper of a whirring electric currency-counting machine and presses a button.

Two-Man sucks in a breath and stares at the machine, stupefied. Vinny displays a wide grin of satisfaction, listening to the fluttery *purr* of the cash-counter flipping through the first stack of bills at warp speed. "Don't you just love that sound?"

Two-Man nods. "Can I give it a try?"

"Sure."

Vinny moves aside to let Two-Man fill the hopper to maximum capacity. He is happy to take over the task, mesmerized, like a child with a new toy.

"If you think *this* is fun, I can't wait to see your face when the girls arrive." Vinny picks up the phone and presses the line to a private concierge. "I need a couple drinks delivered to my office . . . a Vieux Carré and a—" Vinny looks to Two-Man, who is still fascinated by the expeditiously shuffled money, and snaps his fingers.

Two-Man looks up, blinks. "Oh—a Mai Tai."

Vinny flashes him an exasperated look. "And a *Mai Tai*," he says, and hangs up the phone. He fixes his steely eyes on Two-Man.

"What?" Two-Man says defensively. "Can't a guy experiment once in a while?"

During late-night shows in this desert oasis, this land of sin, there are stages in sold-out auditoriums, stages ablaze with glittering rhinestones, sequins, and glowing pink feathers. Elevated platforms where Amazons roam, exotic displays of towering females who whirl and amaze. These stunning topless performers move gracefully beneath extravagant crowns, outlandish headdresses of crystals and giant plumes of ostrich and pheasant. The crowds are drawn in by the razzle-dazzle allure, the mystique, captivated by the fantasy of glamour that these beauties incite.

The small gathering of off-duty showgirls in bathing suits that arrive by invitation to Vinny's luxurious suite are no less magical minus their stage sparkles and feathers. Vinny pours glasses of imported champagne as the room fills with a glorious parade of tall, taut femininity.

"It's bathtime, ladies!" a scantily clad brunette calls out. She opens the hot-water valve of the swanky Roman-style tub and it roars to life.

Two-man stands slack-jawed, in awe of all the bare skin, those long bronze legs on display, and he sees Vinny single out a blonde-haired, blue-eyed doll. Vinny serves her a tall flute of bubbly and intimately caresses her hair. She lowers her chin as he brushes her shiny locks back with his fingers, exposing her neck, and leans in close to whisper something in her ear. She nods and prances across the room to dim the lights. The other girls giggle and clink their glasses, congregating around Vinny and the frothy tub. Two-Man falls into the chair behind him when the blonde tosses him a wink. She approaches with a demure smile and his eyes go wide with excitement. She deposits her glass on a table beside him and bends over to place her lovely hand on his knee.

"H-hello," he says without blinking.

"Hello, big boy," she says, and asks, "Is this seat taken?"

Two-Man's eyes roll back in his head as he inhales her perfume. "Humina, humina, humina," he utters as she lowers her curves into his lap and begins unbuttoning his shirt. Two-Man looks to find Vinny, who is already in the tub surrounded by five smiling ladies and the soft glow of neon. Vinny raises his glass in a toast as if to say, *Let the experimentation begin!*

Tuesday
July 2, 1957

Driving fast on Route 66, Vinny is racing the dawn under a waxing crescent moon when he hears a familiar news signal and turns the volume knob for the radio announcer to bark louder.

"An update on Hurricane Audrey, the destructive storm that pounded the coastlines of Louisiana and Texas last week with winds of one hundred forty-five to one hundred fifty miles per hour, pushing a storm surge of twelve feet, left widespread devastation in its wake. Property damage is estimated to be in the hundreds of millions. A large number of residents are still missing. The death toll is now three hundred ninety and climbing. In other news . . ."

Vinny's brows draw together. He snaps off the radio and accelerates, passing a sign that says WINSLOW. Rolling through downtown in the feeble light of dawn, Vinny veers left, easing into a parallel parking spot beneath a lit café sign.

As he opens the glass door, a bell jingles to announce his arrival. A young, fair-haired waitress in a bubblegum pink uniform looks up from the task of filling ketchup bottles and smiles, her eyes suddenly bright at the sight of his handsome face.

"The cook isn't here yet. Can I get you a cup of coffee, mister?" she asks, abandoning her chore with youthful bounce.

"You got a phone?"

"It's on the wall." She points to a corridor that leads to the restrooms. "You can't miss it. Ugliest phone in Arizona."

Vinny reaches into his pocket for some loose change. When he rounds the corner into the hall, he stops, blinks, and raises his eyebrows at the blue Art Deco payphone glaring at him.

He steps backward and looks at the waitress. "I think I might need that coffee first."

"I tried to warn you." She laughs, shakes her head, and pours him a cup of hot caffeine all the way to the brim. "Cream? Sugar?"

He looks deep into her eyes and sits in front of the steaming coffee cup. "Did you just call me 'sugar'?"

She blushes profusely, unable to break from his gaze. "I . . . uh," she murmurs.

He picks up his cup and slowly blows on his coffee. "No, black is fine," he says, and lowers his eyes, setting her free.

"Oh," she snorts, and bats at him with a cleaning cloth. "You were just funnin."

Vinny tosses her a playful wink and notices a stack of pie plates behind her. "What kind of pie do you have?"

"There is an apple and a cherry. I made the cherry myself," she announces, her chin in the air.

"Then I shall have a slice of your cherry."

She blushes again. "Coming right up."

Vinny drinks his coffee, delighted to watch the young girl from behind as she prepares a sticky wedge of cherry mess topped with a flaky lattice crust. She tucks a fork deep in the filling and presents it to him. Propping her chin upon a laced-finger hammock, she waits for him to take a bite.

He obliges. "Mmmmm," he hums, rolling his eyes back in exaggerated ecstasy.

"A mixture of sweet and tart," she says proudly.

"I bet you are." Vinny licks his lips.

"Oh, be-*have*," she giggles. A flash of irritation crosses her delicate features as the short-order cook and morning regulars start to trickle in. She clears her throat and scribbles on an order pad. "Can I get you anything else?"

"I'll just finish my pie and be on my way."

"Forget-me-not," she says, amused, tears off a check, and places it face down on the counter.

"Huh?"

"The color of that ugly phone over there. Forget-me-not blue."

"Oh, yeah." Vinny hops from the stool to jingle the loose change in his pocket. He walks back to the phone, plunks a dime into the slot, and yanks *0* on the rotary dial.

"City and extension, please," the operator says.

"New Orleans. The Hotel Monteleone."

"Deposit one dollar and twenty-five cents, please."

Vinny cringes, not from the cost but from the unwanted attention each coin drop brings.

"Hotel Monteleone, Al speaking."

"Hey, Big Al, it's Gator. Can you patch me through?"

"Sure. Hold on a sec."

Vinny jabs his foot against the wall, listening to the phone ring.

"Hello?" Chick answers.

"Is everyone all right?"

"Yes, of course. I did exactly what you told me to. Camille is still sleeping. You want me to wake her?"

"No. I'm on my way."

"Good. We'll all be glad to see you."

"I appreciate you taking care of them for me."

"Sure. That's what friends do."

"Look, I have a few stops on the way—at the rate I'm going, I might not be there until tomorrow or the next day," Vinny says, pulling the curly cord—in that same forget-me-not blue—far enough to peek at the waitress.

"Take your time," Chick replies. "They're in good hands."

"Has she said anything about what happened to Mouse?"

"No, not yet."

"Did the doctor come and take a look?"

"Yes. She was completely uncooperative. He left us with directions and pills."

Vinny drags his fingertips across his eyebrow and sighs. "I'll deal with it when I get there." He returns the handset to the cradle, the coins crashing into the collection tray.

Chick isn't surprised when the line goes dead. He knows his friend Gator cares nothing for goodbyes.

The fair-headed waitress is rosy-cheeked, wrapped up in a fluffy white robe, her hair is long and loose. His kiss is still fresh on her lips when she smiles and waves goodbye to Vinny from the front porch of her small rental home. He pulls the car out of her long driveway. She stares at his taillights until they rise and fall over the hill in the distance. On her way back into the cozy living space, she lets the screen door spank and steps on the bubblegum pink uniform that lies crumpled on the floor just inside the doorway. People in these parts tend to trust their friends and neighbors, so there was no *click* of a lock when she closed the door behind her. Locking doors becomes a new trend in Navajo County two days later when the local police discover her body lifeless on the floor with deep ligature marks around her neck.

Thursday
July 4, 1957

Camille struggles beneath Vinny's bear-like hug.

"I missed you, too—now let go! You're crushing my hair!"

Standing close by, Chick rocks from foot to foot, eager for his belated hello. Letting go of Camille, Vinny swings an arm out to make contact with Chick's outstretched hand.

After nearly an hour of their spontaneous patter and a triangular rotation of exchanges, the well of pertinent information begins to run dry, and the gaps of silence become increasingly prominent and awkward. Vinny leans against the stiff, inadequate sofa cushion, his hand on his chest, watching Chick and Camille struggle to find something, anything, no matter how trivial, to avoid discussing the elephant. He taps his fingers on his collarbone, impatient.

"Which one of you is going to tell me what I want to know?" he finally demands.

Chick and Camille flash terrified looks at each other.

Chick drops his eyes and clears his throat. "The story I got from the doorman is that someone dumped Mouse on the curb in front of the hotel just after dark on Monday. Her head was covered with a cloth and her hands were bound. She was pretty banged up and scratched."

Chick hesitates and looks to Camille. She covers her mouth and looks away.

"And?" Vinny huffs. His hand rotates to reel in whatever uncomfortable details are hooked at the end of the line.

Chick looks down again. "The doorman said that she was screaming and crying and didn't make much sense at all."

Vinny cuts his eyes to Camille. "You told me she was doing good."

Camille flinches. "She *was*. In fact, she was the happiest I've ever seen her."

"Where were you when the police came?"

"I was processing a permanent wave. I couldn't just up and leave." Camille narrows her eyes. "Where were *you*?"

Vinny throws himself forward in his seat and frowns, looking at the floor and contemplating a hex placed upon him long ago, wondering if this was somehow his fault. "Has she talked since? Anything coherent at all?"

Chick's eyebrows draw together. "Most of it sounded like gibberish by the time I got here." He sighs and suddenly recalls one detail. "She kept repeating 'Dion, Dion.' "

Vinny jerks his head back in confusion. "Wait . . . like Dion-who-works-in-the-kitchen Dion?"

Chick shrugs.

Camille's eyes avoid Vinny's gaze. She bites down hard on her lip.

"What do *you* know about this?" Vinny asks her sharply.

Camille squeezes her eyes shut. "I didn't see any harm in it . . ."

"Any harm in *what*, exactly?" he asks, bouncing a knee.

"With them being friends."

Vinny jumps up from the couch. He paces the floor, rubbing his neck. "How close are we talking?"

"All I know is that Dion invites her to go for walks and she comes back laughing and smiling. They like spending time together. What crime is there in that?"

"It depends on who is looking at it, Camille. This is the South, and there are still laws about these kinds of things."

"There's a law about having *friends*?"

Vinny shakes his head. "I should have kept you in school. You mean to tell me you've never heard of anti-miscegenation laws? The government wants to keep us segregated for a *reason*, Camille."

"They walk to the river to have sandwiches on his lunch break. How in the hell is that against the law?"

"Can they eat together in a restaurant?" he asks.

She doesn't answer.

"Well, *can* they?"

"I guess not," Camille admits, and lowers her head. "Doesn't make it right."

"How could you not tell me this was happening?"

"She's a grown woman." She looks back up defiantly. "What are *you* gonna do about it?"

"I'm gonna have a long conversation with Dion, that's what I'm gonna do."

"That might be difficult," Chick says reluctantly.

Vinny turns on him. "Why's that?"

"Because no one has seen him since that day."

Vinny walks over to the window. He searches the distant clear sky for broad turkey-vulture wings soaring in wobbly circles, a suspicion rising that he may not be the only one who feeds the wildlife of south Louisiana.

"Where are you going?" Camille says, as Vinny charges across the room toward the bedroom door.

"I need to see Mouse."

"She's going to be loopy," Chick warns. "She had a dose of that medicine just before you came in."

Somberly, Vinny steps into the sour-smelling bedroom where Mouse has spent the last few days convalescing, sedated and resting peacefully. He lowers himself onto the bedside, smooths her oily hair from her battered face, and examines the bruises which are starting to heal—fading carnival colors of purple, gold, and green.

Mouse stirs, pulls her drugged eyes to quarter-mast, and blinks her droopy lids at Vinny. She crinkles her nose and reaches out to touch his face.

"What a fine-looking man you are, Jack Johnson," she slurs, and passes out, slumped to the side of her pillow.

"Silly woman, what kind of drugs do they have you on? 'Jack Johnson'?" He snorts, glancing at the pill bottle on the nightstand. Wanting to improve her comfort, Vinny gently lifts her, causing her to yelp in agony.

Chick and Camille arrive in the doorway with worried faces.

"Why hasn't she been bathed?" Vinny asks them.

"She was a raving lunatic," Camille says defensively. "The doctor said it was more important to keep her calm."

"Have neither of you heard of a sponge bath?" he asks, unfastening Mouse's clothing.

Both caregivers' sorry eyes drop away with no good excuse.

"Don't just stand there! Help me undress her. I don't want to hurt her any more than we have to." As Vinny slowly turns Mouse's ailing body, he recoils from the rancid smell of infection coming from an oozy stain on the back of her shirt.

"I'll go get some warm water and soap," Camille says, and rushes away.

Mouse whimpers in pain, writhing in her loose conscious state, as Vinny gingerly peels the cloth away to reveal two words—*Nigger Lover*—etched into the tender pale flesh of her back.

Chick's gasp is followed by the sound of a ceramic bowl breaking at Camille's feet. She stands in shock; her eyes flood with tears for her mother's suffering and her own defiant ignorance.

"Let's get her to the bathroom," Vinny says, refusing to let his anger get in the way of the care that Mouse needs.

"I was here when it happened. Hell, I gave a statement to the police," the bartender tells Chick, and shakes his head. "Poor Dion is *still* missing, and those officers didn't seem to give a damn about what happened."

Chick stares down at his whiskey sour. "To either of them," he says.

Vinny slams his empty glass on the varnished wood and glares out into the lobby at the clueless Fourth of July merrymakers staggering back to their rooms.

"Independence Day, my ass!" he roars, perched on a stool next to Chick at the Carousel Bar.

"Another Vieux Carré?" the bartender offers Vinny just before last call.

He nods.

With no known target to hunt and no way to smother his flames of rage, Vinny braves the night by dousing them with bottles of cognac and rye whiskey—a valiant effort to drown a bellicose compulsion for revenge upon an enemy he will never be able to destroy. Jim Crow laws are the product of a virulent societal mindset that seems to mutate over time, persisting, surviving in ignorant spaces between the ears of some, blindly obeyed by many, and cunningly shrouded within the formal and technical language of political legalese.

Sunday

October 20, 1957

Carlos arrives, breathless, in the doorway of his office at a quarter past eight. He looks anxiously at Vinny and Two-Man waiting in front of his desk.

Vinny sits up, perturbed. "You're late."

"Did we exterminate?" Carlos asks, waving his finger around the room.

"Yeah, we swept the room already," Two-Man says. "No bugs."

Carlos takes a few careful steps forward and lifts a lamp to take another look.

Vinny's eyes flick skyward. "I promise you it's clean. No one is listening."

"This is too delicate a matter to take any chances." Carlos puts the telephone in a large bottom drawer of the desk and closes it.

Two-Man shares a half-grin with Vinny, amused by Carlos's paranoia.

Too wired to sit, Carlos leans against the desk and faces them with the "gather 'round, children" body language of an overly caffeinated kindergarten teacher on the first day of school.

"Just tell us," says Vinny.

"I got word from Lansky. The commission has sanctioned a job for you."

"And . . . ?" Vinny says, his impatience growing.

Carlos gives both men a dramatic glance.

"I'm going to rip your face off," Vinny warns.

Carlos frowns at him for taking all the fun out of his presentation, then, resignedly, reveals: "The commission has decided to cut Anastasia loose."

Vinny clenches his jaw and glances at Two-Man, who peers back in shock, one hand over his mouth. His hand falls away. "Are you fucking serious . . . you want us to whack the hitman's hitman?"

Carlos nods. "Turns out our Gator is slated to wear that crown—Luciano just gave Lansky the final nod from Naples." He takes a few deep breaths, watching Vinny and Two-Man stare vacantly across the room. He bows his head with compassion. "I know Albert was the first guy to hire you—"

Vinny interrupts his trip down memory lane. "We're going to need two tossables, and fast."

"You got it." Carlos hops into action, arming himself with a pencil. "I'll arrange whatever weapons you need."

Two-Man throws his hands up. "I can't do it."

Vinny turns to Two-Man. "If we don't do this, they'll just find someone else."

"That's the truth," Carlos confirms. "Who better than to have two of your favorite earners do the deed?"

Two-Man swallows hard and bites the inside of his cheek.

Vinny gives him a stern look and says firmly, "It's time for you to get back up on the horse."

Two-Man squirms at the suggestion. "I couldn't bear to have him know it was me."

"Don't be daft," Vinny scoffs. "I got plenty of ways around that issue."

Carlos inhales sharply, and his features twist. "There *is* this one pesky thing I forgot to mention . . ."

Vinny shifts and raises an eyebrow. "Sometime today would be nice," he says, drumming his fingers on the chair.

"They want it *out loud*."

Vinny's fingers are suddenly still. He curls his lip. "Broad daylight?"

"I know it's not your favorite scenario . . . but I didn't think it was a deal-breaker."

Vinny gives Carlos a look of sardonic disbelief. "Decide that all by yourself, did ya?" He wrinkles his nose for a moment as he considers the logistics. "I'll need a few days to get set up. I know where he'll be and I know what to do."

Friday
October 25, 1957

Strong beams of morning light wash across the windshield of Albert Anastasia's chauffeured car as it turns to enter the underground garage of the Park Sheraton Hotel in Midtown Manhattan, Seventh Avenue, just as it has many times before.

In the hotel foyer at a quarter after ten, Albert greets another patron and steps across the threshold of Grasso's barbershop. He peels off his dark blue overcoat, gray hat, and brown suit coat, depositing them onto the nearest pegs of the freestanding coat-rack behind the privacy partition.

The barber stands by all-purpose hydraulic chair number four, holding a candy-striped cloth, and says, "The usual?"

"Gimme the works," Albert replies. He angles the upholstered chair in view of the street and sits atop the thick cushion, expecting a cut, a shave, and his shoes buffed.

"Sure thing," the barber says. He drapes the generously sized cutting cape around Albert's neck and hovers a scissor over comb to snip away at the excess hair.

Albert's driver appears at his chairside with an uneasy smile. "It's my mother's birthday," the driver says. "If it's all right with you, I'd like to go order a cake and some flowers."

Albert nods and waves him away.

Preparing Albert's skin for a close shave, the barber reclines his client in the chair and wraps his face in a steamy white towel, leaving only his nose exposed. Rocked and lulled by the gentle brushstrokes of the boy polishing his brown leather shoes to a high shine, Albert relaxes, his face swathed in eucalyptus-scented warmth, his eyes closed.

Two men—unlikely twins with an indisputable difference in height and weight—wearing matching heavy overcoats, fedoras, sunglasses, and well-placed scarves slip into the lobby entrance of the barbershop and around the partition. With gloved trigger-hands, they draw revolvers and, with the barrels of their cocked guns, motion the shop workers away from the intended target. Customers and employees quietly flee to safety.

Sensing something amiss, Albert sits upright. The towel slips from his face and he instinctively reaches for a sidearm—a sidearm that he no longer carries. He roars with anger and lunges at the assassins as they aim to fire, stunned when his hands smash into their mirrored reflection—fooled by a wall of glass and silver.

The killers open fire on him and disappear, leaving Albert's body in a state of surrender, bloodstained and riddled with bullets, left to collapse lifeless on the unswept floor.

"Meet you at the station," Vinny says as he and Two-Man separate, blending into the activity on the street—losing the scarves, guns, and glasses along the way, now just two guys taking a brisk stroll down the city sidewalk—long gone before the morgue wagon arrives with an official to confirm what everyone on the scene already knew.

"The Lord High Executioner is dead," the coroner pronounces.

"He lived and died by the gun," sighs the detective to the coroner. "Unfortunately, that leaves us doing all the goddamned paperwork."

Under the fixed gaze of majestic stone eagles, Vinny leans against a granite column outside of Penn Station, smoking a cigarette. His eyes explore the mammoth building with childlike wonder until Two-Man arrives to join him for the 3:40 p.m. Lake Shore Limited to Chicago.

Two-Man squints upward. "What are we looking at?"

After a pause, Vinny replies, "How many people do you think walk by these grand old bones and never really take a good look at it?"

Two-Man removes his hat, takes a step back, and cranes his neck. He gives a slow shake of his head. "Huh . . . never gave it that much thought."

"When was the last time you had your eyes checked?" Vinny asks sharply, and pulls the heavy glass door open to cross the threshold.

Newly amazed by the architectural feat of marble, glass, and ironwork, Two-Man shrugs. "I dunno. Why?"

Vinny frowns, humming pensively in the back of his throat. Without another word, he starts across the cavernous light-filled rotunda of Penn Station's terminal. He heads to the nearest retail kiosk, the sound of Two-Man's heavy gallop close behind him.

Vinny scans the latest newsprint and turns his attention to the small pile of nut-filled candy bars Two-Man is building on the counter.

Vinny leans in. "I seriously think you need to get some specs or something."

Two-Man pays and takes his bag of chocolate-coated goodies. "You really think so?"

"After today, I *know* so. I made a doctor's appointment for you tomorrow afternoon in Chicago." Vinny forces a smile. "You're welcome."

Two-Man unwraps a Chicken Dinner candy bar. "You know I don't like doctors. The last one told me that I needed to lose weight."

Vinny raises his eyebrows pointedly at his choice of snack. "You don't say?"

Two-Man looks around and lowers his voice. "I eat when I'm upset, all right?"

"I don't know why you're so upset." Vinny looks around and lowers his voice. "Not one of the bullets in Albert's body were from your gun."

Two-Man's shoulders sag, and he swallows hard. "None?"

"Not a-one," Vinny confirms.

"Dang," Two-Man says with anguish, and takes a bite of his consolatory treat.

Lounging in the upper bunk in his sleeper car, fingertips on the window, Vinny slowly inhales on an old harmonica, releasing a soft, mournful wail, witness to the day slipping away over the Hudson. He says goodbye to the last tendrils of sunset, revisiting old memories of less comfortable train travel, listening to the wheels rumble and clatter on the tracks below and feeling them in his bones. A deep part of him stirs; an inexplicable yearning awakens—an aching hunger for something he has yet to taste. But just when Vinny's soul is about to voice its wishes, Two-Man slides the door open, returning after his long visit to the dining car.

"Do you think it was the coats that made us look short?" he asks, re-securing the door.

Vinny moves restlessly in his bunk and shields his face from Two-Man's pout. "Don't tell me you're still sore about the witnesses getting our heights wrong?"

"I'm a tall guy, and ladies dig on tall guys."

" 'Dig'?" Vinny asks, peeking through his fingers.

"Yeah, it's a thing the kids are saying."

Vinny rolls his eyes. "Credit for a kill often comes with a sentence, and I think I've got that all out of my system now," he says, maneuvering down from the upper berth. He runs his hand through his hair and smooths his clothes, stepping toward the door.

"You leaving?" Two-Man says, his brow creased with disappointment.

"Yeah, I want to go explore for a while."

The train cars rock and sway, speeding down the tracks through the black of night, while Vinny tries to summon a temporary elixir for what ails him in the arms of a lonely female passenger.

Taking full advantage of the last perk of the overnight train ride, Two-Man snorts. "Why do you always inhale your food?" he asks, noting that Vinny's side of the Saturday brunch table has already been cleared. "You should slow down and savor the taste of life once in a while." He drags the last bite of French toast through a puddle of syrup and chews with reverence.

Disengaged, Vinny stares out of the dining-car window as the Chicago skyline develops in the distance. At 12:03 p.m., the mile-weary train lets out one last pneumatic exhalation as it settles to a stop in Chicago's Union Station.

Thursday
November 14, 1957

After explaining the mysteries of the master gland located at the base of the human brain to Joe Barbara and an amused Vinny, Two-Man says, "Thanks for throwing this get-well party for me."

The trio stand on the front stoop of Joe's large stone house, admiring the sprawling acreage on McFall Road. Joe lifts his bushy eyebrows, folds his arms, and flashes a smirk at Vinny.

"Yep," Vinny says with a condescending shake of his head. "This summit is all about *you*, pal."

"A pituitary lesion," Joe says, rubbing his jaw with mock intrigue. "And to think we all thought you were just a bad shot when you missed Frank's melon."

"Turns out I'm not a bad shot after all," Two-Man says, puffing up his chest. "The doctor says the growth is pressing on my optic nerve. He can go in and snip it right off of there, and I'll be good as new."

"Sounds dangerous," Joe says.

Vinny snorts. "No more dangerous than fucking up a hit in broad daylight—a hit on the One-Man Army himself."

Two-Man shuffles, embarrassed. "I was lucky that Gator here was convinced that something was wrong."

Vinny sniffs. "You mean other than being a bad shot?"

Two-Man narrows his eyes at Vinny and swats at the air in his direction. "You'll see when I'm all better."

"No, *you'll* see when you're all better," Joe teases, and he and Vinny burst into laughter.

"All right, all right, I see how you want to be—making fun of the less fortunate."

"Oh, come on, we're just fucking with you," Joe says. He reaches out to pat Two-Man on the shoulder, but the big guy turns away. Joe shoves his hands in his pockets, shrugging. "I'm sure everyone will be glad to hear that your procedure is scheduled and you can get back to work."

"Sure they will," Two-Man grunts.

Joe shrugs again and looks to change the subject. "I'm sure glad you and Gator were able to come early to prep the steaks. No one knows their way around a spice rack quite like you do."

Two-Man's stomach growls. "You had me at grilled meat."

Joe Barbara's face brightens. "Look! Here come the fellas!" He rubs his paws together, priming them for exuberant handshaking, and smiles at the out-of-state guests arriving in their expensive cars, a gathering of Mafiosi arranged to quell any dissension within the factions of the organized crime syndicate post-Anastasia. "There are refreshments out back, gentlemen," Barbara announces, beaming.

Soon the intoxicating smoky vapors of sizzling beef permeate the backyard air. Staying true to his antisocial nature, Vinny adheres to the outskirts of the patio, enjoying the warmth of the stocked barbecue pit, avoiding conversation. His attention is drawn to an expansive wall of woods that borders the Apalachin estate, the half-naked trees whispering to him in a chilly November blast.

After a burst of laughter, Vinny turns to scan the gathering crowd and begins to back away warily until his shoes find the crunchy grass.

Two-Man walks up beside him. "What is it? What do you see?"

Vinny slams the back of his hand against Two-Man's chest. "It's what I *don't* see. We gotta get out of here."

"But we didn't eat yet."

Vinny pops a hard look in his direction. "I'm gonna leave your ass in exactly one minute."

"What's the big hurry?"

Vinny grabs Two-Man's wide chin and points it in the direction of the small crowd of men in tailored silk suits. "Do you see Lansky?"

"No."

"Do you see Giancana?"

"Uh-uh."

"Do you see Costello?"

Two-Man's eyes expand with fear. "We gotta get the fuck outta here," he whispers.

Sensing the trap, Vinny takes another minute to survey the situation without drawing any unwanted attention. In case of surveillance, he touches his lips to hide his words. "I feel like we're running out of time, and the car is likely blocked. We need to leave on foot, like now." He points off to the side of an auxiliary building. "You head left. I'll go right."

Feigning a casual stroll, the two wander off separately and meet up on the other side of the auxiliary building.

"Okay, now follow me," Vinny whispers to Two-Man. "I'm pretty sure the road is this way." In single file, the two well-dressed men push through crackling brush and trudge through thick blankets of slippery, decaying leaves to reach a bend in the winding country road.

When a commercial delivery truck filled with Charles Chips finally comes by and its brakes squeak, Vinny says, "Be cool and let me do the talking."

The passenger's door slides open. "You fellas need a lift?" the youthful driver asks, adjusting his cap.

"We just need to get to a phone, if that's all right."

"Sure—if you guys don't mind sitting in the bay," the truck driver says apologetically. He settles back down on the pedestal driver's seat and waves them inside. "Hop on in. I could use the company. These quiet roads tend to lull me to sleep." The truck driver notices the soiled bottoms of Two-Man's pant legs as he climbs into the vehicle.

"Car trouble," Two-Man blurts.

The truck driver's friendly features melt. He bites his lip and takes another look in his rearview mirror. He didn't remember seeing any stranded cars recently. As Vinny passes, they share a strained smile.

The truck comfortably climbs into third gear, passing two state trooper cars parked on the side of the road. "Must be nap time," the truck driver snarks uneasily.

"Or a doughnut convention," Vinny says, seeing another police car arriving, ready to pounce and crash the big barbecue.

Friday
November 15, 1957

An orderly mops the vinyl floor in an infirmary corridor at the Naval Air Facility in Atsugi, Japan. His face brightens when he hears the familiar *swoosh, swoosh, swoosh* of the sensible cushioned shoes that hug the attractive feet of his favorite shift nurse as she approaches, her nurse's cap happily standing at attention atop her neatly pinned hair.

"How can you shoot yourself in the elbow?" he asks her as she passes.

The swooshing stops abruptly and she turns to him with a friendly sparkle in her eye. "You know, I asked myself that very thing when they brought him in," she admits, hugging Lee Harvey Oswald's redacted medical chart to her chest, and her head tilts. "Who knew being a radar operator was so hazardous?"

He leans forward and places a stiff hand next to his mouth. "I don't think it's supposed to be, and a derringer's not standard issue . . . the MPs paid him a visit yesterday."

"I guess we'll never know. He's getting out today. I have his discharge papers right here." She winks, pats the back of the clipboard, and resumes her swooshing down the hall to Oswald's room.

The orderly inhales the last of her jasmine fragrance and pushes the cotton mop around with a contented smile.

Outside the Naval Hospital Yokosuka infirmary window, as Lee signs the standardized paperwork, a U-2 spy plane rises into the sky above a flat canopy of black pine trees, heading out on another CIA mission, this time minus one of the essential overflight technicians blessed with enough security clearance to monitor its top-secret whereabouts—a technician with a left elbow that's still on the mend.

Saturday
January 25, 1958

Carlos arrives at the special-guest table, located front and center at the tawdry Sho Bar on Bourbon Street, where Vinny, Two-Man, and Jack "Ruby" Rubenstein wait in a smoke-filled room for the *feature du jour*–burlesque queen, Blaze Starr–to thrill the crowd.

"You fellas are in for a treat!" Carlos grins as he talks around a Cuban cigar and slaps Two-Man on the back. "This big lug might have a stroke after all." Carlos reaches to nudge Jack. "Huh, Ruby?"

"More likely a heart attack," laughs Ruby.

Two-Man flares his nostrils and turns his fully recovered eyes to Carlos.

Carlos jerks away and removes the cigar from his mouth. "What? Did they remove your sense of humor along with that booger on your brain?" He laughs, taking a seat as the lights go dim.

Jazz music plays and the stage light centers on a narrow brocade chaise lounge in search of the main attraction–Blaze Starr. She appears onstage, head crowned by a small white furry hat, matching the fluffy fur boa that drapes her bare shoulders. Seductive shtick underway, Blaze swings her rounded hips, her body slinking and swaying back and forth in front of the lounger, teasing the audience with her shimmy and shake. She wears a silver strapless wrap-style dress, and her hands are smoothly sheathed in long black satin gloves.

On one gloved fingertip she dangles a small purse.

Ruby cups his hands around his mouth and yells, "Show me some skin!"

Coquettishly, Blaze sheds her boa. She drops the small purse, and with the help of her teeth, she slowly removes her gloves and tosses them into the audience.

The second glove lands on Two-Man's head, blocking part of his enamored face. Two-Man brings the satiny glove to his nose and inhales the intoxicating vanilla scent.

Blaze gives him a smile and a little wave before removing her hat and messing up her hair with a look of exaggerated ecstasy. Fanning herself with the hat, Blaze lifts her silvery skirt higher and higher, revealing her black undergarments and thigh-high stockings, and tosses the hat over the crowd. Tantalizing the wolves in the room, she lifts her boa from the stage floor and drags it across her skin, straddling the long narrow strip of fur, briefly thrusting and gyrating with it placed between her legs before letting it drop once again. Fingers combing through her hair, Blaze smiles at her engrossed audience and then slowly unzips and wriggles her way free of the outer silver shell.

Amused, Vinny reaches over to lift Two-Man's jaw that has fallen open. Barely noticing, Two-Man licks his lips, eyes glued to the next garment to go: the black satin skirt-slip.

Next, Blaze slides a stretch-lace garter free from her thigh and catapults it into the darkened seating area. Only her black corset and panty set remain. Slowly, she unsnaps the clips holding her stockings in place.

"Why do they wear so many pieces?!" Two-Man says, and shifts in his chair, impatiently waiting through the infuriatingly slow process of the corset- and stocking-removal while Blaze stretches across the chaise.

Leaning back, she playfully lifts a leg over the armless lounger and lightly bounces in a new straddle position. With a *come hither* look to the audience, she reaches for the purse, fishes a powder puff from its bowels, and begins patting the puff in a sultry zigzag pattern from her neck to her thighs. Her face mimics rapturous delight as she stretches back, extending her body over the couch to twist and thrash.

Two-Man frowns. "Is she all right?"

"She looks more than all right to me!" Carlos laughs and turns to Vinny, but his chair is empty. Carlos's face goes slack. His eyes scan the room, landing on Earl K. Long, the current Louisiana Governor, standing with confidence in the center of the room, flanked by two large men. From the darkness behind them, Carlos can see the glint of the Gator's eyes as he silently stalks his possible prey.

"Well, look what the cat dragged in," Carlos says as Earl approaches the table. He reaches to shake Earl's hand and looks to the now-abandoned stage. "Sorry you missed the show."

"That's all right, Little Man." Earl smiles with a mischievous twinkle in his eye and shakes hands with Two-Man and Ruby, both of whom he has met on prior occasions. "We both know I'm here for the after-party."

"How about I buy you a drink?" Carlos raises a hand to signal a server.

"That won't be necessary." Earl winks and pulls out his wallet. "Tell you what—why don't you let me buy you all a round?" He places a hundred-dollar bill on the table.

Carlos raises his eyebrows. "Since when do you old boys have a problem taking graft?"

Earl lightly elbows Carlos. "You're not going to ruin my good mood tonight, so don't even try."

"Pfft. You can keep your wife's money, Earl. Nobody here is gonna go tattle to Blanche."

Earl rubs his hands together. "So . . . where's the dressing room?"

"Don't you mean '*un*dressing room'?" Ruby sneers. "Follow me."

Carlos looks around for Vinny, but he has left the premises without a trace.

Wednesday
February 12, 1958

G linting crystals of frozen rain are adrift in the morning air, the first measurable snowfall in twenty years, dainty flakes that leave all of New Orleans blanketed in a dazzling layer of white.

Taking cautious steps on slippery concrete, Vinny blocks a chilly gust of wind with the brown sack of groceries he carries to the deteriorating residence of an old friend. He sighs at the small shotgun house with chipping lead paint, a landscape sick with rot and weeds, and other eyesores that go unnoticed by the owner.

Vinny reaches in the doorside mailbox to use the key that is hidden there, then drops it back in place. Christmas barks as he pushes the unlocked door open. Old Joe sits at the kitchen table with his attentive furry friend, patting her side.

"Shhh, girl, you know Vinny," he says.

Christmas whines and rests her head on Joe's knee.

"I wish you could see the snow outside," says Vinny. "There's more than an inch of it."

"More than an inch, you say?" Bewildered, Old Joe rubs Christmas's neck and lifts one of her keen ears to tell her, "Hell done froze."

Vinny searches the cabinet for a pitcher and dumps a frozen concentrated cylinder of orange mush inside. He fills the pitcher a little more than halfway under the faucet, then swirls the contents with a long spoon.

Old Joe sits helplessly, listening to Vinny bang around on a quest for this or that, rinsing, and putting away groceries.

"You don't have to go to all dis trouble."

Vinny discovers a cutting board and dumps a large pile of damp turnip leaves out of a colander. "I hired someone to come cook and clean for you, but she can't start until Monday."

"I can feed myself," Joe says with wounded pride.

"And your doctor made it sound like you've been doing a poor job of that lately."

"I caught the diabetes and I lost a few pounds . . . it's not that big-a deal," Joe replies. He flinches at the sound of Vinny's fist landing hard on the counter.

"It *is* a big deal!" Vinny yells, and Joe can feel his hot temper coming his way. "Isn't blind enough?" he says, slapping the table in front of Joe. "Or do you want to have your legs amputated, too?"

Joe chuckles.

Vinny blinks rapidly and backs away, as if he were going to catch this sudden case of insanity. "I oughtta amputate that hard head of yours," he mutters, and turns to grab a knife. He begins to attack the pile of cruciferous greens, irritated by Joe's insolence as the blind man laughs harder. "Tell me, what's so goddamned funny about this situation?"

Joe snorts loudly. "You think the diabetes did this to my eyes?"

"Well, didn't it?"

Joe wags his head slowly. "Trust me, dis broke-down pancreas had nothing to do with it."

Tuesday
March 4, 1958

Under Hollywood contract—less than a month before he is to report for deferred duty with the United States Army—Elvis Presley causes a stir while filming on location in New Orleans. The debonair crooner ends his workday on Lake Pontchartrain's southern shore by signing autographs, surrounded by a gaggle of squealing girls—a diversion that is graciously welcomed by the city's underbelly.

Elvis's co-star Carolyn Jones narrowly escapes the raucous crowd full of female hormones. Despite suffering a high fever, she crinkles her exotic features and becomes comedic, lifting a pretend cigar to her mouth like Groucho Marx.

"So what am I, chopped liver?" she snarks wearily to her new bodyguard.

The hired muscle smiles, not entirely sure if she's referring to Mr. Presley's attention, that of the adoring fans, or both. He lifts Carolyn's achy frame off the ground, carrying her to the royal red Hudson Hornet parked beneath a huge vine-covered tree. After setting her down gently, as if she were made of glass, he helps her into the front passenger's seat and closes the car door behind her. Carolyn's eyes follow the bodyguard's young, sinuous body as he walks in front of the car.

"My, my, Gator! Aren't you Prince Charming," she says as he slides into the driver's seat.

"Just doing my job, ma'am," Vinny replies.

"Ouch!" she says, touching his toned arm. "Cut it out with the 'ma'am' stuff, would ya?"

Vinny looks down at her weak ivory hand on his arm, and then pierces her gaze with his own. "Your husband has paid me well to keep you comfortable and safe." He flashes a devilish grin, and suddenly Carolyn finds herself caught in the hypnotic trance of his glittering pupils. Her body relaxes, her brain tingles, and her pale hand drops heavily to the seat.

"Now, isn't that better?" he soothes. "Sit back, relax, and enjoy the ride, doll."

Carolyn gives a faint nod of cooperation in the fog of her numb, meditative state. The Hudson pulls away from the tree and gently rolls across the grass onto a worn car path of crushed white shells, following the arrow posted on a rustic cypress sign.

The long wheelbase of the two-door hardtop gives Carolyn a smooth, quiet ride to the front door of the Roosevelt Hotel. In her tenth-floor suite, she is compelled to put a deep dent of recovery in the bed next to her husband, Aaron Spelling, who has been patiently waiting for her.

Saturday
April 5, 1958

"**How come Canada** gets to watch all that cool shit?"

In the corner of Carlos's office, Nofio clicks off the portable nine-inch rabbit-eared Zenith, abandoning his constant adjustments of the antenna's metal stems—along with his hope of finding a broadcast of the massive Ripple Rock explosion. He pouts at having to miss a historical event that would spew debris a thousand feet in the air and demolish a dangerous underwater mountain peak near the Canadian coastline.

Bored, Nofio lingers in front of the desk, reaches into a sack of boiled peanuts labeled HOT, and relaxes back in the chair with a handful to remove the softened shells. He pops one into his mouth and chews, watching Carlos, who is lost in an article in *The Times-Picayune.*

"Hey," says Nofio, "did you hear what happened to Mickey Cohen's guy last night?" He rips the skin off another peanut and discards the husk in a nearby ashtray.

"Huh?" Carlos looks up from the newspaper, eyebrows drawn together. His mind is stuck on foreign affairs, digesting the details of an attack on Havana by a rapidly growing militia led by the bearded rebel leader Fidel Castro (a communist revolutionary pest who threatens the dictatorship rule of Batista with plans to cock block a billion dollars' worth of cash-cow enterprises owned and operated through American interests; a Marxist fly wanting to swim in a bowl of soup owned by big oil, casinos, and trade–those that hold spoons are not amused).

"Come on. You remember Johnny Stomp?"

Carlos rubs his cleft chin for recollection. "You mean John Stompanato, that high-heel chaser in Beverly Hills?"

"He caught himself a starlet." Nofio grins. "Poor Johnny Stomp won't be fleecing any more broads, though–some fourteen-year-old girl shoved a butcher knife into his gut last night."

Carlos's head flinches back slightly. "Is she for hire?" He smirks impishly.

"I'd say she's plenty set. A Tinseltown heiress." Nofio snickers, cleaning his teeth with his tongue. "Hollywood," he says, eyebrows raised with a meddling curiosity as he slowly peels another spicy legume. "Isn't that where your golden boy's been hanging out lately?" He raises his beady eyes to catch a wave of anger crossing Carlos's face.

"Whatcha tryin to say?"

Nofio shrugs and tosses another peanut into his mouth.

"Vinny has way too much class to pin a hit on some little girl, if that's what you're drivin at. Besides, he's too busy." Carlos leans forward and shoves a finger onto the desk as he speaks. "He's out there securing a future, yours and mine. Right now, he's helpin Hoffa run the biggest piggy bank in the goddamned country. We'll be running the whole fuckin show with those kind of numbers at the polls. They're yanking every union leader in California under his Teamster wing. Don't you get it?"

"I guess I don't," Nofio admits, tugging at his earlobe.

Carlos's face brightens and his lips spread wide in an evil grin. "Government is just another numbers game. We round up every schmo in every trade union and we got us a fix in every election there is."

Nofio sucks his teeth and his eyes wander in deep contemplation. "How do we get them union leaders to take the bait?"

"We offer 'em long-term benefits," Carlos says, and taps his pinky ring once on the desk. "The ones we can't convince, we buy."

"And what if they can't be bought?"

"Well . . ." Carlos curls his lips, relaxes back in his chair, and strokes his throat. "If we can't shake 'em or buy 'em . . . we *kill* 'em."

Friday
June 20, 1958

The air in the Bluebird Café heats up when Marine Corps Private Oswald seeks out his superior officer, Sergeant Miguel Rodriguez, for relentlessly picking on him while on duty—an act that in the moment is either a display of profound stupidity in an emerging pattern of ill-conceived absurdities, or a skillfully planned cover story played out in public for memorandum.

"What the hell is your problem with me, anyway?" Oswald slurs, before drunkenly dousing Rodriguez's knee with his glass of Crown and Coke.

Rodriguez shoves Oswald and snarls, "Get your drunk ass away from me, Private!"

Oswald stumbles backward. "How about we take this outside?"

"You can't go around disrespecting a superior officer like that!" yells Staff Sergeant James Milam. He turns to the café staff. "Someone call the MPs!"

Rodriguez blots his pant leg with a cloth napkin. "We don't need to get them involved."

"Come on, ya yellowbelly," Oswald says, and raises his fists. "Put up your dukes and fight me like a man!"

"Boy, your dumb ass is going to get *way* more than KP duty for this!"

Friday
June 27, 1958

Oswald enters the eerily quiet disciplinary building. His shoes *click-clop* across the terrazzo floor.

"Summons," says the military officer on duty, coldly requesting the copy of Oswald's court-martial paperwork. The officer studies the onion-skinned charge sheet for a moment and points Oswald to a nearby bench. "Have a seat. And don't make me hunt you down when it's your turn."

On the edge of the bench, Private Oswald repeatedly swipes the folded edge of his charge sheet with sudden regret, lamenting his decision to refuse legal counsel at the court-martial hearing. Armed with a flimsy defense, he faces serious punitive action.

Oswald's lack of preparation is met with a guilty verdict under the Uniform Code of Military Justice. He is immediately remanded into custody to serve a humiliating four-week prison sentence, and he exits the courtroom as one of a group of temporary convicts loading onto a Naval transport van.

"Move it! Snuggle up tight, nut to butt, ladies!" barks the officer in charge. "I want all you brig rats to keep your cum-dumpsters shut and your dick-beaters to yourselves. You're in my house now!" he yells, and slams the van doors shut.

Saturday
June 28, 1958

Mouse unwraps a towel from her hair and wipes a clear path in the foggy bathroom mirror. She considers her reflection—faded nightgown, dyed hair, and a face she's beginning not to recognize—and leans in to study her eyes.

"There. There's the sadness, old friend," she says to the eyes that have witnessed her happiest moments and all of her darkest days; expressive eyes that are punctuated by sags, crinkles, and creases which refuse to smooth. With her fingertips, Mouse tugs the slackness of her skin back to its origins and then lets it go.

"Oh, well."

She shrugs and grabs a tube of Gleem that was improperly squeezed in the middle. Mouse sighs in defeat at a tube that represents a battle of wills with Camille she stopped fighting a long time ago. With a small glass, she begins pressing the contents of the tube back into place; suddenly she stops and sets the glass down, realizing the desire to fight her way through the simplest of tasks is all gone too.

Life . . . only those in heaven must know the point of it all,

she thinks.

A voice from her past whispers, *"How you think I know, Mouse?"*

Her eyes pan the ceiling. "Beulah . . . ?"

Mouse checks in the cabinet and behind the shower curtain for someone she knows couldn't possibly be there. She knows it's laughable to think Beulah could be hiding in a bar of soap or a jar of beauty cream, but she checks just the same on the off chance of seeing her best friend once more, in whatever form available.

Not knowing whether to feel relief or disappointment, Mouse loads her toothbrush with a dollop of paste and scrubs the surface of her teeth with a rolling motion as random memories float in and out of her head. Completing a familiar pattern, she leans over the sink to rinse until her mouth feels fresh and free of suds and grit.

When she looks again into the mirror, her reflection is not alone. Before her scream can resonate, the intruder, a man with his facial features hidden behind a surgical mask, covers her nose and mouth with a cloth liberally doused in halothane.

Having monitored his nemesis's movements for many weeks, Iosef acts on the sage wisdom recorded by a military tactician from ancient China . . . particularly fixated on a passage that suggests batting your enemy around like a cat does with a mouse. *If your enemy is at rest, make them toil. When full, starve them. If they are settled, make them move.*

The curse Iosef placed on the boy who betrayed his precious Margit was taking far too long to manifest an acceptable outcome, and left another chance at happiness in its wake. Beulah's death surprisingly stung him infinitely more than he expected or wanted to admit. Iosef had allowed his desire for vengeance against Gator to overshadow his budding love for the woman who bore him. An injured soul, so locked into the sport of war that he missed out on a woman who could have delivered him from all the pain. Beulah saw it too, *all of it*, visualizing every path available, when Iosef took her hands on that fateful day. Overwhelming prescience that included a path that would lead her into Iosef's arms, to her own happiness at the expense of others she held so dear, to decisions that she found herself unable to make. She left her own fate to wiser hands and chose to forget, to forget it all, to not be unduly influenced by her own needs, her own cravings, because her willingness to be sacrificed in exchange for her son's absolution was paramount.

Wasn't it?

Vinny arrives in his suite a few days earlier than expected and drops his car keys in a fancy glazed pottery dish—a gift from one of Camille's many admirers, no doubt. He moves cautiously through the far-too-quiet suite; his senses prickle with some patient, long-forgotten danger . . . just before he spots Mouse's foot on the floor in the bathroom doorway. He rushes to her side.

"Oh no, no, no, no, no, no," Vinny repeats, tapping Mouse's ashen face as she lies unresponsive on the cold tiles.

A syringe with traces of a powerful opiate protrudes from her arm—a pain-relieving euphoria gone too far.

He plucks out the needle and tosses it aside and lifts her eyelids to reveal tiny pinpoint pupils. He grabs a towel to wipe a pink froth from her mouth, and checks for breath.

"Come on, come on, wake up, Maureen!"

He presses his ear to her chest, eager to hear a heartbeat . . . but that song has ended.

This isn't my fault, it can't be!

Vinny cries as his mind fills with Iosef's curse.

Unable to coax her spirit back from the ether, Vinny finds himself distraught, at odds with these uncalculated events far beyond his command. Betrayed by death—a power he normally wields with impunity.

Someone's gonna pay.

Tuesday
July 1, 1958

A cicada's call echoes from high in a tree on Metairie Road—a buzzing loud enough to disturb the solemn stillness of a final prayer of rest at Maureen's funeral. Having emerged from his nymphal casing, the cicada proudly pops his tymbals in triumphant song, unaware that this is no time or place for celebration.

Vinny and Camille stand in stoic unison, much like the stained marble slabs that make up the small family mausoleum, beneath a muggy gray melancholic sky. A sea of black funeral garb slowly recedes from the Smith family crypt as mourners turn to leave the heart of the cemetery. Vinny's eyes and ears constantly search the crowd for clues, on the hunt for the unspoken identity of the dealer responsible for this preventable tragedy.

Before the caretaker decides to shove the casket into the entombment, to be interred with the remains of a father Camille can barely recollect, she steps forward with tears of sorrow and places a gloved hand on the glossy oak surface of her mother's final resting place. The only person she has ever fully trusted rests an understanding hand on her shoulder.

"Vinny, she was in so much pain," she cries. Camille covers her mouth with her hand, her eyes squeeze shut, and hot tears spill out onto the glove.

Vinny wraps her in a protective embrace. "No more pain now," he whispers, and nods to the caretaker.

Walking with Camille along the broken sidewalk leading to the car, Vinny's mind is loud and the cicada's call continues, both screaming in vain. His heart is heavy, but his hands are even heavier with a need to give Camille–and Mouse–some form of retribution.

Camille's skin crawls with anxiety; she stops abruptly and shudders. Her body lurches over the grass, heaving to expel the contents of her stomach, but there is nothing but spurts of acidic saliva.

Listening to her cough and spit, Vinny retrieves a handkerchief from his suit and hands it to her. "Are you okay?"

She presses the cloth to her lips, looks at him, and moans in unendurable torment. Suddenly, becoming frenzied, she announces, "It's all my fault! I could've stopped her! I should've *done* something."

His arms reach to encircle her. "Honey, you didn't know–"

Camille writhes in his arms. She breaks free and backs away, her eyes wild. "Oh, but I *did!*" She points an accusatory finger at him. "And so did *you.*"

Vinny stands frozen, blindsided by her indictment. "I didn't, Camille. What are you saying?"

"What system brings the drugs into the city, huh? We all know who the candy man is, don't we, Vinny?"

"Be careful, Camille." He growls and takes a fighting stance. "Your accusation won't land lightly."

"You think I don't know that?"

"What is it that you think you know?" He narrows his flinty eyes and cocks his head to the side to wait for her answer.

She swallows hard, sways, and bites her lip. "I know you're a mid-level thug answering to high-level thugs . . . what more is there to know that won't put me in any more danger than I'm already in?" She chokes and pounds an open hand on her chest several times, and her face contorts in pain. "It was *me*," she cries, and claws at her face. "The drugs were supposed to be for me . . . I got them for *me*," she weeps. Camille staggers a few steps, shaking her head vehemently. She turns and throws her hands in the air in frustration. "I didn't know what else to do. She needed so much . . . too much . . . too much . . ."

Vinny grabs Camille by her shoulders. Refusing to meet his gaze, she slams her eyes shut and he gives her an insistent shake.

"*She* did this. We did not do this!"

"Didn't we, though?" she cries, revealing her teary, bloodshot eyes.

As the cicada's song persists in his ears, Vinny presses his lips together and looks to the infinite sky for clarity. He finally gathers his resolve and sighs. "We can erase this—we've done it before. Whatever we knew or did not know, whatever we did or did not do, *she* put that needle in her arm."

Monday
July 7, 1958

There are legends and myths about hybrid creatures that lurk in the swamps of Louisiana, but deep down we all know the truth ... that we construct grotesque stories of freakish mutation, a diversionary simulacrum of fantastical lore to make the half-human monsters that walk city streets seem a little less scary.

Evil can be a pervasive coldness that radiates through tissue and bone; it spreads and devours warmth from its host and from others in the vicinity, to take on the temperature of their surroundings—just as all cold-blooded animals are expected to do.

Can we blame them?

Somewhere outside of Slidell, the Gator heads deeper along the familiar narrowing Old Pearl River fingers, every bend of the waterway memorized, dodging every cypress knee. He loves the feel of the cool wind and spray blasting his body, the sound of the roaring boat motor as he flies, chasing the glistening moonlight across the flat midnight water.

Surrounded now by dense subtropical fauna, Vinny cuts the engine and listens to the swirling murk caress the aluminum hull and waits for the right moment to dump a meaty treat over the side for his ectothermic friends of the Honey Island Swamp.

Perched on a gnarled, moss-covered branch, a hoot owl watches him float by with large, curious orbs. Below the silvery moss, many other inquisitive witnesses, both poisonous and non-poisonous, crawl, slither, and scurry along the banks and upon half-submerged logs.

Vinny hears the high-pitched croaks of baby alligators, followed by that deep, rumbling growl, and smiles. With a pocket-knife handle between his teeth, he lifts the heavy gift wrapped in burlap; then, supporting the weight with his hip, he retrieves the knife and severs the twisted, knotted cords of twine. He grunts, giving the free edge of material a sharp tug. The headless, handless corpse of an unfortunate male—a Tampa-based smuggler who unwisely gifted supplies that ended up in Camille's possession—rolls out over the side of the boat and into the water.

Vinny playfully slaps the side of the boat, and an apex predator, the big boy of his neighborhood, hears that dinner bell ring. Through a thin carpet of duckweed comes a formidable pair of red glowing eyes that glide along the surface, eerily spaced fifteen inches apart. The adult gator's bony armor lurks nearer to the body, swimming past smaller sets of eyes hoping to have a taste, and opens his broad snout to give a slow, angry hiss of warning. The ferocious reptile's powerful jaw clamps down on a thick muscular leg, followed by the fast splashes of acrobatic twists and twirls in the water, the snapping of bone, the detaching of limbs—evidence savagely destroyed before daylight.

Wednesday
July 23, 1958

"**W**hat *about* the Hudson?" Vinny booms, his eyes pinched with suspicion as he charges into Carlos's office to discover his boss with his ear to the phone.

Bug-eyed Carlos grabs his chest and places his hand over the mouthpiece to complain. "Learn to knock, before you go and give me a fucking heart attack!"

Vinny raises his arms to Carlos in a defiant Italian salute, lowers himself into a chair, and places a foot atop his knee to stare his boss down for discussing his favorite car with some unknown party.

Carlos smirks and swats at the air. "Yeah, I'm listening," he says into the receiver, glaring back at Vinny. "As long as you understand that I need that delivery made and the rest of the job tied in a bow ASAP—no excuses." He compresses his lips, waiting for the party on the other end to respond. "I already told you, I can have it detailed and delivered to Dallas as early as Monday." Carlos raps his knuckles on the desk and sighs, a poor attempt to veil the irritation in his voice. "Dallas, Houston, Miami, it's your choice. How 'bout you think that over and I'll call you back."

Carlos tosses the receiver into the cradle and drops his crimson face into his hands. Vinny watches him take a few deep breaths until the red starts to fade. Carlos spreads his fingers to peek out at Vinny's smooth, expressionless face.

"You gonna tell me or what?" Vinny says.

Carlos lowers his arms in defeat. "This guy is someone we need up in Baton Rouge. He happens to have a strong desire for that vehicle, and we are going to give it to him."

"Oh we are, are we? And why, pray tell, would *we* do a thing like that?"

Carlos watches Vinny about to shove a cigarette between his lips, change his mind, and instead fidget with the unlit stick in his young, skillful fingers. "*We* need him to do *us* a huge favor, and that was the price," Carlos says, just before his stomach lets out an audible growl.

"But why the Hudson?" Vinny sniffs, detecting a faint odor of a rat having been in the room.

Carlos shrugs. "Someone must have mentioned it to him. How 'bout we discuss the details ova lunch?" He stands up, and the cigarette between Vinny's knuckles snaps in half. Carlos lets out a one-syllable laugh and his eyebrows draw tightly together. "You growing attached to things now?" He quickly waves the insinuation away. "No hard loss, my friend—you'll get another sleek set of wheels, just like you always do."

"She's *custom*," Vinny says, and bites down on his bottom lip so hard he can taste blood.

"And that's the big draw now, isn't it? We all just want to own a tailored dream."

"Or we simply take someone else's."

"Says the man with the clear conscience." Carlos laughs, pulling his car keys out of his deep pocket. "How 'bout we go down to the Ford dealership after lunch and take a gander at one of them new Thunderbirds?"

Wednesday
August 13, 1958

Upon release from his punishment in the Atsugi Naval Air Facility brig, Lee squints behind a raised hand as he steps into the searing light of day, embittered by the humiliating experience. Forty-eight days of hard labor and confinement left him with bigger arms and an increasingly calloused heart against a system of militarism; each sullen step he takes leads him further away from monolithic Western society and further into a new perversion of political ideology.

This is to be the entry into Ozzie Rabbit's official file in the absence of concrete proof or witness. The truth is such a malleable chronicle in the world of global espionage, a built-in failsafe, a hollow archipelago of narrative assembled to deflect further analysis, where the conclusive reality is whatever perception it provides the average onlooker.

Are you watching?

"Were you paying attention?"

Angleton turns his long bony frame to stare at Lee Harvey Oswald and Iosef Popescu pointedly before pausing the playback on a top-secret newsreel of Operation Blue Bat. The Bell & Howell sits humming, at the ready, to continue projecting footage of an authorized military intervention meant to till foreign soil, to prepare, to plant seeds for a harvest, a boon for a future military-industrial complex, images of US airborne battlegroups' July landing in Beirut and a film to explain how a far-reaching strategy might affect missions slated for the fledgling NASA space program.

Lee is proudly wearing his neatly starched uniform (which is faintly perfumed by jet fuel) for the on-base meeting. "Sir, yes, sir," he answers, as eager as a first-day recruit.

Mildly impressed, Angleton then looks to Iosef, who wields a different, more relaxed set of credentials.

"We study Soviet enemy," Iosef says, and lifts the cover of a binder filled with coded field directives for infiltrating the USSR to gather intel and an introduction to a future assignment at Michoud Assembly Facility in New Orleans. "We train hard and understand need for rockets that put big eye in space." Iosef shares a strong nod with Lee. "The two of us are not unlike quilters guild, sewing together scraps of patchwork fabric until we form good cover."

Angleton's darting eyes probe the two men for signs of weakness or insecurity. "Piercing the iron curtain will be no small task, Private Oswald. You will have to maintain focus on your objectives no matter what. Do you understand what we're asking of you?"

"Yes, sir, I do. I'm ready to be whatever my country asks of me."

"Whatever, without question?"

Lee lifts his chest higher, filled with purpose and belonging. "Without question, sir."

"Good," Angleton says. The thin flesh of his cadaverous face rises to further accentuate his high cheek bones, a cross between a smile and a sneer. "Go ahead and start laying more groundwork for defection. It must look plausible."

Lee nods in fervent obedience. "Authentic. Will do, sir."

"Can you believe in your own lies and still keep your wits about you? There will be no room for mistakes. You must be unshakable," Angleton says, keenly aware that even the best covert operative can succumb to moments of fear and doubt. "If you are to get caught, we simply cannot help you. Do you understand?"

"Sir, yes, sir," Lee says with enthusiasm. "I'll stick to the script. They won't break me, sir."

"Did you have any questions or concerns about setting the latest cultural reports to memory?"

"No, but my Russki dialect still needs work."

Angleton gives a wry smile and hands Lee a round-trip travel packet for New Orleans. "We've found a way to overcome that issue. You're going to meet with a friend in your home town who can help with a crash course. In just a few days, there will no longer be a language barrier for you."

"A few days?" Lee's forehead wrinkles with uncertainty.

Angleton claps the soldier on the back. "Don't worry—you still have months yet to prepare and practice."

Meanwhile, fourteen hours behind in New Orleans, Vinny is already on duty under a blanket of clouds hiding the summer stars. Nothing but darkness in the Hudson's rearview mirror as he rolls up to a secluded intersection. He cranks down the window to breathe in the sticky humid air and leans on the steering wheel, fascinated by a crab inching its way across the road in the bright headlight beams, its claws in the air as if to claim no part in what Vinny is about to do.

"Get a load of this little guy," Vinny says, addressing the overly intoxicated body of an uncooperative state official slumped against the passenger-side window. He shakes his head and reaches over to tap the guy's cheek. "That's one weak liver you have there, pal."

The man moans. Vinny pats him down and recovers a key that opens a post office box in Chalmette.

Driving along the newly paved Wisner, near Mirabeau Avenue, Vinny punches the gas and skitters for about nine hundred feet before the car loses contact with the road and sails into the air, plunging upside down into Bayou St. John. As the partially submerged vehicle sinks farther and farther down to the bayou's murky floor, Vinny escapes, swimming against rushing, swirling water, before the Hudson hits a final depth of around fifteen feet. He swims away from the car to safety at the water's edge, the unconscious passenger still inside, his ankle firmly secured in place with a braided strip of sausage-casing tied to the seat anchor.

Dripping, Vinny sits in pinch-lipped misery, letting his favorite car drown, eyes glued to the surface until the last bubble is released and the last ripple is stilled.

He pushes up to stand defiant above the moon's peaceful

reflection on the black fluid canvas.

"If I can't have her, no one can."

When the body is discovered bloated and afloat a week later, no evidence of the restraint is left to be identified, and the poor state official is swiftly declared to be a victim of his own drunken stupidity.

Friday
September 5, 1958

"**I just came** by to pick up the rest of my things," Camille explains into the telephone handset pressed between her shoulder and her ear, her hands busy rummaging through Vinny's belongings, searching his office area for something that eludes her. "Yes. I *know* you 'found perfection,' you said that already." She giggles, sitting down at the desk, and rolls her eyes as she listens to Chick blather on about some silly car he saw earlier today.

"Do you know if Vinny's still looking?" he asks her.

Camille tugs at the top desk drawer and it refuses to budge. Locked. Her smile fades. "I wouldn't know," she says matter-of-factly into the receiver. "We haven't talked much since I moved out."

"Are you two ever going to bury the hatchet?"

"I'm willing to," she admits, sliding a letter opener into the slender gap above the drawer. "When he decides to treat me like an adult."

Chick laughs. "Maybe he will when you *are*."

"I'm eighteen, Dumbo."

"Since when?!"

"August twenty-third!" she huffs smartly, trying to pop the latch. "Older every year, like clockwork."

"Why wasn't I invited to the party?"

"You were. I figured your invitation got lost in the mail," she says, falling to her knees to get a better look at the lock.

"Well, now I owe you a drink."

"Been there, done that. We had our own little private party back in July, didn't we?"

"Err . . . y—yeah, I guess we did," Chick stammers. He remembers only bits and pieces of that drunken night of tears, rum, and skin—a foggy recollection of a soothing mutual compassion that went, admittedly, a little too far. "Was I . . . did I . . . are you okay?"

" 'Okay'?" Camille asks with an air of innocence, and smiles. She can almost hear the blood rush to his cheeks through the telephone wire. And maybe to somewhere else, somewhere lower.

"I mean . . . have you forgiven me?"

"There's really nothing to forgive, Chick. I wasn't hurt or taken advantage of, if that's what you're wondering. You were kind and gentle."

"Does Vinny know?"

"You're still breathing, aren't you?"

'Should we tell him?"

"What for? You plannin to ask him for my hand or somethin?"

"Is . . . is that what you want me to do?"

"Oh, for heaven's sake, Chick!" Camille laughs. "Quite the lovestruck romantic, aren't you? I do hope that the man I marry isn't quite so wishy-washy about the task."

"I don't know what to say."

Camille takes another stab at the lock and wonders why it always looks so easy on the silver screen. She slumps in defeat. "How about a belated birthday present?"

"Oh, yes, of course. And I am truly sorry that I missed your party."

Her eyes widen as she hears Vinny enter the suite, whistling. Heart pounding, she rises to her feet and tosses the letter opener back onto the blotter where she found it. "My sophisticated friends threw a blowout. You wouldn't have enjoyed it . . . there wasn't any cake or ice cream."

"You're right, that doesn't sound like much fun to me."

Vinny appears and gives the signal for *I'm not here.*

"He just walked in, Chick, did you need to speak with him?" Camille says, absently touching her hair with one hand and holding the receiver in front of Vinny with the other as they exchange an evil eye. Vinny shakes his head in refusal; she touches the handset to his chest with fluttering artificial lashes and a satisfied grin.

Vinny drops his head and places the handset to his ear. "What do you want?" he growls.

"Did you pick out a new ride yet?" Chick says to Vinny with a hint of exuberance.

"Not yet, why?"

"Because I've found a dressed-up machine that's the most!"

"The most what . . . the most lettuce?"

"Trust me, I can get you this cherry ride for two dimes and a song."

Vinny gives a snort of doubt. "Is this 'steal' supposed to be for you or for me?"

"Well . . ."

"Thanks, but no thanks, pal. I doubt that we share the same taste in wheels."

"Oh, come on, just give her a look . . . please?"

"What happened to the Rocket?"

"Oh, she's fine . . . I'm going to save her for the dragway."

"Who are you trying to kid with that bullshit? I know you don't have the stomach for racing anymore . . . and we both know why, don't we?"

The offhanded insult is punctuated by Chick's pained silence. Chick listens to Vinny's even breaths, half expecting him to apologize and half expecting a dial tone, but in the end comes neither.

"Where'd you get the nuggets for a new ride?" Vinny asks.

"Oh . . . I have a steady gig now. You should hop the bus in the morning and come hang out for a day or two."

"*Me*, on a bus to *Houma?*" Vinny asks with a sardonic chuckle. "And give me one good reason I should do that."

"There's a festival this weekend . . . we could stir up some fun."

"Hmmm," Vinny says, while straightening the desktop blotter that is ever so slightly askew.

Saturday
September 6, 1958

Somehow knowing that his own procrastination in replacing a murdered car makes that window seat on the morning bus to Houma even more ill-fitting and ridiculous.

What in the hell am I doing?

he asks himself, and is about to get up to leave when the aisle becomes obstructed by a wide skirt of felt swinging from the narrow hips of a budding teenage girl. He waits for her to pass so he can escape. She spies the empty spot beside him, a handsome stranger—way more appealing than the other available options. But now Vinny's getaway plan is foiled as she uses her purse to claim the seat next to him. She tosses her fine wave of brown hair as if she were Marilyn Monroe as she peels a thin decorative sweater from her as-yet-unremarkable frame.

"I don't know what I was thinking putting this blasted thing on in this heat," she says airily before completing her invasion of his privacy.

Vinny's muscles coil, and he feels a sudden, inexplicable regret. He considers rudely barreling past her and heading for the nearest breakfast café—when he hears the bus doors seal and the engine rev.

Stuck on this ride to Houma, he settles in and closes his eyes to pretend that he is traveling to a place of magic and wonder. Unlike the bland female companion who occupies the space beside him, his sleepy brain conjures up a curvaceous and alluring woman-child. A figure that is a mysterious blend of Margit and Elizabeth, angelic virgin and sultry vixen, a mate that can only exist in dreams.

The imagery dissolves when the girl's shrill voice pierces Vinny's pleasant escape. "Is a friend supposed to meet you here?"

So close, so close!

Some say a person does not come to life until they know what it is to be in love . . . that you can want someone so bad that you dream them into being . . . and that when a heart is brave, the bonds of love can be forged before two people meet.

Vinny's eyes are sealed, still searching to see that dreamy figure once more.

THE GATOR
LEAVES NOTHING BEHIND
PART I

 The Disturbing History Saga

Inspired by actual events

The insidious seduction of a college-bound girl by a hell-bent abuser . . .

At fifteen, Mary Lou Poche is known in her small town of Houma, Louisiana, for her profound beauty and intelligence. She and her best friend, Gayle Gautreau, believe their futures are as bright as the Southern sun.

On September 6th, 1958, Mary and Gayle strike out on their first adventure to the fall festival—alone—where they meet a mysterious psychic who sends Mary reeling from the revelation of events that will affect her for years to come. In the reading, the psychic speaks of secret keys that will unlock Mary's safety and of a difficult choice between two men. The Creole psychic woman says, "Choose de right one an' you will know peace and success . . . choose de wrong one an' you will suffer in bondage many a year."

Is the reading purely whimsical entertainment . . . or a frightening glimpse of things to come?

Now available @ www.boleybooks.com & Amazon!

THE GATOR LEAVES NOTHING BEHIND
PART II

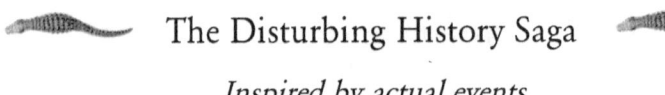 The Disturbing History Saga

Inspired by actual events

"Choose de right one an' you will know peace and success . . .
Choose de wrong one an' you will suffer in bondage many a year."

A chance meeting set the spinning threads of destiny in motion in the bayou-side community of Houma, Louisiana, where a young woman's quiet struggle builds to horrific heights. Mary Poche finds herself facing a diabolical threat, a nemesis she never expected: her husband.

Back in September of 1958, Mary was delivered a fate-filled message about dangerous choices and two men who would enter her life. The mysterious details of that Creole woman's warning fade fast from Mary's memory as the busy school days go by, yet her future continues to align, inescapable.

Mary has a brilliant mind with a clear road to her educational ambitions, but life is about to throw her into a maze of relationships, hormones, desires, and dangers she never saw coming. She finds herself lured, caught amidst the attention of a boy and a man. One has a questionable future and one has a mysterious past; both are a possible threat to her safety.

She's afraid of losing her head and her heart to love . . . but what if the stakes are much higher?

Now available @ www.boleybooks.com & Amazon!

The story unfolds, questions are answered,
and fate will not be denied in . . .

THE DISTURBING
HISTORY SAGA

MORE SECRETS REVEALED . . .

. . . coming soon—sign up for pre-order information
and extras at

www.boleybooks.com.

AFTERWORD

History has always fascinated me—my own included. In this book, I was able to delve into both. There have been many, many books written in the years since JFK was assassinated; I didn't want my book to feel like it was covering the same tired ground as all the others, so I added layers of other histories (and an ounce or two of make-believe). I stacked them carefully for you, like a deck of trick cards.

As I studied and delved into research for my first series of novels, The Disturbing History Saga, I was inspired to include many historical facts and plausible morsels. I felt by stirring in several real-world ingredients that it would make the story more delicious. Wrapping my fiction up in some truth would add more fun, color, and depth. I read countless blog posts, news articles, and books in order to have them blend together well—some areas perhaps a little *too* well; please don't confuse the two. Not every factual detail was easy to find or easy to corroborate (but you may be surprised to learn how much of it *was*—and the rest tirelessly hunted down by me, my fans, my editors Nicole and Spencer, and Lee Alessi as mentioned in my acknowledgments), and we now know that not everything is Google-able.

So many were gracious enough to help me during this odyssey, but I had the last call in what went in and what didn't, and I apologize if I missed the mark—I promise it wasn't for lack of trying. I never had any intention of offending friends, relatives, history buffs, or any other people with these flights of my imagination; what you hold in your hands is simply (or perhaps not-so-simply, considering the ten-plus years it took to get here) my artistic interpretation of the past, written entirely for your entertainment.

Please enjoy!

If you would like to take a deeper look behind the scenes and learn more about the history that inspired my books, sign up for my email list, and you will receive a free gift filled with the insider's scoop. If I didn't address something that you are interested in, you find an error, or have more questions about any of my work, please email me at kami@boleybooks.com and I will answer as quickly as I can.

Thank you for reading!

In gratitude,

Kami Boley

04/21/2019

ACKNOWLEDGMENTS

As you may know, it takes more than one person to birth a book. I wanted to take a moment to thank the people who help make my dreams possible.

First and foremost, I would like to thank my daughter, **Kirstie Rae Schieffler**, and my husband, **James Boley**, for improving my life, and all the other wonderful miracles they perform (like having the compassion and patience to put up with me on my toughest days).

I also owe a debt of gratitude to the following:

Spencer Hamilton—For getting my jokes, for understanding the soul of my stories, for smacking some words out of my hands even when I resisted, helping me dig for that one right word, for polishing my story to a high shine, and for all the hand-holding—he deserves a standing ovation. If you have a manuscript that needs to get ready for publication, I highly recommend that you contact Spencer's freelance editing service without delay—Nerdy Wordsmith—at www.nerdywordsmith.com.

Sandeep Likhar—For being a deeply kind soul who often contemplates the world with me, as well as formatting all of my prose to make it an enjoyable experience for my readers. I highly recommend his services, and all self-publishing professionals should visit his website at www.LikharPublishing.in.

Nicole Eva Fraser—For her expert guidance and steadfast belief in me, for being a dear friend and my biggest fan. I laid all of my tangled first-draft work at her feet. I honestly could not have finished this or any book without the care and support of this lovely lady. She gave my book the wisdom of her experience as an editor and a strong female perspective. Nicole's books are also available on Amazon.

Lee Alessi—A special thanks for his shared love of details and history, for kindly helping me track down those hard-to-find nuggets of information.

Jim Molinelli—Thank you for lending your expertise in repairing my construction verbiage.

My Fearless Ninja Readers: Toni Palermo, Kathleen Doring, Morgan Day Jackson, Konnilaree Sanders, and **Lee Alessi**—For the kindness and willingness to share their eyes and their honesty as my critical readers. These hawk-eyed connoisseurs spent precious time combing through my advance reader copy for things we overlooked. Your efforts are deeply appreciated.

Dr. Wagner's Honey Island Swamp Tours—For fortifying my waterway knowledge.

Damonza—For delivering another gorgeous book cover I can be proud of, and a special thanks to **Chrissy**.

A huge shoutout to all of my Pen Pals! (the lovely people on the Boley Books email list)—thank you all for supporting my work and having my back whenever I need interaction, help, or feedback. I get lonely and you guys are my besties!

The awesome peeps who interact with me on Litsy, Facebook,

Twitter, LinkedIn, Goodreads, and other social media platforms, especially those who assist me with difficult research issues—I appreciate all of your time, valuable feedback, and efforts!

. . . and last but not least, **I THANK YOU!**

Readers breathe life into a writer's words, so I wanted to take this opportunity to thank you for your purchase and for the support in making my dream of being a full-time author a reality.

I am an **Independent Author**, which makes me a tiny voice in a big world. If you enjoyed this book, please leave a review on Amazon, Litsy, and Goodreads—help me spread the experience to others.

I love a good story, and I'm already working on my next one. Please follow my writing journey at **www.boleybooks.com**.

WANT MORE?

Other Titles by **Kami Boley**:

Novels:

The Gator Leaves Nothing Behind – Part I

The Gator Leaves Nothing Behind – Part II

Children's Books:

Bree the Tree

A Piggy Named Mort

The Adventures of Benny and Jenny

About the Author

The author **Kami Boley** was born in Houma, Louisiana, in 1973. At

 a young age, she discovered a deep passion for books and writing. As a young adult, she put that dream on hold to devote her time and energy to working as a cosmetologist so she could provide for a new love in her life, her daughter, Kirstie. Now that Kirstie is grown, Kami is ready to share her stories. Some stories will be for children, some will be for adults—but as she creates them, you will be able to find them all at www.boleybooks.com.